Crime in the 24th Century

Ben Reich, owner of the most powerful business in the solar system, plans and executes a fantastic crime in order to save himself from ruin. In his ruthless struggle to escape the consequences, he encounters a formidable opponent—Lincoln Powell, a mind-reading detective.

Powell is in love with a girl whom Reich has hurt. He is determined, at all costs, to get revenge. He will stop at nothing to prove Reich's guilt.

Here is a thrilling novel of a fantastic manhunt in the 24th century and a killer who tries to outwit a fool-proof interplanetary police force.

More Science Fiction from SIGNET

THE
DEMOLISHED
MAN

by

ALFRED BESTER

A SIGNET BOOK from
NEW AMERICAN LIBRARY
TIMES MIRROR

To Horace Gold

*I*N THE ENDLESS UNIVERSE there is nothing new, nothing different. What may appear exceptional to the minute mind of man may be inevitable to the infinite Eye of God. This strange second in a life, that unusual event, those remarkable coincidences of environment, opportunity, and encounter . . . all may be reproduced over and over on the planet of a sun whose galaxy revolves once in two hundred million years and has revolved nine times already.

There are and have been worlds and cultures without end, each nursing the proud illusion that it is unique in space and time. There have been men without number suffering from the same megalomania; men who imagined themselves unique, irreplaceable, irreproducible. There will be more . . . more plus infinity. This is the story of such a time and such a man . . .

THE DEMOLISHED MAN.

Explosion! Concussion! The vault doors burst open. And deep inside, the money is racked ready for pillage, rapine, loot. Who's that? Who's inside the vault? Oh God! The Man With No Face! Looking. Looming. Silent. Horrible. Run . . . Run . . .

Run, or I'll miss the Paris Pneumatique and that exquisite girl with her flower face and figure of passion. There's time if I run. But that isn't the Guard before the gate. Oh Christ! The Man With No Face. Looking. Looming. Silent. Don't scream. Stop screaming . . .

But I'm not screaming. I'm singing on a stage of sparkling marble while the music soars and the lights burn. But there's no one out there in the amphitheater. A great shadowed pit . . . empty except for one spectator. Silent. Staring. Looming. The Man With No Face.

And this time his scream had sound.

Ben Reich awoke.

He lay quietly in the hydropathic bed while his heart shuddered and his eyes focused at random on objects in the room, simulating a calm he could not feel. The walls of green jade, the nightlight in the porcelain mandarin whose head nodded interminably if you touched him, the multi-clock that radiated the time of three planets and six satellites, the bed itself, a crystal pool flowing with carbonated glycerine at ninety-nine point nine Fahrenheit.

The door opened softly and Jonas appeared in the gloom, a shadow in puce sleeping suit, a shade with the face of a horse and the bearing of an undertaker.

"Again?" Reich asked.

"Yes, Mr. Reich."

"Loud?"

"Very loud, sir. And terrified."

"God damn your jackass ears," Reich growled. "I'm never afraid."

"No, sir."

"Get out."

"Yes, sir. Good night, sir." Jonas stepped back and closed the door.

Reich shouted: "Jonas!"

The valet reappeared.

"Sorry, Jonas."

"Quite all right, sir."

"It isn't all right," Reich charmed him with a smile. "I'm treating you like a relative. I don't pay enough for the privilege."

"Oh no, sir."

"Next time I yell at you, yell right back. Why should I have all the fun?"

"Oh, Mr. Reich . . ."

"Do that and you get a raise." The smile again. "That's all, Jonas. Thank you."

"Thank you, sir." The valet withdrew.

Reich arose from the bed and toweled himself before the cheval mirror, practicing the smile. "Make your enemies by choice," he muttered, "not by accident." He stared at the reflection: the heavy shoulders, narrow flanks, long corded legs . . . the sleek head with wide eyes, chiseled nose, small sensitive mouth scarred by implacability.

"Why?" he asked. "I wouldn't change looks with the devil. I wouldn't change places with God. Why the screaming?"

He put on a gown and glanced at the clock, unaware that he was noting the time panorama of the solar system with an unconscious skill that would have baffled his ancestors. The dials read:

A.D. 2301

VENUS	EARTH	MARS
Mean Solar Day 22	February 15	Duodecember 35
Noon + 09	0205 Greenwich	2220 Central Syrtis

MOON	IO	GANYMEDE	CALLISTO	TITAN	TRITON
2D3H	1D1H	6D8H	13D12H	15D3H	4D9H
		(eclipsed)		(transit)	

Night, noon, summer, winter . . . without bothering to think, Reich could have rattled off the time and season for any meridian on any body in the solar system. Here in New York it was a bitter winter morning after a bitter night of dreaming. He would give himself a few minutes of analysis with the Esper psychiatrist he retained. The screaming had to stop.

"E for Esper," he muttered. "Esper for Extra Sensory Perception . . . For Telepaths, Mind Readers, Brain Peepers. You'd think a mind-reading doctor could stop the screaming. You'd think an Esper M.D. would earn his money and peep inside your head and stop the screaming. Those damned

8

mindreaders are supposed to be the greatest advance since Homo sapiens evolved. E for Evolution. Bastards! E for Exploitation!"

He yanked open the door, shaking with fury.

"But I'm not afraid!" he shouted. "I'm never afraid."

He stepped down the corridor, clacking his sandals sharply on the silver floor, ke-tat-ke-tat-ke-tat-ke-tat, indifferent to the slumber of his house staff, unaware that this early morning skeletal clack awakened twelve hearts to hatred and dread. He thrust open the door of his analyst's suite, entered and at once lay down on the couch.

Carson Breen, Esper Medical Doctor 2, was already awake and ready for him. As Reich's staff analyst he slept the "nurse's sleep" in which he remained en rapport with his patient and could only be awakened by his needs. That one scream had been enough for Breen. Now he was seated alongside the couch, elegant in embroidered gown (his job paid twenty thousand credits a year) and sharply alert (his employer was generous but demanding).

"Go ahead, Mr. Reich."

"The Man With No Face again," Reich growled.

"Nightmares?"

"You lousy blood-sucker, peep me and find out. No. Sorry. Childish of me. Yes, nightmares again. I was trying to rob a bank. Then I was trying to catch a train. Then someone was singing. Me, I think. I'm trying to give you the pictures best I can. I don't think I'm leaving anything out . . ." There was a long pause. Finally Reich blurted: "Well? You peep anything?"

"You persist that you cannot identify The Man With No Face, Mr. Reich?"

"How can I? I never see it. All I know is—"

"I think you can. You simply will not."

"Listen," Reich burst out in guilty rage. "I pay you twenty thousand. If the best you can do is make idiotic statements . . ."

"Do you mean that, Mr. Reich, or is it simply a part of the general anxiety syndrome?"

"There is no anxiety," Reich shouted. "I'm not afraid. I'm never—" He stopped himself, realizing the inutility of ranting while the deft mind of the peeper searched underneath his overturning words. "You're wrong anyway," he said sulkily. "I don't know who it is. It's a Man With No Face. That's all."

"You've been rejecting the essential points, Mr. Reich. You must be made to see them. We'll try a little free association. Without words, please. Just think. Robbery . . ."

9

"Jewels - watches - diamonds - stocks - bonds - sovereigns - counterfeiting - cash - bullion - dort . . ."

"What was that last again?"

"Slip of the mind. Meant to think bort . . . uncut, gem stones."

"It was not a slip. It was a significant correction; or, rather, alteration. Let's continue. Pneumatique . . ."

"Long - car - compartments - air - conditioned . . . That doesn't make sense."

"It does, Mr. Reich. A phallic pun. Read 'Heir' for 'air' and you'll see it. Continue, please."

"You peepers are too damned smart. Let's see. Pneumatique . . . train - underground - compressed air - ultra sonic speed—'We transport You Into Transports,' slogan of the—What the devil is the name of that company? Can't remember. Where'd the notion come from anyway?"

"From the pre-conscious, Mr. Reich. One more trial and you'll begin to understand. Amphitheater . . ."

"Seats - pits - balcony - boxes - stalls - horse stalls - Martian horses - Martian Pampas . . ."

"And there you have it, Mr. Reich. Mars. In the past six months, you've had ninety-seven nightmares about The Man With No Face. He's been your constant enemy, frustrator, and inspirer of terror in dreams that contain three common denominators . . . Finance, Transportation, and Mars. Over and over again . . . The Man With No Face, and Finance, Transportation, and Mars."

"That doesn't mean anything to me."

"It must mean something, Mr. Reich. You must be able to identify this terrifying figure. Why else would you attempt to escape by rejecting his face?"

"I'm not rejecting anything."

"I offer as further clues the altered word 'Dort' and the forgotten name of the company that coined the slogan 'We Transport You Into—' "

"I tell you I don't know who it is." Reich arose abruptly from the couch. "Your clues don't help., I can't make any identification."

"The Man With No Face does not fill you with fear because he's faceless. You know who he is. You hate him and fear him, but you know who he is."

"You're the peeper. You tell me,"

"There's a limit to my ability, Mr. Reich. I can read your mind no deeper without help."

"What do you mean, help? You're the best E.M.D. I could hire. If—"

"You're neither thinking nor meaning that, Mr. Reich.

10

You deliberately hired a 2nd Class Esper in order to protect yourself in such an emergency. Now you're paying the price of your caution. If you want the screaming to stop, you'll have to consult one of the 1st Class men . . . Say, Augustus Tate or Gart or Samuel @kins . . ."

"I'll think about it," Reich muttered and turned to go. As he opened the door, Breen called: "By the way . . . 'We Transport You Into Transports' is the slogan of the D'Courtney Cartel. How does that tie in with the alteration of 'bort' to 'dort'? Think it over."

"The Man With No Face!"

Without staggering, Reich slammed the door across the path from his mind to Breen and then lurched down the corridor toward his own suite. A wave of savage hatred burst over him. *"He's right. It's D'Courtney who's giving me the screams. Not because I'm afraid of him. I'm afraid of myself. Known all along. Known it deep down inside. Known that once I faced it I'd have to kill that D'Courtney bastard. It's no face because it's the face of murder."*

Fully dressed and in his wrong mind, Reich stormed out of his apartment and descended to the street where a Monarch Jumper picked him up and carried him in one graceful hop to the giant tower that housed the hundreds of floors and thousands of employees of Monarch's New York Office. Monarch Tower was the central nervous system of an incredibly vast corporation, a pyramid of transportation, communication, heavy industry, manufacture, sales distribution, research, exploration, importation. Monarch Utilities & Resources, Inc. bought and sold, traded and gave, made and destroyed. Its pattern of subsidiaries and holding companies was so complex that it demanded the fulltime services of a 2nd Class Esper Accountant to trace the labyrinthine flow of its finances.

Reich entered his office, followed by his chief (Esper 3) secretary and her staff, bearing the litter of the morning's work.

"Dump it and jet," he growled.

They deposited the papers and recording crystals on his desk and departed hastily but without rancour. They were accustomed to his rages. Reich seated himself behind his desk, trembling with a fury that was already goring D'Courtney. Finally he muttered: "I'll give the bastard one more chance."

He unlocked his desk, opened the drawer-safe and withdrew the Executive's Code Book, restricted to the executive heads of the firms listed quadruple A-1-* by Lloyds. He found most of the material he required in the middle pages of the book:

QQBA	. . . .	PARTNERSHIP
RRCB	. . . .	BOTH OUR
SSDC	. . . .	BOTH YOUR
TTED	. . . .	MERGER
UUFE	. . . .	INTERESTS
VVGF	. . . .	INFORMATION
WWHG	. . . .	ACCEPT OFFER
XXIH	. . . .	GENERALLY KNOWN
YYJI	. . . .	SUGGEST
ZZKJ	. . . .	CONFIDENTIAL
AALK	. . . .	EQUAL
BBML	. . . .	CONTRACT

Marking his place in the code book, Reich flipped the v-phone on and said to the image of the inter-office operator: "Get me Code."

The screen dazzled and cut to a smokey room cluttered with books and coils of tape. A bleached man in a faded shirt glanced at the screen, then leaped to attention.

"Yes, Mr. Reich?"

"Morning, Hassop. You look like you need a vacation." *Make your enemies by choice.* "Take a week at Spaceland. Monarch expense."

"Thank you, Mr. Reich. Thank you very much."

"This one's confidential. To Craye D'Courtney. Send —" Reich consulted the Code Book. "Send YYJI TTED RRCB UUFE AALK QQBA. Get the answer to me like rockets. Right?"

"Right, Mr. Reich. I'll jet."

Reich cut off the phone. He jabbed his hand once into the pile of papers and crystals on his desk, picked up a crystal and dropped it into the play-back. His chief secretary's voice said: "Monarch Gross off two points one one three four per cent. D'Courtney Gross up two point one one three oh per cent . . ."

"God damn him!" Reich growled. "Out of my pocket into his." He snapped off the play-back and arose in an agony of impatience. It would take hours for the reply to come. His whole life hung on D'Courtney's reply. He left his office and began to roam through the floors and departments of Monarch Tower, pretending the remorseless personal supervision he usually exercised. His Esper secretary unobtrusively accompanied him like a trained dog.

"*Trained bitch!*" Reich thought. Then aloud: "I'm sorry. Did you peep that?"

"Quite all right, Mr. Reich. I understand."

"Do you? I don't. Damn D'Courtney!"

In Personnel they were testing, checking, and screening the usual mass of job applicants . . . clerks, craftsmen, specialists, middle bracket executives, top echelon experts. All of the preliminary elimination was done with standardized tests and interviews, and never to the satisfaction of Monarch's Esper Personnel Chief who was stalking through the floor in an icy rage when Reich entered. The fact that Reich's secretary had sent an advance telepathic announcement of the visit made no difference to him.

"I have allotted ten minutes per applicant for my final screening interview," the Chief was snapping to an assistant. "Six per hour, forty-eight per day. Unless my percentage of final rejections drops below thirty-five, I am wasting my time; which means you are wasting Monarch's time. I am not employed by Monarch to screen out the obviously unsuitable. That is your work. See to it." He turned to Reich and nodded pedantically. "Good morning, Mr. Reich."

"Morning. Trouble?"

"Nothing that cannot be handled once this staff understands that Extra Sensory Perception is not a miracle but a skill subject to wage-hour limitations. And what is your decision on Blonn, Mr. Reich?"

Secretary: *"He hasn't read your memo yet."*

"May I point out, young woman, that unless I am used with maximum efficiency I am wasted. The Blonn memo has been on Mr. Reich's desk for three days."

"Who the hell is Blonn?" Reich asked.

"First, the background, Mr. Reich: There are approximately one hundred thousand (100,000) 3rd Class Espers in the Esper Guild. An Esper 3 can peep the conscious level of a mind—can discover what a subject is thinking at the moment of thought. A 3rd is the lowest class of telepath. Most of Monarch's security positions are held by 3rds. We employ over five hundred . . ."

"He knows all this. Everybody does. Get to the point, long-wind!"

"Permit me, if I may, to arrive at the point in my own way. Next, there are approximately ten thousand 2nd Class Espers in the Guild," the Personnel Chief continued frostily. "They are experts like myself who can penetrate beneath the conscious level of the mind to the preconscious. Most 2nds are in the professional class . . . physicians, lawyers, engineers, educators, economists, architects and so on."

"And you all cost a fortune," Reich growled.

"Why not? We have unique service to sell. Monarch appreciates the fact. Monarch employs over one hundred 2nds at present."

"Will you get to the point?"

"Finally there are less than a thousand 1st Class Espers in the Guild. The 1sts are capable of deep peeping, through the conscious and preconscious layers down to the unconscious . . . the lowest levels of the mind. Primordial basic desires and so forth. These, of course, hold premium positions. Education, specialized medical service . . . analysts like Tate, Gart, @kins, Moselle . . . criminologists like Lincoln Powell of the Psychotic Division . . . Political Analysts, State Negotiators, Special Cabinet Advisors, and so on. Thus far Monarch Utilities has never had occasion to hire a 1st."

"And?" Reich muttered.

"The occasion has arisen, Mr. Reich, and I believe Blonn may be available. Briefly . . ."

"It says here."

"Briefly, Mr. Reich, Monarch is hiring so many Espers that I have suggested we set up a special Esper Personnel Department, headed by a 1st like Blonn, to devote itself exclusively to interviewing telepaths."

"He's wondering why you can't handle it."

"I have given you the background to explain why I cannot handle the job, Mr. Reich. I am a 2nd Class Esper. I can telepath normal applicants rapidly and efficiently, but I cannot handle other Espers with the same speed and economy. All Espers are accustomed to using mind-blocks of varying effectiveness depending on their rating. It would take me one hour per 3rd for an efficient screening interview. It would take me three hours per 2nd. I could not possibly peep through the mind-block of a 1st. We must hire a 1st like Blonn for this work. The cost will be enormous, of course, but the necessity is urgent."

"What's so urgent?" Reich said.

"For heaven's sake! Don't give him that picture! That isn't diversion. It's waving a red flag. He's sore enough now."

"I have my job to do, Madam." To Reich, the Chief said: "The fact is, sir, we are not hiring the best Espers. The D'Courtney Cartel has been taking the cream of the Espers away from us. Over and over again, through lack of proper facilities, we have been mouse-trapped by D'Courtney into bidding for inferior people while D'Courtney has quietly appropriated the best."

"Damn you!" Reich shouted. "Damn D'Courtney. All right. Set it up. And tell this Blonn to start mouse-trapping D'Courtney. You'd better start, too."

Reich tore out of Personnel and over to Sales-city. The same unpleasant information was waiting for him. Monarch Utilities & Resources was losing the gut-fight with the D'Court-

14

ney Cartel. It was losing the fight in every sector-city—Advertising, Engineering, Research, Public Relations. There was no escaping the certainty of defeat. Reich knew his back was to the wall.

He returned to his own office and paced in a fury for five minutes. "It's no use," he muttered. "I know I'll have to kill him. He won't accept merger. Why should he? He's licked me and he knows it. I'll have to kill him and I'll need help. Peeper help."

He flipped on the v-phone and told the operator: "Recreation."

A sparkling lounge appeared on the screen, decorated in chrome and enamel, equipped with game tables and a bar dispenser. It appeared to be and was used as a recreation center. It was, in fact, headquarters of Monarch's powerful espionage division. The Recreation Director, a bearded scholar named West, looked up from a chess problem, then rose to attention.

"Good morning, Mr. Reich."

Warned by the formal 'Mister,' Reich said: "Good morning, Mr. West. Just a routine check. Paternalism, you know. How's amusement these days?"

"Modulated, Mr. Reich. However, I must complain, sir. I think there's entirely too much gambling going on." West stalled in a fussy voice until two bona fide Monarch clerks innocently finished their drinks and departed. Then he relaxed and slumped into his chair. "All clear, Ben. Shoot."

"Has Hassop broken the confidential code yet, Ellery?"

The peeper shook his head.

"Trying?"

West smiled and nodded.

"Where's D'Courtney?"

"En route to Terra, aboard the 'Astra'."

"Know his plans? Where he'll be staying?"

"No. Want a check?"

"I don't know. It depends . . ."

"Depends on what?" West glanced at him curiously. "I wish the Telepathic Pattern could be transmitted by phone, Ben. I'd like to know what you're thinking at."

Reich smiled grimly. "Thank God for the phone. At least we've got that protection from mind readers. What's your attitude on crime, Ellery?"

"Typical."

"Of anybody?"

"Of the Guild. The Guild doesn't like it, Ben."

"So what's so hot about the Esper Guild? You know the value of money, success . . . Why don't you clever-up? Why do you let the Guild do your thinking?"

15

"You don't understand. We're born in the Guild. We live with the Guild. We die in the Guild. We have the right to elect Guild officers, and that's all. The Guild runs our professional lives. It trains us, grades us, sets ethical standards, and sees that we stick to them. It protects us by protecting the layman, the same as medical associations. We have the equivalent of the Hippocratic Oath. It's called the Esper Pledge. God help any of us if we break it . . . . as I judge you're suggesting I should."

"Maybe I am," Reich said intently. "Maybe I'm hinting it could be worth your while to break the peeper pledge. Maybe I'm thinking in terms of money . . . more than you or any 2nd Class peeper ever sees in a lifetime."

"Forget it, Ben. Not interested."

"So you bust your pledge. What happens?"

"We're ostracized."

"That's all? Is that so awful? With a fortune in your pocket? Smart peepers have broken with the Guild before. They've been ostracized. So what? Clever-up, Ellery."

West smiled wryly: "You wouldn't understand, Ben."

"Make me understand."

"Those ousted peepers you mention . . . like Jerry Church. They weren't so smart. It's like this . . ." West considered. "Before surgery really got started, there used to be a handicapped group called deaf-mutes."

"No-hear no-talk?"

"That's it. They communicated by a manual sign language. That meant they couldn't communicate with anybody but deaf-mutes. Understand? They had to live in their own community or they couldn't live at all. A man goes crazy if he can't talk to friends."

"So?"

"Some of them started a racket. They'd tax the more successful deaf-mutes for weekly hand-outs. If the victim refused to pay, they'd ostracize him. The victim always paid. It was a choice of paying or living in solitary until he went mad."

"You mean you peepers are like deaf-mutes?"

"No, Ben. You normals are the deaf-mutes. If we had to live with you alone, we'd go mad. So leave me alone. If you're nursing something dirty, I don't want to know."

West cut off the phone in Reich's face. With a roar of rage, Reich snatched up a gold paper-weight and hurled it into the crystal screen. Before the shattered fragments finished flying, he was in the corridor and on his way out of the building.

16

His peeper secretary knew where he was going. His peeper chauffeur knew where he wanted to go. Reich arrived in his apartment and was met by his peeper house-supervisor who at once announced early luncheon and dialed the meal to Reich's unspoken demands. Feeling slightly less violent, Reich stalked into his study and turned to his safe, a shimmer of light in the corner.

It was simply a honey-comb paper rack tuned out of temporal phase with a single-cycle beat. Each second when the safe phase and the temporal phase coincided, the rack pulsed with a brilliant glow. The safe could only be opened by the pore-pattern of Reich's left index finger which was irreproducible.

Reich placed the tip of his finger in the center of the glow. It faded and the honey-comb rack appeared. Holding his finger in place, he reached up and took down a small black notebook and a large red envelope. He removed his index finger and the safe pulsed out of phase again.

Reich flipped through the pages of the notebook . . . ABDUCTION . . . ANARCHISTS . . . ARSONISTS . . . BRIBERY (PROVEN) . . . BRIBERY (POTENTIAL) . . . Under (POTENTIAL) he found the names of fifty-seven prominent people. One of them was Augustus Tate, Esper Medical Doctor 1. He nodded with satisfaction.

He tore open the red envelope and examined its contents. It contained five sheets of closely written pages in a handwriting that was centuries old. It was a message from the founder of Monarch Utilities and the Reich clan. Four of the pages were lettered: PLAN A, PLAN B, PLAN C, PLAN D. The fifth was headed INTRODUCTION. Reich read the ancient spidery cursive slowly:

> To those who come after me: The test of intellect is the refusal to belabor the obvious. If you have opened this letter we understand one another. I have prepared four general murder plans which may help you. I bequeath them to you as part of your Reich inheritance. They are outlines. The details must be filled in by yourself as your time, your environment, and necessity require.

> Caution: The essence of murder never changes. In every era it remains the conflict of the killer against society with the victim as the prize. And the ABC of conflict with society remains constant. Be audacious, be brave, be confident and you will not fail. Against these assets society can have no defense.

> Geoffry Reich

17

Reich leafed through the plans slowly, filled with admiration for the first of his line who had had the fore-thought to prepare for every possible emergency. The plans were out-dated but they kindled imagination; and ideas began forming and crystallizing to be considered, discarded, and instantly replaced. One phrase caught his attention:

> If you believe yourself a natural killer, avoid planning too carefully. Leave most to your instinct. Intellect may fail you, but the killer instinct is invincible.

"The killer instinct," Reich breathed. "By God, I've got that."

The phone chimed once and then the automatic switched on. There was a quick chatter and tape began to stutter out of the recorder. Reich strode to the desk and examined it. The message was short and deadly:

CODE TO REICH: REPLY WWHG.

"WWHG. 'Offer refused.' Refused! REFUSED! I knew it!" Reich shouted. "All right, D'Courtney. If you won't let it be merger, then I'll make it murder."

2

Augustus Tate, E.M.D. 1, received Cr. 1,000 per hour of analysis . . . not a high fee considering that a patient rarely required more than an hour of the doctor's devastating time; but it placed his income at Cr. 8,000 a day or well over Cr. 2 million a year. Few people knew what proportion of that income was paid into the Esper Guild for the education of other Telepaths and the furthering of the Guild's Eugenic plan to bring Extra Sensory Perception to everyone in the world.

Augustus Tate knew, and the 95% he paid was a sore point with him. Consequently, he belonged to "The League of Esper Patriots," an extreme right-wing political group within the Guild, dedicated to the preservation of the autocracy and incomes of the upper grade Espers. It was this membership that placed him in Ben Reich's BRIBERY (POTENTIAL) category. Reich marched into Tate's exquisite consultation room, glanced once at Tate's tiny frame—a figure slightly out of proportion but carefully realigned by tailors. Reich sat down and grunted: "Peep me quick."

He glared in concentration at Tate while the elegant little

peeper examined him with a glittering eye and spoke in quick bursts: "You're Ben Reich of Monarch. Ten billion credit firm. Think I should know you. I do. You're involved in a death struggle with the D'Courtney Cartel. Right? You're savagely hostile toward D'Courtney. Right? Offered merger this morning. Coded message: YYJI TTED RRCB UUFE AALK QQBA. Offer refused. Right? In desperation you have resolved to—" Tate broke off abruptly.

"Go ahead," Reich said.

"To murder Craye D'Courtney as the first step in taking over his cartel. You want my help. . . . Mr. Reich, this is ridiculous! If you keep on thinking like this, I'll have to commit you. You know the law."

"Clever-up, Tate. You're going to help me break the law."

"No, Mr. Reich. I'm not in a position to help you."

"You say that? A 1st Class Esper? And I'm supposed to believe it? I'm supposed to believe you're incapable of outwitting any man, any group, the whole world?"

Tate smiled. "Sugar for the fly," he said. "A characteristic device of—"

"Peep me," Reich interrupted. "It'll save time. Read what's in my mind. Your gift. My resources. An unbeatable combination. My God! It's lucky for the world I'm willing to stop at one murder. Together we could rape the universe."

"No," Tate said with decision. "This won't do. I'll have to commit you, Mr. Reich."

"Wait. Want to find out what I'm offering you? Read me deeper. How much am I willing to pay? What's my top limit?"

Tate closed his eyes. His mannequin face tightened painfully. Then his eyes opened in surprise. "You can't be serious," he exclaimed.

"I am," Reich grunted. "And what's more, you know it's an offer in good faith, don't you?"

Tate nodded slowly.

"And you're aware that Monarch plus D'Courtney can make the offer good."

"I almost believe you."

"You can believe me. I've been financing your League of Esper Patriots for five years. If you've peeped me deep enough you know why. I hate the damned Esper Guild as much as you do. Guild ethics are bad for business . . . lousy for making money. Your League is the organization that can break the Esper Guild some day . . ."

"I've got all that," Tate said sharply.

"With Monarch and D'Courtney in my pocket I can do better than help your faction break the Guild. I can make you President of a new Esper Guild for life. That's an unconditional guarantee. You can't do it alone, but you can do it with me."

Tate closed his eyes and murmured: "There hasn't been a successful premeditated murder in 79 years. Espers make it impossible to conceal intent before murder. Or, if Espers have been evaded before the murder, they make it impossible to conceal the guilt afterwards."

"Esper evidence isn't admitted in court."

"True, but once an Esper discovers guilt he can always uncover objective evidence to support his peeping. Lincoln Powell, the Prefect of the Police Psychotic Division, is deadly." Tate opened his eyes. "D'you want to forget this conversation?"

"No," Reich growled. "Look it over with me first. Why have murders failed? Because mind-readers patrol the world. What can stop a mind-reader? Another one. But no killer ever had the sense to hire a good peeper to run interference for him; or if he had the sense, he couldn't make the deal. I've made the deal."

"Have you?"

"I'm going to fight a war," Reich continued. "I'm going to fight one sharp skirmish with society. Let's look at it as a problem in strategy and tactics. My problem's simply the problem of any army. Audacity, bravery, and confidence aren't enough. An army needs Intelligence. A war is won with Intelligence. I need you for my G-2."

"Agreed."

"I'll do the fighting. You'll provide the Intelligence. I'll have to know where D'Courtney will be, where I can strike, when I can strike. I'll take care of the killing myself, but you'll have to tell me when and where the opportunity will be."

"Understood."

"I'll have to invade first . . . cut through the defensive network surrounding D'Courtney. That means reconnaissance from you. You'll have to check the normals, spot the peepers, warn me and block their mind-reading if I can't avoid them. I'll have to retreat after the killing through another network of normals and peepers. You'll have to help me fight a rear-guard action. You'll have to remain on the scene after the murder. You'll find out whom the police suspect and why. If I know suspicion is directed against myself, I can divert it. If I know it's directed against someone else, I can clinch it. I can fight this war and win this war with your Intelligence. Is that the truth? Peep me."

After a long pause, Tate said: "It's the truth. We can do it."

"Will you do it?"

20

Tate hesitated, then nodded with finality. "Yes. I'll do it."

Reich took a deep breath. "Right. Now here's the course I'm plotting. I think I can set up the killing with an old game called 'Sardine.' It will give me the opportunity to get at D'Courtney, and I've figured out a trick to kill him; I know how to fire an antique explosive gun without bullets."

"Wait," Tate interrupted sharply. "How are you going to keep all this intent concealed from stray peepers? I can only screen you when I'm with you. I won't be with you all the time."

"I can work up a temporary mind-block. There's a song-writer down on Melody Lane I can swindle into helping me."

"It may work," Tate said after a moment's peeping. "But one thing occurs to me. Suppose D'Courtney is protected? Do you expect to shoot it out with his bodyguards?"

"No. I'm hoping it won't be necessary. A physiologist named Jordan has just developed visual knock-out drops for Monarch. We intended using it for strike riots. I'll use it on D'Courtney's guards."

"I see."

"You'll be working with me all along . . . doing reconnaissance and intelligence, but I need one piece of information first. When D'Courtney comes to town he's usually the guest of Maria Beaumont."

"The Gilt Corpse?"

"The same. I want you to find out if D'Courtney intends staying with her this trip. Everything depends on that."

"Easy enough. I can locate D'Courtney's destination and plans for you. There's to be a social gathering tonight at Lincoln Powell's house. D'Courtney's physician will probably be there. He's on Terra for a week's visit. I'll start the reconnaissance through him."

"And you're not afraid of Powell?"

Tate smiled contemptuously. "If I were, Mr. Reich, would I trust myself in this bargain with you? Make no mistake. I'm no Jerry Church."

"Church!"

"Yes. Don't act surprised. Church, the 2nd. He was kicked out of the Guild ten years ago for that little junket of his with you."

"Damn you. Got that from my mind, eh?"

"Your mind and history."

"Well, it won't repeat itself this time. You're tougher and smarter than Church. Need anything special for Powell's party? Women? Clothes? Jewels? Money? Just call on Monarch."

"Nothing, but thank you very much."

21

"Criminal but generous, that's me." Reich smiled as he arose to go. He did not offer to shake hands.

"Mr. Reich!" Tate called suddenly.

Reich turned at the door.

"The screaming will continue. The Man With No Face is not a symbol of murder."

"What? Oh Christ! The nightmares? Still? You God damned peeper. How did you get that? How did you—"

"Don't be a fool. D'you think you can play games with a 1st?"

"Who's playing, you bastard? What about the nightmares?"

"No, Mr. Reich, I won't tell you. I doubt if anyone but a 1st can tell you, and naturally you would not dare to consult another after this conference."

"For God's sake, man! Are you going to help me?"

"No, Mr. Reich." Tate smiled malevolently. "That's my little weapon. It keeps us on a parity basis. Balance of power, you understand. Mutual dependence ensures mutual faith. Criminal but peeper . . . that's me."

Like all upper-grade Espers, Lincoln Powell. Ph.D.1, lived in a private house. It was not a question of conspicuous consumption, but rather a problem of privacy. Although thought transmission was too faint to penetrate masonry, the average plastic apartment unit was too flimsy to block this transmission. Life in any such multiple dwelling was life in an inferno of naked emotion for an Esper.

Powell, the Police Prefect, could afford a small limestone maisonette on Hudson Ramp overlooking the North River. There were only four rooms; upstairs a bedroom and study, downstairs a living room and kitchen. There was no servant in the house. Like most upper-grade Espers, Powell required large quantities of solitude. He preferred to do for himself. He was in the kitchen, checking over the refreshment-dials in preparation for the party, whistling a plaintive, crooked tune.

He was a slender man in his late thirties, tall, loose, slow-moving. His wide mouth seemed perpetually on the verge of laughter, but at the moment he wore an expression of sad disappointment. He was lecturing himself on the follies and stupidities of his worst vice.

The essence of the Esper is his responsiveness. His personality always takes color from his surroundings. The trouble with Powell was an enlarged sense of humor, and his response was invariably exaggerated. He had attacks of what he called

22

"Dishonest Abe" moods. Someone would ask Lincoln Powell an innocent question, and Dishonest Abe would answer. His fervent imagination would cook up the wildest tall-story and he would deliver it with straight-faced sincerity. He could not suppress the liar in him.

Only this afternoon, Police Commissioner Crabbe had inquired about a routine blackmail case, and simply because he'd mispronounced a name, Powell had been inspired to fabricate a dramatic account involving a make-believe crime, a daring midnight raid, and the heroism of an imaginary Lieutenant Kopenick. Now the Commissioner wanted to award Lieutenant Kopenick a medal.

"Dishonest Abe," Powell muttered bitterly. "You give me a stiff pain."

The house-bell chimed. Powell glanced at his watch in surprise (it was too early for company) and then directed *Open in C-sharp* at the TP lock-sensor. It responded to the thought pattern, as a tuning fork will vibrate to the right note, and the front door slid open.

Instantly came a familiar sensory impact: Snow/mint/tulips/taffeta.

Mary Noyes. Come to help the bachelor prepare for the party? Blessings!

"Hoped you'd need me, Linc."

*"Every host needs a hostess. Mary, what am I going to do for Canapes*ᵒˣ*?"*

"Just invented a new recipe. I'll make it for you. Roast chutney &."

"&?"

"That's telling, my love."

She came into the kitchen, a short girl physically, but tall and swaying in thought; a dark girl exteriorly, but frost white in pattern. Almost a nun in white, despite the swarthy texture of externals; but the mind is the reality. You are what you think.

"I wish I could re-think, darling. Have my psyche reground!"

"Change your (I kiss you as you are) self, Mary?"

"If I only (You never really do, Linc) could. I'm so tired of tasting you tasting mint every time we meet."

"Next time I'll add brandy and ice. Shake well. Voila! Stinger-Mary."

"Do that. Also $ℕ𝕆𝕎 "

"Why strike out the snow? I love snow."

"But I love you."

"And I love you, Mary."

"Thanks, Linc." But he said it. He always said it. He never thought it. She turned away quickly. The tears within her scalded him.

"Again, Mary?"

"Not again. Always. Always." And the deeper levels of her mind cried: "I love you, Lincoln. I love you. Image of my father: Symbol of security: Of warmth: Of protecting passion: Do not reject me always . . . always . . . for ever . . ."

"Listen to me, Mary . . ."

"Don't talk, Please, Linc. Not in words. I couldn't bear it if words came between us."

"You're my friend, Mary. Always. For every disappointment. For every elation."

"But not for love."

"No, dear heart. Don't let it hurt you so. Not for love."

"I have enough love, God pity me, for both of us."

"One, God pity us, is not enough for both, Mary."

"You must marry an Esper before you're forty, Linc. The Guild insists on that. You know it."

"I know it."

"Then let friendship answer. Marry me, Lincoln. Give me a year, that's all. One little year to love you. I'll let you go. I won't cling. I won't make you hate me. Darling, it's so little to ask . . . so little to give . . ."

The door-bell chimed. Powell looked at Mary helplessly. "Guests," he murmured and directed Open in C-sharp at the TP lock-sensor. At the same instant she directed Close a fifth above. The harmonies meshed and the door remained shut.

"Answer me first, Lincoln."

"I can't give you the answer you want, Mary."

The door-bell chimed again.

He took her shoulders firmly, held her close and looked deep into her eyes. "You're a 2nd. Read me as deeply as you can. What's in my mind? What's in my heart? What's my answer?"

He removed all blocks. The thundering plunging depths of his mind cascaded over her in a warm, frightening torrent . . . terrifying, yet magnetic and desirable; but . . . "Snow. Mint. Tulips. Taffeta," she said wearily. "Go meet your guests, Mr. Powell. I'll make your canapes. It's all I'm good for."

He kissed her once, then turned toward the living room and opened the front door. Instantly, a fountain of brilliance sparkled into the house, followed by the guests. The Esper party began.

24

Frankly   Canapes?   Why
 Ellery,   Thanks delicious. Yes.
  I   Mary, they're   Tate,
   don't   I'm
    think   treating
We   you'll Canapes? D'Courtney.
Brought be   I
 Galen   working   expect
  along   for   him
   to   Monarch   in
   help him celebrate. much   town
     He's   longer.   very
      just   The   shortly.
      taken his Guild Exam
   If   is   and
  you're   just   been
interested   about   classed
  Powell, we're ready   2nd.
        to
      run rule
      you Monarch's
     for   espionage
    Guild Canapes? unethical.
   President.
       Canapes?
        Why yes.
         Thank
      Canapes?   you,
          Mary . . .

"@kins! Chervil! Tate! Have a heart! Will you people take a look at the pattern (?) we've been weaving . . ."

The TP chatter stopped. The guests considered for a moment, then burst into laughter.

"This reminds me of my days in the kindergarten. A little mercy for your host, please. I'll jump my tracks, if we keep on weaving this mish-mash. Let's have some order. I don't even ask for beauty."

"Just name the pattern, Linc."

"What'll you have?"

"Basket-weave? Math curves? Music? Architectural design?"

"Anything. Anything. Just so long as you don't make my brains itch."

Sorry, Lincoln.	We weren't party-minded	Enough
Tate	thought	Esper
but	Alan	Men
I'm	Seaver	remaining
Not that a Pres	was ever elected still	unmarried
at	coming	can
liberty	but	ruin
To be generous,	I feel Al's a man to loa	the
reveal	don't	Guild's
anything	TP	entire
about	him	eugenic
D'Courtney is	arriving according to	plan
	yet	

There was another burst of laughter when Mary Noyes was left hanging with that unreticulated "yet." The door-bell chimed again, and a Solar Equity Advocate 2 entered with his girl. She was a demure little thing, surprisingly attractive outwardly, and new to the company. Her TP pattern was naive and not deeply responsive. Obviously a 3rd.

"Greetings. Greetings. Abject apologies for the delay. Orange blossoms & wedding rings are the excuse. I proposed on the way over."

"And I'm afraid I accepted," the girl said, smiling.

"Don't talk," the lawyer shot at her. "This isn't a 3rd Class brawl, I told you not to use words."

"I forgot," she blurted again, and then heated the room with her fright and shame. Powell stepped forward and took the girl's trembling hand.

"Ignore him, he's a 2nd-come-lately snob. I'm Lincoln Powell, your host. I Sherlock for the cops. If your fiancé beats you, I'll help him regret it. Come and meet your fellow freaks . . ." He conducted her around the room. "This is Gus Tate, a quack-one. Next to him, Sam & Sally @kins. Sam's another of the same. She's a baby-sitter-two. They're just in from Venus. Here on a visit . . ."

"H-How—I mean, how do you do?"

"That fat man sitting on the floor is Wally Chervil, architect-two. The blonde sitting in his (lap)² is June, his wife. June's an editor-two. That's their son, Galen, talking to Ellery West. Gally's a tech-undergrad-three . . ."

Young Galen Chervil indignantly started to point out that he'd just been classed 2nd and hadn't needed to use words in over a year. Powell cut him off and below the girl's perceptive threshold explained the reason for the deliberate mistake.

"Oh," said Galen. "Yep, brother and sister 3rds, that's us. And am I glad you're here. These deep peepers were beginning to scare me."

"Oh, I don't know. I was scared at first, but I'm not any more."

"And this is your hostess, Mary Noyes."

"Hello, Canapes?"

"Thank you. They look delicious, Mrs. Powell."

"Now how about a game?" Powell interposed quickly. "Rebus, anyone?"

Outside, huddled in the shadow of the limestone arch, Jerry Church pressed against the garden door of Powell's house, listening with all his soul. He was cold, silent, immobile, and starved. He was resentful, hating, contemptuous, and starved. He was an Esper 2 and starved. The bend sinister of ostracism was the source of his hunger.

Through the thin maple panel filtered the multiple TP pattern of the party; a weaving, ever-changing, exhilarating design. And Church, Esper 2, living on a sub-marginal diet of words for the past ten years, was starved for his own people— for the Esper world he had lost.

"The reason I mentioned D'Courtney is that I've just come across a case that might be similar."

That was Augustus Tate, sucking up to @kins.

"Oh really? Very interesting. I'd like to compare notes. Matter of fact, I made the trip to Terra because D'Courtney is coming here. Too bad D'Courtney won't—well, be available." @kins was obviously being discreet and it smelled as though Tate was after something. Maybe not, Church speculated, but there was some elegant block and counter-blocking going on, like duellists fencing with complicated electrical circuits.

"Look here, peeper. I think you've been pretty snotty to that poor girl."

"Listen to him shoot off his mind," Church muttered. "Powell, that holy louse who had me kicked out, preaching down his big nose at the lawyer."

"Poor girl? You mean dumb girl, Powell. My God! How gauche can you get?"

"She's only a 3rd. Be fair."

"She gives me a pain."

"Do you think it's decent . . . marrying a girl when you feel that way about her?"

"Don't be a romantic ass, Powell. We've got to marry peepers. I might as well settle for a pretty face."

The Rebus game was going on in the living room. The Noyes girl was busy building a camouflaged image with an old poem:

<pre>
The   vast,
sea   and
is   out   Glimmering
calm   in   the   stand,
tonight,   tranquil   bay   England
The   Come   to   the window   of
tide   sweet   is   the night   cliffs
is   air.   Only   the
full   from   the   gone;
the   long   line   is
moon   of spray   and
lies   Gleams
fair   light
</pre>
Upon the straights;—on the French coast the

What the devil was that? An eye in a glass? Eh? Oh. Not a glass. A stein. Eye in a stein. Einstein. Easy.

"What d'you think of Powell for the job, Ellery?" That was Chervil with his phoney smile and his big fat pontifical belly.

"For Guild President?"

"Yes."

"Damned efficient man. Romantic but efficient. The perfect candidate if only he'd get married."

"That's the romance in him. He's having trouble locating a girl."

"Don't all you deep peepers? Thank God I'm not a 1st."

And then a smash of glass crashing in the kitchen and Preacher Powell again, lecturing that little snot, Gus Tate.

"Never mind the glass, Gus. I had to drop it to cover for you. You're radiating anxiety like a nova."

"The devil I am, Powell."

"The devil you're not. What's all this about Ben Reich?"

The little man was really on guard. You could feel his mental shell hardening.

"Ben Reich? What brought him up?"

"You did, Gus. It's been moiling in your mind all evening. I couldn't help reading it."

"Not me, Powell. You must be tuning another TP."

Image of a horse laughing.

"Powell, I swear I'm not—"

"Are you mixed up with Reich, Gus?"

"No." But you could feel the blocks bang down into place.

"Take a hint from an old hand, Gus. Reich can get you into trouble. Be careful. Remember Jerry Church? Reich ruined him. Don't let it happen to you."

Tate drifted back to the living room; Powell remained in

the kitchen, calm and slow-moving, sweeping up broken glass. Church lay frozen against the back door, suppressing the seething hatred in his heart. The Chervil boy was showing off for the lawyer's girl, singing a love ballad and paralleling it with a visual parody. College stuff. The wives were arguing violently in sine curves. @kins and West were interlacing cross-conversation in a fascinatingly intricate pattern of sensory images that made Church's starvation keener.

"Would you like a drink, Jerry?"

The garden door opened. Powell stood silhouetted in the light, a bubbling glass in his hand. The stars lit his face softly. The deep hooded eyes were compassionate and understanding. Dazed, Church climbed to his feet and timidly took the proffered drink.

"Don't report this to the Guild, Jerry. I'll catch hell for breaking the taboo. I'm always breaking rules. Poor Jerry . . . We've got to do something for you. Ten years is too long."

Suddenly Church hurled the drink in Powell's face, then turned and fled.

3

At nine Monday morning, Tate's mannequin face appeared on the screen of Reich's v-phone.

"Is this line secure?" he asked sharply.

In answer Reich simply pointed to the Warranty Seal.

"All right," Tate said. "I think I've done the job for you, I peeped @kins last night. But before I report, I must warn you. There's a chance of error when you deep peep a 1st. @kins blocked pretty carefully."

"I understand."

"Craye D'Courtney arrives from Mars on the 'Astra' next Wednesday morning. He will go at once to Maria Beaumont's town house where he will be a secret and hidden guest for exactly one night . . . No more."

"One night," Reich muttered. "And then? His plans?"

"I don't know. Apparently D'Courtney is planning some form of drastic action—"

"Against me!" Reich growled.

"Perhaps. According to @kins, D'Courtney is under some kind of violent strain and his adaptation pattern is shattering. The Life Instinct and Death Instinct have defused. He is regressing under the emotional bankruptcy very rapidly . . ."

"God damn it! My life depends on this," Reich raged. "Talk straight."

"It's quite simple. Every man is a balance of two opposed drives . . . The Life Instinct and the Death Instinct. Both drives have the identical purpose . . . to win Nirvana. The Life Instinct fights for Nirvana by smashing all opposition. The Death Instinct attempts to win Nirvana by destroying itself. Usually both instincts fuse in the adapted individual. Under strain they defuse. That's what's happening to D'Courtney."

"Yes, by God! And he's jetting for me!"

"@kins will see D'Courtney Thursday morning in an effort to dissuade him from whatever he contemplates. @kins is afraid of it and determined to stop it. He made a flying trip from Venus to cut D'Courtney off."

"He won't have to stop it. I'll stop it myself. He won't have to protect me. I'll protect myself. It's self-defense, Tate . . . not murder! Self-defense! You've done a good job. This is all I need."

"You need much more, Reich. Among other things, time. This is Monday. You'll have to be ready by Wednesday."

"I'll be ready," Reich growled. "You'd better be ready too."

"We can't afford to fail, Reich. If we do—it's Demolition. You realized that?"

"Demolition for both of us. I realize that." Reich's voice began to crack. "Yes, Tate, you're in this with me, and I'm in it straight to the finish . . . all the way to Demolition."

He planned all through Monday, audaciously, bravely, with confidence. He pencilled the outlines as an artist fills a sheet with delicate tracery before the bold inking-in; but he did no final inking. That was to be left for the killer-instinct on Wednesday. He put the plan away and slept Monday night . . . and awoke screaming, dreaming again of The Man With No Face.

Tuesday afternoon, Reich left Monarch Tower early and dropped in at the Century Audio-bookstore on Sheridan Place. It specialized mostly in piezo-electric crystal recordings . . . tiny jewels mounted in elegant settings. The latest vogue was brooch-operas for M'lady. ("She Shall Have Music Wherever She Goes.") Century also had shelves of obsolete printed books.

"I want something special for a friend I've neglected," Reich told the salesman.

He was bombarded with merchandise.

"Not special enough," he complained. "Why don't you

people hire a peeper and save your clients this trouble? How quaint and old-fashioned can you get?" He began sauntering around the shop, tailed by a retinue of anxious clerks.

After he had dissembled sufficiently, and before the worried manager could send out for a peeper salesman, Reich stopped before the bookshelves.

"What's this?" he inquired in surprise.

"Antique books, Mr. Reich." The sales staff began explaining the theory and practice of the archaic visual book while Reich slowly searched for the tattered brown volume that was his goal. He remembered it well. He had glanced through it five years ago and made a note in his little black opportunity book. Old Geoffry Reich wasn't the only Reich who believed in preparedness.

"Interesting. Yes. Fascinating. What's this one?" Reich pulled down the brown volume. " 'Let's Play Party.' What's the date on it? Not really. You mean to say they had parties that long ago?"

The staff assured him that the ancients were very modern in many astonishing ways.

"Look at the contents," Reich chuckled. " 'Honcymoon Bridge' . . . 'Prussian Whist' . . . 'Post Office' . . . 'Sardine.' What in the world could that be? Page ninety-six. Let's have a look."

Reich flipped pages until he came to a bold-face heading: HILARIOUS MIXED PARTY GAMES. "Look at this," he laughed, pretending surprise. He pointed to the well-remembered paragraph.

SARDINE
One player is selected to be It. All the lights are extinguished and the It hides anywhere in the house. After a few minutes, the players go to find the It, hunting separately. The first one who finds him does not reveal the fact but hides with him wherever he may be. Successively each player finding the Sardines joins them until all are hidden in one place and the last player, who is the loser, is left to wander alone in the dark.

"I'll take it," Reich said. "It's exactly what I need."

That evening he spent three hours carefully defacing the remains of the volume. With heat, acid, stain, and scissors, he mutilated the game instructions; and every burn, every cut, every slash, was a blow at D'Courtney's writhing body. When his proxy murders were finished, he had reduced every game to incomplete fragments. Only "Sardine" was left intact.

Reich wrapped the book, addressed it to Graham, the appraiser, and dropped it into the airslot. It went off with a puff

31

and a bang and returned an hour later with Graham's official sealed appraisal. Reich's mutilations had not been detected.

He had the book gift-wrapped with the appraisal enclosed (as was the custom) and slotted it to Maria Beaumont's house. Twenty minutes later came the reply: "Darling! Darling! Darling! I thot you'd forgotten (evidently Maria had written the note herself) little ol sexy me. How 2 divine. Come to Beaumont House tonite. We're having a party. We'll play games from your sweet gift." There was a portrait of Maria centered in the star of a synthetic ruby enclosed in the message capsule. A nude portrait, naturally.

Reich answered: "Devastated. Not tonight. One of my millions is missing."

She answered: "Wednesday, you clever boy. I'll give you one of mine."

He replied: "Delighted to accept. Will bring guest. I kiss all of yours." And went to bed.

And screamed at The Man With No Face.

Wednesday morning, Reich visited Monarch's Science-city ("Paternalism, you know.") and spent a stimulating hour with its bright young men. He discussed their work and their glowing futures if they would only have faith in Monarch. He told the ancient dirty joke about the celibate pioneer who made the emergency landing on the hearse in deep space (and the corpse said: "I'm just one of the tourists!") and the bright young men laughed subserviently, feeling slightly contemptuous of the boss.

This informality enabled Reich to drift into the Restricted Room and pick up one of the visual knock-out capsules. They were cubes of copper, half the size of fulminating caps, but twice as deadly. When they were broken open, they erupted a dazzling blue flare that ionized the Rhodopsin—the visual purple in the retina of the eye—blinding the victim and abolishing his perception of time and space.

Wednesday afternoon, Reich went over to Melody Lane in the heart of the theatrical district and called on Psych-Songs, Inc. It was run by a clever young woman who had written some brilliant jingles for his sales division and some devastating strike-breaking songs for Propaganda back when Monarch needed everything to smash last year's labor fracas. Her name was Duffy Wyg&. To Reich she was the epitome of the modern career girl—the virgin seductress.

"Well, Duffy?" He kissed her casually. She was as shapely as a sales-curve, pretty, but a trifle too young.

"Well, Mr. Reich?" She looked at him oddly. "Some day I'm going to hire one of those Lonely-Heart Peepers to case your kiss. I keep thinking you don't mean business."

"I don't."

"Dog."

"A man has to make up his mind early, Duffy. If he kisses girls he kisses his money goodbye."

"You kiss me."

"Only because you're the image of the lady on the credit."

"Pip," she said.

"Pop," he said.

"Bim," she said.

"Bam," he said.

"I'd like to kill the bem who invented that fad," Duffy said darkly. "All right, handsome. What's your problem?"

"Gambling," Reich said. "Ellery West, my Rec director, is complaining about the gambling in Monarch. Says there's too much. Personally I don't care."

"Keep a man in debt and he's afraid to ask for a raise."

"You're entirely too smart, young lady."

"So you want a no-gamble-type song?"

"Something like that. Catchy. Not too obvious. More a delayed action than a straight propaganda tune. I'd like the conditioning to be more or less unconscious."

Duffy nodded and made quick notes.

"And make it a tune worth hearing. I'll have to listen to God knows how many people singing and whistling and humming it."

"You louse. All my tunes are worth hearing."

"Once."

"That's a thousand extra on your tab."

Reich laughed. "Speaking of monotony . . ." he continued smoothly.

"Which we weren't."

"What's the most persistent tune you ever wrote?"

"Persistent?"

"You know what I mean. Like those advertising jingles you can't get out of your head."

"Oh. Pepsis, we call 'em."

"Why?"

"Dunno. They say because the first one was written centuries ago by a character named Pepsi. I don't buy that. I wrote one once . . ." Duffy winced in recollection. "Hate to think of it even now. Guaranteed to obsess you for a month. It haunted me for a year."

"You're rocketting."

"Scout's honor, Mr. Reich. It was 'Tenser, Said The Tensor.' I wrote it for that flop show about the crazy mathematician. They wanted nuisance value and they sure got it. People got so sore they had to withdraw it. Lost a fortune."

"Let's hear it."

"I couldn't do that to you."

"Come on, Duffy. I'm really curious."

"You'll regret it."

"I don't believe you."

"All right, pig," she said, and pulled the punch panel toward her. "This pays you back for that no-guts kiss."

Her fingers and palm slipped gracefully over the panel. A tune of utter monotony filled the room with agonizing, unforgettable banality. It was the quintessence of every melodic cliche Reich had ever heard. No matter what melody you tried to remember, it invariably led down the path of familiarity to "Tenser, Said The Tensor." Then Duffy began to sing:

> Eight, sir; seven, sir;
> Six, sir; five, sir;
> Four, sir; three, sir;
> Two, sir; one!
> Tenser, said the Tensor.
> Tenser, said the Tensor.
> Tension, apprehension,
> And dissension have begun.

"Oh my God!" Reich exclaimed.

"I've got some real gone tricks in that tune," Duffy said, still playing. "Notice the beat after 'one'? That's a semicadence. Then you get another beat after 'begun.' That turns the end of the song into a semi-cadence, too, so you can't ever end it. The beat keeps you running in circles, like: Tension, apprehension, and dissension have begun. RIFF. Tension, apprehension, and dissension have begun. RIFF. Tension, appre—"

"You little devil!" Reich started to his feet, pounding his palms on his ears. "I'm accursed. How long is this affliction going to last?"

"Not more than a month."

"Tension, apprehension, and diss—I'm ruined. Isn't there any way out?"

"Sure," Duffy said. "It's easy. Just ruin me." She pressed herself against him and planted an earnest young kiss. "Lout," she murmured. "Pig. Boob. Dolt. When are you going to drag me through the gutter? Clever-up, dog. Why aren't you as smart as I think you are?"

"I'm smarter," he said and left.

As Reich had planned, the song established itself firmly in his mind and echoed again and again all the way down to the street. *Tenser, said the Tensor. Tenser, said the Tensor. Tension, apprehension, and dissension have begun. RIFF.* A perfect mind-block for a non-Esper. What peeper could get past that? *Tension, apprehension, and dissension have begun.*

34

"Much smarter," murmured Reich, and flagged a Jumper to Jerry Church's pawnshop on the upper west side.

Tension, apprehension, and dissension have begun.

Despite all rival claims, pawnbroking is still the oldest profession. The business of lending money on portable security is the most ancient of human occupations. It extends from the depths of the past to the uttermost reaches of the future, as unchanging as the pawnbroker's shop itself. You walked into Jerry Church's cellar store, crammed and littered with the debris of time, and you were in a museum of eternity. And even Church himself, wizened, peering, his face blackened and bruised by the internal blows of suffering, embodied the ageless money-lender.

Church shuffled out of the shadows and came face to face with Reich, standing starkly illuminated in a patch of sunlight slanting across the counter. He did not start. He did not acknowledge Reich's identity. Brushing past the man who for ten years had been his mortal enemy, he placed himself behind the counter and said: "Yes, please?"

"Hello, Jerry."

Without looking up, Church extended his hand across the counter. Reich attempted to clasp it. It was snatched away.

"No," Church said with a snarl that was half-hysterical laugh. "Not that, thank you. Just give me what you want to pawn."

It was the peeper's sour little trap, and he had tumbled into it. No matter.

"I haven't anything to pawn, Jerry."

"As poor as that? How the mighty have fallen. But we must expect it, eh? We all fall. We all fall." Church glanced sidelong at him, trying to peep him. Let him try. *Tension, apprehension, and dissension have begun.* Let him get through the crazy tune rattling in his head.

"All of us fall," Church said. "All of us."

"I expect so, Jerry. I haven't yet. I've been lucky."

"I wasn't lucky," the peeper leered. "I met you."

"Jerry," Reich said patiently. "I've never been your bad luck. It was your own luck that ruined you. Not—"

"You God damned bastard," Church said in a horribly soft voice. "You God damned eater of slok. May you rot before you die. Get out of here. I want nothing to do with you. Nothing! Understand?"

"Not even my money?" Reich withdrew ten gleaming sovereigns from his pocket and placed them on the counter. It was a subtle touch. Unlike the credit, the sovereign was the coin of the underworld. *Tension, apprehension, and dissension have begun . . .*

"Least of all your money. I want your heart cut open. I want your blood spilling on the ground. I want the maggots eating the eyes out of your living head . . . But I don't want your money."

"Then what do you want, Jerry?"

"I told you!" the peeper screamed. "I told you! You God damned lousy—"

"What do you want, Jerry?" Reich repeated coldly, keeping his eyes on the wizened man. *Tension, apprehension, and dissension have begun.* He could still control Church. It didn't matter that Church had been a 2nd. Control wasn't a question of peeping. It was a question of personality. *Eight, sir; seven, sir; six, sir; five, sir* . . . He always had . . . He always would control Church.

"What do you want?" Church asked sullenly.

Reich snorted. "You're the peeper. You tell me."

"I don't know," Church muttered after a pause. "I can't read it. There's crazy music mixing everything up . . ."

"Then I'll have to tell you. I want a gun."

"A what?"

"G-U-N. Gun. Ancient weapon. It propels projectiles by explosion."

"I haven't anything like that."

"Yes, you do, Jerry. Keno Quizzard mentioned it to me some time ago. He saw it. Steel and collapsible. Very interesting."

"What do you want it for?"

"Read me, Jerry, and find out. I haven't anything to hide. It's all quite innocent."

Church screwed up his face, then quit in disgust. "Isn't worth the trouble," he mumbled and shuffled off into the shadows. There was a distant slamming of metal drawers. Church returned with a compact nodule of tarnished steel and placed it on the counter alongside the money. He pressed a stud and the lump of metal sprang open into steel knuckle-rings, revolver and stiletto. It was a XXth Century knife-pistol . . . the quintessence of murder.

"What do you want it for?" Church asked again.

"You're hoping it's something that can lead to black-mail, eh?" Reich smiled. "Sorry. It's a gift."

"A dangerous gift." The ostracized peeper gave him that sidelong glance of snarl and laugh. "Ruination for someone else, eh?"

"Not at all, Jerry. It's a gift for a friend of mine. Dr. Augustus Tate."

"Tate!" Church stared at him.

"Do you know him? He collects old things."

"I know him. I know him." Church began to chuckle

36

asthmatically. "But I'm beginning to know him better. I'm beginning to feel sorry for him." He stopped laughing and shot a penetrating glance at Reich. "Of course. This will make a lovely gift for Gus. A perfect gift for Gus. Because it's loaded."

"Oh? Is it loaded?"

"Oh yes indeed. It's loaded. Five lovely cartridges." Church cackled again. "A gift for Gus." He touched a cam. A cylinder snapped out of the side of the gun displaying five chambers filled with brass cartridges. He looked from the cartridges to Reich. "Five serpent's teeth to give to Gus."

"I told you this was innocent," Reich said in a hard voice. "We'll have to pull those teeth."

Church stared at him in astonishment, then he trotted down the aisle and returned with two small tools. Quickly he wrenched each of the bullets from the cartridges. He slid the harmless cartridge cases back into the chambers, snapped the cylinder home and then placed the gun alongside the money.

"All safe," he said brightly. "Safe for dear little Gus." He looked at Reich expectantly. Reich extended both hands. With one he pushed the money toward Church. With the other he drew the gun toward himself. At that instant, Church changed again. The air of chirpy madness left him. He grasped Reich's wrists with iron claws and bent across the counter with blazing intensity.

"No, Ben," he said, using the name for the first time. "That isn't the price. You know it. Despite that crazy song in your head, I know you know it."

"All right, Jerry," Reich said steadily, never relaxing his hold on the gun. "What is the price? How much?"

"I want to be reinstated," the peeper said. "I want to get back into the Guild. I want to be alive again. That's the price."

"What can I do? I'm not a peeper. I don't belong to the Guild."

"You're not helpless, Ben. You've got ways and means. You could get to the Guild. You could have me reinstated."

"Impossible."

"You can bribe, blackmail, intimidate . . . bless, dazzle, fascinate. You can do it, Ben. You can do it for me. Help me, Ben. I helped you, once."

"I paid through the nose for that help."

"And I? What did I pay?" the peeper screamed. "I paid with my life!"

"You paid with your stupidity."

"For God's sake, Ben. Help me. Help me or kill me. I'm dead already. I just haven't the guts to commit suicide."

After a pause, Reich said brutally: "I think the best thing for you, Jerry, would be suicide."

The peeper flung himself back as though he had been branded. In his bruised face his eyes stared glassily at Reich.

"Now tell me the price," Reich said.

Quite deliberately, Church spat on the money, then levelled a glance of burning hatred at Reich. "There will be no charge," he said, and turned and disappeared into the shadows of the cellar.

4

Until it was destroyed for reasons lost in the misty confusion of the late XXth Century, the Pennsylvania Station in New York City was, unknown to millions of travellers, a link in time. The interior of the giant terminal was a replica of the mighty Baths of Caracalla in ancient Rome. So also was the sprawling mansion of Madame Maria Beaumont, known to her thousand most intimate enemies as The Gilt Corpse.

As Ben Reich glided down the east ramp with Dr. Tate at his side and murder in his pocket, he communicated with his senses in staccatto spurts. The sight of the guests on the floor below . . . The glitter of uniforms, of dress, of phosphorescent flesh, of beams of pastel light swaying on stilt legs . . . *Tenser, said the Tensor* . . .

The sound of voices, of music, of annunciators, of echoes . . . *Tension, apprehension, and dissension* . . . The wonderful potpourri of flesh and perfume, of food, of wine, of gilt ostentation . . . *Tension, apprehension* . . .

The gilt trappings of death . . . Of something, by God, which has failed for seventy years . . . A lost art . . . As lost as phlebotomy, chirurgery, alchemy . . . I'll bring death back. Not the hasty, crazy killing of the psychotic, the brawler . . . but the normal, deliberate, planned, cold-blooded—

"For God's sake!" Tate murmured. "Be careful, man. Your murder's showing."

Eight, sir; seven, sir . . .

"That's better. Here comes one of the peeper secretaries. He screens the guests for crashers. Keep singing."

A slender, willowy young man, all gush, all cropped golden hair, all violet blouse and silver culottes: "Dr. Tate! Mr. Reich! I'm speechless. Actually. I can't utter word one. Come in! Come in!"

Six, sir; five, sir . . .

Maria Beaumont clove through the crowd, arms outstretched, eyes outstretched, naked bosom outstretched . . .

38

her body transformed by pneumatic surgery into an exaggerated East Indian figure with puffed hips, puffed calves and puffed gilt breasts. To Reich she was the painted figurehead of a pornographic ship . . . the famous Gilt Corpse.

"Ben, darling creature!" She embraced him with pneumatic intensity, contriving to press his hand into her cleavage. "It's too too wonderful."

"It's too too plastic, Maria," he murmured in her ear.

"Have you found that lost million yet?"

"Just laid hands on it now, dear."

"Be careful, audacious lover. I'm having every morsel of this divine party recorded."

Over her shoulder, Reich shot a glance at Tate. Tate shook his head reassuringly.

"Come and meet everybody who's everybody," Maria said. She took his arm. "We'll have ages for ourselves later."

The lights in the groined vaults overhead changed again and shifted up the spectrum. The costumes changed color. Skin that had glowed with pink nacre now shone with eerie luminescence.

On his left flank, Tate gave the prearranged signal: Danger! Danger! Danger!

Tension, apprehension, and dissension have begun. RIFF. Tension, apprehension, and dissension have begun . . .

Maria was introducing another effete, all gush, all cropped copper hair, all fuchsia blouse and Prussian blue culottes.

"Larry Ferar, Ben. My other social secretary. Larry's been dying to meet you."

Four, sir; three, sir . . .

"Mr. Reich! But too thrilled. I can't utter word one."

Two, sir; one!

The young man accepted Reich's smile and moved on. Still circling in convoy, Tate gave Reich a reassuring nod. Again the overhead lights changed. Portions of the guests' costumes appeared to dissolve. Reich, who had never succumbed to the fashion of wearing ultra-violet windows in his clothes, stood secure in his opaque suit, watching with contempt the quick roving eyes around him, searching, appraising, comparing, desiring.

Tate signalled: Danger! Danger! Danger!

Tenser, said the Tensor . . .

A secretary appeared at Maria's elbow, "Madame," he lisped, "a slight contretemps."

"What is it?"

"The Chervil boy. Galen Chervil."

Tate's face constricted.

"What about him?" Maria peeped through the crowd.

"Left of the fountain. An impostor, Madame. I have

39

peeped him. He has no invitation. He's a college student. He bet he could crash the party. He intends to steal a picture of you as proof."

"Of me!" Maria said, staring through the windows in young Chervil's clothes. "What does he think of me?"

"Well, Madame, he's extremely difficult to probe. I think he'd like to steal more from you than your picture."

"Oh, would he?" Maria cackled delightedly.

"He would, Madame. Shall he be removed?"

"No." Maria glanced once more at the muscular young man, then turned away. "He'll get his proof."

"And it won't be stolen," Reich said.

"Jealous! Jealous!" she squawked. "Let's dine."

In response to Tate's urgent sign, Reich stepped aside momentarily.

"Reich, you've got to give it up."

"What the hell . . . ?"

"The Chervil boy."

"What about him?"

"He's a 2nd."

"God damn!"

"He's precocious, brilliant . . . I met him at Powell's last Sunday. Maria Beaumont never invites peepers to her house. I'm only in on your pass. I was depending on that."

"And this peeper kid has to be the one to crash. God damn!"

"Give it up, Reich."

"Maybe I can stay away from him."

"Reich, I can block the social secretaries. They're only 3rds. But I can't guarantee to handle them and a 2nd too . . . even if he is only a kid. He's young. He may be too nervous to do any clever peeping. But I can't promise."

"I'm not quitting," Reich growled. "I can't. I'll never get a chance like this again. Even if I knew I could, I wouldn't quit. I couldn't. I've got the stink of D'Courtney in my nostrils. I—"

"Reich, you'll never—"

"Don't argue. I'm going through with it." Reich turned his scowl full on Tate's nervous face. "I know you're looking for a chance to squirm out of this; but you won't. We're trapped in this together, right down the line, from here to Demolition."

He shaped his distorted face into a frozen smile and rejoined his hostess on a couch alongside one of the tables. It was still the custom for couples to feed one another at these affairs, but the gesture that had originated in oriental courtesy and generosity had degenerated into erotic play. The morsels of food were accompanied by tongue touched to fingers and were as often offered between the lips. The wine was tasted mouth to mouth. Sweets were given more intimately.

Reich endured it all with a seething impatience, waiting for the vital word from Tate. Part of Tate's Intelligence work was to locate D'Courtney's hiding place in the house. He watched the little peeper drift through the crowd of diners, probing, prying, searching, until he at last returned with a negative shake of his head and gestured toward Maria Beaumont. Clearly Maria was the only source of information, but she was now too excited by sensuality to be easily probed. It was another in a never-ending series of crises that had to be met by the killer-instinct. Reich arose and crossed toward the fountain. Tate intercepted him.

"What are you up to, Reich?"

"Isn't it obvious? I've got to get the Chervil boy off her mind."

"How?"

"Is there any way but one?"

"For God's sake, Reich, don't go near the boy."

"Get out of my way." Reich radiated a burst of savage compulsion that made the peeper recoil. He signaled in fright and Reich tried to control himself. "It's taking chances, I know, but the odds aren't as long as you think. In the first place, he's young and green. In the second place, he's a crasher and scared. In the third place, he can't be flying full jets or he wouldn't have let the fag secretaries peep him so easily."

"Have you got any conscious control? Can you double-think?"

"I've got that song on my mind and enough trouble to make doublethinking a pleasure. Now get the hell out of the way and stand by to peep Maria Beaumont."

Chervil was eating alone alongside the fountain, clumsily attempting to appear to belong.

"Pip," said Reich.

"Pop," said Chervil.

"Bim," said Reich.

"Bam," said Chervil.

With the latest fad in informality disposed of, Reich eased himself down alongside the boy. "I'm Ben Reich."

"I'm Gally Chervil, I mean . . . Galen. I—" He was visibly impressed by the name of Reich.

Tension, apprehension, and dissension . . .

"That damned song," Reich muttered. "Heard it for the first time the other day. Can't get it out of my mind. Maria knows you're a phoney, Chervil."

"Oh no!"

Reich nodded. *Tension, apprehension . . .*

"Should I start running?"

"Without the picture?"

"You know about that too? There must be a peeper in the house."

"Two of them. Her social secretaries. People like you are their job."

"What about that picture, Mr. Rcich? I've got fifty credits riding on the line. You ought to know what a bet means. You're a gamb—I mean, financier."

"Glad I'm not a peeper, eh? Never mind. I'm not insulted. See that arch? Go straight through and turn right. You'll find a study. The walls are lined with Maria's portraits, all in synthetic stones. Help yourself. She'll never miss one."

The boy leaped up, scattering food. "Thanks, Mr. Reich. Some day I'll do you a favor."

"Such as?"

"You'd be surprised. I happen to be a—" He caught himself and blushed. "You'll find out, sir. Thanks again." He began weaving his way across the floor toward the study.

Four, sir; three, sir; two, sir; one!

Reich returned to his hostess.

"Naughty lover," she said. "Who've you been feeding? I'll tear her eyes out."

"The Chervil boy," Reich answered. "He asked me where you keep your pictures."

"Ben! You didn't tell him!"

"Sure did," Reich grinned. "He's on his way to get one now. Then he'll take off. You know I'm jealous."

She leaped from the couch and sailed toward the study.

"Bam," said Reich.

By eleven o'clock, the ritual of dining had aroused the company to a point of intensity that required solitude and darkness for release. Maria Beaumont had never failed her guests, and Reich hoped she would not fail tonight. She had to play the Sardine game. He knew it when Tate returned from the study with concise directions for locating the hidden D'Courtney.

"I don't know how you got away with it," Tate whispered. "You're broadcasting bloodlust on every wavelength of the TP band. He's here. Alone. No servants. Only two bodyguards provided by Maria. @kins was right. He's dangerously sick . . ."

"To hell with that. I'll cure him. Where is he?"

"Go through the west arch. Turn right. Up stairs. Through overpass. Turn right. Picture Gallery. Door between paintings of the Rape of Lucrece and the Rape of the Sabine Women . . ."

"Sounds typical."

"Open the door. Up a flight of steps to an anteroom.

42

Two guards in the anteroom. D'Courtney's inside. It's the old wedding suite her grandfather built."

"By God! I'll use that suite again. I'll marry him to murder. And I'll get away with it, little Gus. Don't think I won't."

The Gilt Corpse began to clamor for attention. Flushed and shining with perspiration, standing in the glare of a pink light on the dais between the two fountains, Maria clapped her hands for silence. Her moist palms beat together, and the echoes roared in Reich's ears: Death. Death. Death.

"Darlings! Darlings! Darlings!" she cried. "We're going to have so much fun tonight. We're going to provide our own entertainment." A subdued groan went up from the guests and a drunken voice shouted: "I'm just one of the tourists."

Through the laughter, Maria said: "Naughty lovers, don't be disappointed. We're going to play a wonderful old game; and we're going to play it in the dark."

The company cheered up as the overhead lights began to dim and disappear. The dais still blazed, and in the light, Maria produced a tattered volume. Reich's gift.

Tension . . .

Maria turned the pages slowly, blinking at the unaccustomed print.

Apprehension . . .

"It's a game," Maria cried, "called 'Sardine.' Isn't that too adorable?"

She took the bait. She's on the hook. In three minutes I'll be invisible. Reich felt his pockets. The gun. The Rhodopsin. Tension, apprehension, and dissension have begun.

"One player," Marie read, "is selected to be It. That's going to be me. All the lights are extinguished and the It hides anywhere in the house." As Maria struggled through the directions, the great hall was reduced to pitch darkness with the exception of the single pink beam on the stage.

"Successively each player finding the Sardine joins them until all are hidden in one place, and the last player, who is the loser, is left to wander alone in the dark." Maria closed the book. "And darlings, we're all going to feel sorry for the loser because we're going to play this funny old game in a darling new way."

As the last light on the dais melted away, Maria stripped off her gown and displayed the astonishing nude body that was a miracle of pneumatic surgery.

"We're going to play Sardine like this!" she cried.

The last light blinked out. There was a roar of exultant laughter and applause, followed by a multiple whisper of cloth drawn across skin. Occasionally there came the sound of a rip, then muttered exclamations and more laughter.

Reich was invisible at last. He had half an hour to slip

up into the house, find and kill D'Courtney, and then return to the game. Tate was committed to pinning the peeper secretaries out of the line of his attack. It was safe. It was foolproof except for the Chervil boy. He had to take that chance.

He crossed the main hall and jostled into bodies at the west arch. He went through the arch into the music room and turned right, groping for the stairs.

At the foot of the stairs he was forced to climb over a barrier of bodies with octopus arms that tried to pull him down. He ascended the stairs, seventeen eternal steps, and felt his way through a close tunnel overpass papered with velour. Suddenly he was seized and a woman crushed herself against him.

"Hello, Sardine," she whispered in his ear. Then her skin became aware of his clothes. "Owww!" she exclaimed, and felt the hard outlines of the gun in his breast pocket. "What's that?" He slapped her hand away. "Clever-up, Sardine," she giggled. "Get out of the can."

He divested himself of her and bruised his nose against the dead-end of the overpass. He turned right, opened a door and found himself in a vaulted gallery over fifty feet long. The lights were extinguished here too, but the luminescent paintings, glowing under ultra-violet spotlights, filled the gallery with a virulent glow. It was empty.

Between a livid Lucrece and a horde of Sabine Women was a flush door of polished bronze. Reich stopped before it, removed the tiny Rhodopsin Ionizer from his back pocket and attempted to poise the copper cube between his thumbnail and forefinger. His hands were trembling violently. Rage and hatred boiled inside him, and his death-lust shot image after image of an agonized D'Courtney through his mind's eye.

"Christ!" he cried. "He'd do it to me. He's tearing at my throat. I'm fighting for survival." He made his orisons in fanatical multiples of three and nine. "Stand by me, dear Christ! Today, tomorrow, and yesterday. Stand by me! Stand by me! Stand by me!"

His fingers steadied. He poised the Rhodopsin cap, then thrust open the bronze door, revealing nine steps mounting to an anteroom. Reich snapped his thumbnail against the copper cube as though he were trying to flip a penny to the moon. As the Rhodopsin cap flew up into the anteroom, Reich averted his eyes. There was a cold purple flash. Reich leaped up the stairs like a tiger. The two Beaumont House guards were seated on the bench where he had caught them. Their faces were sagging, their vision destroyed, their time sense abolished.

If anyone entered and found the guards before he was finished, he was on the road to Demolition. If the guards revived before he was finished, he was on the road to Demo-

44

lition. No matter what happened, it was a final gamble with Demolition. Leaving the last of his sanity behind him, Reich pushed open a jewelled door and entered the wedding suite.

5

Reich found himself in a spherical room designed as the heart of a giant orchid. The walls were curling orchid petals, the floor was a golden calyx; the chairs, tables and couches were orchid and gold. But the room was old. The petals were faded and peeling; the golden tile floor was ancient and the tesselations were splitting. There was an old man lying on the couch, musty and wilted, like a dried weed. It was D'Courtney, stretched out like a corpse.

Reich slammed the door in rage. "You're not dead already, you bastard," he exploded. "You can't be dead."

The faded man started up, stared, then arose painfully from the couch, his face breaking into a smile.

"Still alive," Reich cried exultantly.

D'Courtney stepped toward Reich, smiling, his arms outstretched as though welcoming a prodigal son. Alarmed again, Reich growled: "Are you deaf?"

The old man shook his head.

"You speak English," Reich shouted. "You can hear me. You can't understand me. I'm Reich. Ben Reich of Monarch."

D'Courtney nodded, still smiling. His mouth worked soundlessly. His eyes glistened with sudden tears.

"What the hell is the matter with you? I'm Ben Reich. Ben Reich! Do you know me? Answer me."

D'Courtney shook his head and tapped his throat. His mouth worked again. Rusty sounds came; then words as faint as faint as dust: "Ben . . . Dear Ben . . . Waited so long. Now . . . Can't talk. My throat . . . Can't talk." Again he attempted to embrace Reich.

"Arrgh! Keep off, you crazy idiot." Bristling, Reich stepped around D'Courtney like an animal, his hackles raised, the murder boiling in his blood.

D'Courtney's mouth formed the words: "Dear Ben . . ."

"You know why I'm here. What are you trying to do? Make love to me?" Reich laughed. "You crafty old pimp. Am I supposed to turn soft for your chewing?" His hand lashed out.

The old man reeled back from the slap and fell into an orchid chair that looked like a wound.

"Listen to me—" Reich followed D'Courtney and stood over him. He began to shout incoherently. "This payoff's been on the fire for years. And you want to rob me with a Judas kiss. Does murder turn the other cheek? If it does, embrace me, brother killer. Kiss death! Teach death love. Teach Godliness and shame and blood and—No. Wait. I—" He stopped short and shook his head like a bull trying to cast off a halter of delirium.

"Ben," D'Courtney whispered in horror. "Listen, Ben . . ."

"You've been at my throat for ten years. There was room enough for both of us. Monarch and D'Courtney. All the room in time and space, but you wanted my blood, eh? My heart. My guts in your lousy hands. The Man With No Face!"

D'Courtney shook his head in bewilderment. "No, Ben. No . . ."

"Don't call me Ben. I'm no friend of yours. Last week I gave you one more chance to wash in decency. Me. Ben Reich. I asked for armistice. Begged for peace. Merger. I begged like a screaming woman. My father would spit on me if he were alive. Every fighting Reich would blacken my face with contempt. But I asked for peace, didn't I? Eh? Didn't I?" Reich prodded D'Courtney savagely. "Answer me."

D'Courtney's face was blanched and staring. Finally he whispered: "Yes. You asked . . . I accepted."

"You what?"

"Accepted. Waiting for years. Accepted."

"Accepted!"

D'Courtney nodded. His lips formed the letters: "WWHG."

"What? WWHG? Acceptance?"

The old man nodded again.

Reich shrieked with laughter. "You clumsy old liar. That's refusal. Denial. Rejection. War."

"No, Ben. No . . ."

Reich reached down and yanked D'Courtney to his feet. The old man was frail and light, but his weight bruised Reich's arm, and the touch of the old skin burned Reich's fingers.

"So it's to be war, is it? Death?"

D'Courtney shook his head and tried to make signs.

"No merger. No peace. Death. That's the choice, eh?"

"Ben . . . No."

"Will you surrender?"

"Yes," D'Courtney whispered. "Yes, Ben. Yes."

"Liar. Clumsy old liar." Reich laughed. "But you're dangerous. I can see it. Protective mimicry. That's your trick. You imitate the idiots and trap us at your leisure. But not me. Never."

"I'm not . . . your enemy, Ben."

"No," Reich spat. "You're not because you're dead. You've been dead ever since I came into this orchid coffin. Man With No Face! Can you hear me screaming for the last time? You're finished forever!"

Reich tore the gun out of his breast pocket. He touched the stud and it opened like a red steel flower. A faint groan escaped from D'Courtney when he saw the weapon. He backed away in horror. Reich caught him and held him fast. D'Courtney twisted in Reich's grasp, his face pleading, his eyes glazed and rheumy. Reich transferred his grasp to the back of D'Courtney's thin neck and wrenched the head toward him. He had to fire through the open mouth for the trick to work.

At that instant, one of the orchid petals swung open, and a half-dressed girl burst into the room. In a blaze of surprise, Reich saw the corridor behind her, a bedroom door standing open at the far end; the girl, nude under a frost silk gown hastily thrown on, yellow hair flying, dark eyes wide in alarm . . . A lightning flash of wild beauty.

"Father!" she screamed. "For God's sake! Father!"

She ran toward D'Courtney. Reich swung quickly between them, never relaxing his hold on the old man. The girl stopped short, backed away, then darted to the left around Reich, screaming. Reich pivoted and cut viciously at her with the stiletto. She eluded him but was driven back on the couch. Reich thrust the point of the stiletto between the old man's teeth and forced his jaws open.

"No!" she cried. "No! For the love of Christ! Father!"

She stumbled around the couch and ran toward her father again. Reich thrust the gun muzzle into D'Courtney's mouth and pulled the trigger. There was a muffled explosion and a gout of blood spurted from the back of D'Courtney's head. Reich let the body drop and leaped for the girl. He caught her while she fought and screamed.

Reich and the girl were screaming together. Reich shook with galvanic spasms that forced him to release the girl. The girl fell forward to her knees and crawled to the body. She moaned in pain as she snatched the gun from the mouth where it still hung. Then she crouched over the twitching body, silent, fixed, staring into the waxen face.

Reich gasped for breath and beat his knuckles together painfully. When the roaring in his ears subsided, he propelled himself toward the girl, trying to arrange his thoughts and make split second alterations in his plans. He had never counted on a witness. No one mentioned a daughter. God damn Tate! He would have to kill the girl. He—

She turned and shot a terror-stricken glance over her shoulder. Again that lightning flash of yellow hair, dark eyes, dark brows, wild beauty. She leaped to her feet, darted out of his sodden grasp, ran to the jewelled door, flung it open and ran into the anteroom. As the door slowly closed, Reich had a glimpse of the guards still slumped on the bench and the girl running silently down the stairs with the gun in her hands . . . with Demolition in her hands.

Reich started. The clogged blood began pounding through his veins again. He reached the door in three strides, ran through and tore down the steps to the picture gallery. It was empty but the door to the overpass was just closing. And still no sound from her. Still no alarm. How long before she started screaming the house down?

He raced down the gallery and entered the overpass. It was still pitch dark. He blundered through, reached the head of the stairs that led down to the music room and paused again. Still no sound. No alarm.

He went down the steps. The dark silence was terrifying. Why didn't she scream? Where was she? Reich crossed toward the west arch and knew he was at the edge of the main hall by the quiet splash of the fountains. Where was the girl? In all that black silence, where was she? And the gun! Christ! The tricked gun!

A hand touched his arm. Reich jerked in alarm. Tate whispered: "I've been standing by. It took you exactly—"

"You son of a bitch!" Reich burst out. "There was a daughter. Why didn't you—"

"Be quiet," Tate snapped. "Let me peep it." After fifteen seconds of burning silence, he began to tremble. In a terrified voice he whined: "My God. Oh, my God . . ."

His terror was the catalyst. Reich's control returned. He began thinking again. "Shut up," he growled. "It isn't Demolition yet."

"You'll have to kill her too, Reich. You'll—"

"Shut up. Find her, first. Cover the house. You got her pattern from me. Locate her. I'll be waiting at the fountain. Jet!"

He flung Tate from him and staggered to the fountain. At the jasper rim he bent and bathed his burning face. It was burgundy. Reich wiped his face and ignored the muffled sounds that came from the other side of the basin. Evidently some other person or persons unknown were bathing in wine.

He considered swiftly. The girl must be located and killed. If she still had the gun when Tate found her, the gun would be used. If she didn't? What? Strangle her? No . . . The fountain. She was naked under that silk gown. It could be stripped off. She could be found drowned in the fountain . . .

just another guest who had bathed in wine too long. But it had to be soon . . . soon . . . soon . . . Before this damned Sardine game was ended. Where was Tate? Where was the girl?

Tate came blundering up through the darkness, his breath wheezing.

"Well?"

"She's gone."

"You weren't gone long enough to find a louse. If this is a double-cross—"

"Who could I cross? I'm on the same road you are. I tell you her pattern's nowhere in the house. She's gone."

"Anyone notice her leave?"

"No."

"Christ! Out of the house!"

"We'd better leave too."

"Yes, but we can't run. Once we get out of here, we'll have the rest of the night to find her, but we've got to leave as though nothing's happened. Where's The Gilt Corpse?"

"In the projection room."

"Watching a show?"

"No. Still playing Sardine. They're packed in there like fish in a can. We're almost the last out here in the house."

"Wandering alone in the dark, eh? Come on."

He gripped Tate's shaking elbow and marched him toward the projection room. As he walked he called plaintively: "Hey . . . Where is everybody? Maria! Ma-ri-aaa! Where's everybody?"

Tate emitted a hysterical sob. Reich shook him roughly. "Play up! We'll be out of here in five minutes. Then you can start worrying."

"But if we're trapped in here, we won't be able to get the girl. We'll—"

"We won't be trapped. ABC, Gus. Audacious, brave, and confident." Reich pushed open the door of the projection room. There was darkness in here, too, but the heat of many bodies. "Hey," he called. "Where is everybody? I'm all alone."

No answer.

"Maria. I'm all alone in the dark."

A muffled sputter, then a burst of laughter.

"Darling, darling, darling!" Maria called. "You've missed all the fun, poor dear."

"Where are you, Maria? I've come to say good night."

"Oh, you can't be leaving."

"Sorry, dear. It's late. I've got to swindle a friend tomorrow. Where are you, Maria?"

"Come up on the stage, darling."

Reich walked down the aisle, felt for the steps and mounted the stage. He felt the cool perimeter of the projection globe behind him. A voice called: "All right. Now we've got him. Lights!"

White light flooded the globe and blinded Reich. The guests seated in the chairs around the stage started to whoop with laughter, then howled in disappointment.

"Oh Ben, you cheat," Maria screeched. "You're still dressed. That isn't fair. We've been catching everybody divinely flagrante."

"Some other time, Maria dear." Reich extended his hand before him and began the graceful bow of farewell. "Respectfully, Madame. I give you my thanks for—" He broke off in amazement. On the gleaming white lace of his cuff an angry red spot appeared.

In stunned silence, Reich saw a second, then a third red splotch appear on the lace. He snatched his hand back and a red drop spattered on the stage before him, to be followed by a slow, inexorable stream of gleaming crimson droplets.

"That's blood!" Maria screamed. "That's blood! There's someone upstairs bleeding. For God's sake, Ben . . . You can't leave me now. Lights! Lights! Lights!"

6

At 12:30 A.M., the Emergency Patrol arrived at Beaumont House in response to precinct notification: "GZ. Beaumont. YLP-R" which, translated, meant: "An Act or Omission, forbidden by law has been reported at Beaumont House, 9 Park South."

At 12:40, the Park precinct Captain arrived in response to Patrol report: "Criminal Act possible Felony-AAA."

At 1:00 A.M., Lincoln Powell arrived at Beaumont House in response to a frantic call from a deputy inspector: "I tell you, Powell, it's Felony Triple-A. I'll swear it is. The wind's been knocked out of me. I don't know whether to be grateful or scared; but I know none of us is equipped to handle it."

"What can't you handle?"

"Look here, Powell. Murder's abnormal. Only a distorted TP pattern can produce death by violence. Right?"

"Yes."

"Which is why there hasn't been a successful Triple-A in over seventy years. A man can't walk around with a distorted

50

pattern, maturing murder, and go unnoticed these days. He'd have as much chance of going unnoticed as a man with three heads. You peepers always pick 'em up before they go into action."

"We try to . . . when we contact them."

"And there are too many peeper screens to pass in normal living these days for you to be avoided. A man would have to be a hermit to do that. How can a hermit kill?"

"How indeed?"

"Now here's a killing that must have been carefully planned . . . and the killer was never noticed. Never reported. Even by Maria Beaumont's peeper secretaries. That means there couldn't have been anything to notice. He must have a passable pattern and yet be abnormal enough to murder. How the hell can we resolve a paradox like that?"

"I see. Any prospects?"

"We've got a pay-load of inconsistencies to iron out. One, we don't know what killed D'Courtney. Two, his daughter's disappeared. Three, somebody robbed D'Courtney's guards of one hour and we can't figure how. Four—"

"Don't count any higher. I'll be right over."

The great hall of Beaumont House blazed with harsh white light. Uniformed police were everywhere. The white-smocked technicians from Lab were scurrying like beetles. In the center of the hall, the party guests (dressed) were assembled in a rough corral, milling like a herd of terrified steers at a slaughter house.

As Powell came down the east ramp, tall and slender, black and white, he felt the wave of hostility that greeted him. He reached out quickly to Jackson Beck, police Inspector 2: *"What's the situation Jax?"*

"Scramble."

Switching to their informal police code of scrambled images, reversed meanings and personal symbols, Beck continued: *"Peepers here. Play it safe."* In a micro-second he brought Powell up to date.

"I see. Nasty. What's everybody doing lumped out on the floor? You staging something?"

"The villain-friend act."

"Necessary?"

"It's a rotten crowd. Pampered. Corrupt. They'll never co-operate. You'll have to do some tricky coaxing to get anything out of them; and this case is going to need it. I'll be the villain. You be their friend."

"Right. Good work. Start recording."

Halfway down the ramp, Powell halted. The humor de-

51

parted from his mouth. The friendliness disappeared from his deep dark eyes. An expression of shocked indignation appeared on his face.

"Beck," he snapped. His voice cracked through the echoing hall. There was dead silence. Every eye turned in his direction.

Inspector Beck faced Powell. In a brutal voice, he said: "Here, sir."

"Are you in charge, Beck?"

"I am, sir."

"And is this your concept of the proper conduct of an investigation? To herd a group of innocent people together like cattle?"

"They're not innocent," Beck growled. "A man's been killed."

"All in this house are innocent, Beck. They will be presumed to be innocent and treated with every courtesy until the truth is uncovered."

"What?" Beck sneered. "This gang of liars? Treated with courtesy? This rotten, lousy, high-society pack of hyenas . . ."

"How dare you! Apologize at once."

Beck took a deep breath and clenched his fists angrily.

"Inspector Beck, did you hear me? Apologize to these ladies and gentlemen at once."

Beck glared at Powell, then turned to the staring guests. "My apologies," he mumbled.

"And I'm warning you, Beck," Powell snapped. "If anything like this happens again, I'll break you. I'll send you straight back to the gutter you came from. Now get out of my sight."

Powell descended to the floor of the hall and smiled at the guests. Suddenly he was again transformed. His bearing conveyed the subtle suggestion that he was at heart one of them. There was even a tinge of fashionable corruption in his diction.

"Ladies and gentlemen: Of course I know you all by sight. I'm not that famous so let me introduce myself. Lincoln Powell, Prefect of the Psychotic Division. Prefect and Psychotic. Two antiquated titles, eh? We won't let them bother us." He advanced toward Maria Beaumont with hand outstretched. "Dear Madame Maria, what an exciting climax for your wonderful party. I envy all of you. You'll make history."

A pleased rustle ran through the guests. The lowering hostility began to fade. Maria took Powell's hand dazedly, mechanically beginning to preen herself.

"Madame . . ." He confused and delighted her by kissing her brow with paternal warmth. "You've had a trying time, I know. These boors in uniform."

52

"Dear Prefect . . ." She was a little girl, clinging to his arm. "I've been so terrified."

"Is there a quiet room where we can all be comfortable and endure this exasperating experience?"

"Yes. The study, dear Prefect Powell." She was actually beginning to lisp.

Powell snapped his fingers behind him. To the Captain who stepped forward, he said: "Conduct Madame and her guests to the study. No guards. The ladies and gentlemen are to be left in privacy."

"Mr. Powell, sir . . ." The Captain cleared his throat. "About Madame's guests. One of them arrived after the felony was reported. An attorney, Mr. ¼maine."

Powell found Jo ¼maine, Attorney-At-Law 2, in the crowd. He shot him a telepathic greeting.

"Jo?"

"Hi."

"What brings you to this Blind Tiger?"

"Business. Called by my cli(Ben Reich)ent."

"That shark? Makes me suspicious. Wait here with Reich. We'll get squared off."

"That was an effective act with Beck."

"Hell. You cracked our scramble?"

"Not a chance. But I know you two. Gentle Jax playing a thick cop is one for the books."

Beck broke in from across the hall where he was apparently sulking: *"Don't give it away, Jo."*

"Are you crazy?" It was as though ¼maine had been requested not to smash every sacred ethic of the Guild. He radiated a blast of indignation that made Beck grin.

All this during the second in which Powell again kissed Maria's brow with chaste devotion and gently disengaged himself from her tremulous grasp.

"Ladies and gentlemen: we'll meet again in the study."

The crowd of guests moved off, conducted by the Captain. They were chattering with renewed animation. It was all beginning to take on the aspect of a fabulous new form of entertainment. Through the buzz and the laughter, Powell felt the iron elbows of a rigid telepathic block. He recognized those elbows and permitted his astonishment to show.

"Gus! Gus Tate!"

"Oh. Hello, Powell."

"You? Lurking & Slinking?"

"Gus?" Beck popped out. *"Here? I never tagged him."*

"What the devil are you hiding for?"

Chaotic response of anger, chagrin, fear of lost reputation, self-deprecation, shame—

"Sign off, Gus. Your pattern's trapped in a feed-back.

53

Won't do you any harm to let a little scandal rub off on you. Make you more human. Stay here & help. Got a hunch I can use another 1st. This one is going to be a Triple-A stinker."

After the hall cleared, Powell examined the three men who remained with him. Jo ¼maine was a heavy-set man, thick, solid, with a shining bald head and a friendly blunt-featured face. Little Tate was nervous and twitchy . . . more so than usual.

And the notorious Ben Reich. Powell was meeting him for the first time. Tall, broad-shouldered, determined, exuding a tremendous aura of charm and power. There was kindliness in that power, but it was corroded by the habit of tyranny. Reich's eyes were fine and keen, but his mouth seemed too small and sensitive and looked oddly like a scar. A magnetic man, with something vague inside him that was repellent.

He smiled at Reich. Reich smiled back. Spontaneously, they shook hands.

"Do you take everybody off guard like this, Reich?"

"The secret of my success," Reich grinned. He understood Powell's meaning. They were en rapport.

"Well, don't let the other guests see you charm me. They'll suspect collusion."

"Not you, they won't. You'll swindle them, Powell. You'll make 'em all feel they're in collusion with you."

They smiled again. An unexpected chemotropism was drawing them together. It was dangerous. Powell tried to shake it off. He turned to ¼maine: "Now then, Jo?"

"About the peeping, Linc . . ."

"Keep it up on Reich's level," Powell interrupted. "We're not going to pull any fast ones."

"Reich called me in to represent him. No TP, Linc. This has got to stay on the objective level. I'm here to see that it does. I'll have to be present at every examination."

"You can't stop peeping, Jo. You've got no legal right. We can dig out all we can—"

"Provided it's with the consent of the examinee. I'm here to tell you whether you've got that consent or not."

Powell looked at Reich. "What happened?"

"Don't you know?"

"I'd like your version."

Jo ¼maine snapped: "Why Reich's in particular?"

"I'd like to know why he hollered so quick for a lawyer. Is he mixed up in this mess?"

"I'm mixed up in plenty," Reich grinned. "You don't run Monarch without building a stock-pile of secrets that have got to be protected."

54

"But murder isn't one of them?"

"Get out of there, Lincl"

"Stop throwing blocks, Jo. I'm just peeping around a little because I like the guy."

"Well, like him on your own time . . . not mine."

"Jo doesn't want me to love you," Powell smiled to Reich. "I wish you hadn't called a lawyer. It makes me suspicious."

"Isn't that an occupational disease?" Reich laughed.

"No." Dishonest Abe took over and answered smoothly. "You'd never believe it, but the occupational disease of detectives is Laterality. That's right-handedness or left-handedness. Most detectives suffer from strange changes of Laterality. I was naturally left-handed until the Parsons Case when I—"

Abruptly, Powell choked off his lie. He took two steps away from his fascinated audience and sighed deeply. When he turned back to them, Dishonest Abe was gone.

"I'll tell you about that another time," he said. "Tell me what happened after Maria and the guests saw the blood dripping down on your cuff."

Reich glanced at the bloodstains on his cuff. "She yelled bloody murder and we all went tearing upstairs to the Orchid Suite."

"How could you find your way in the dark?"

"It was light. Maria yelled for lights."

"You didn't have any trouble locating the suite with the light on, eh?"

Reich smiled grimly. "I didn't locate the suite. It was secret. Maria had to lead the way."

"There were guards there . . . knocked out or something?"

"That's right. They looked dead."

"Like stone, eh? They hadn't moved a muscle?"

"How would I know?"

"How indeed?" Powell looked hard at Reich. "What about D'Courtney?"

"He looked dead too. Hell, he was dead."

"And everybody was standing around staring?"

"Some were in the rest of the suite, looking for the daughter."

"That's Barbara D'Courtney. I thought nobody knew D'Courtney and his daughter were in the house. Why look for her?"

"We didn't know. Maria told us and we looked."

"Surprised to find her gone?"

"We were beyond surprise."

"Any idea where she went?"

"Maria said she'd killed the old man and rocketed."

"Would you buy that?"

55

"I don't know. The whole thing was crazy. If the girl was lunatic enough to sneak out of the house without a word and go running naked through the streets, she may have had her father's scalp in her hand."

"Would you permit me to peep you on all this for background and detail?"

"I'm in the hands of my lawyer."

"The answer is no," ¼maine said. "A man's got the constitutional right to refuse Esper Examination without prejudice to himself. Reich is refusing."

"And I'm in one hell of a mess," Powell sighed and shrugged. "Well, let's start the investigation."

They turned and walked toward the study. Across the hall, Beck scrambled into police code and asked: *"Linc, why'd you let Reich make a monkey out of you?"*

"Did he?"

"Sure he did. That shark can stiff you any time."

"Well you better get your knife ready, Jax. This shark is ripe for Demolition."

"What?"

"Didn't you hear the slip when he was busy stiffing me? Reich didn't know there was a daughter. Nobody did. He didn't see her. Nobody did. He could infer that the murder made her run out of the house. Anybody could. But how did he know she was naked?"

There was a moment of stunned silence, and then, as Powell went through the north arch into the study, a broadcast of fervent admiration followed him: *"I bow, Linc. I bow to the Master."*

The "study" of Beaumont House was constructed on the lines of a Turkish Bath. The floor was a mosaic of jacinth, spinel and sunstone. The walls, cross-hatched with gold wire cloisons were glittering with inset synthetic stones . . . ruby, emerald, garnet, chrysolite, amethyst, topaz . . . all containing various portraits of the owner. There were scatter rugs of velvet, and scores of chairs and lounges.

Powell entered the room and walked directly to the center, leaving Reich, Tate, and ¼maine behind him. The buzz of conversation stopped, and Maria Beaumont struggled to her feet. Powell motioned her to remain seated. He looked around him, accurately gauging the mass psyche of the assembled sybarites, and measuring the tactics he would have to use. At length he began.

"The law," he remarked, "makes the silliest damned fuss about death. People die by the thousands every day; but simply because someone has had the energy and enterprise to assist old D'Courtney to his demise, the law insists upon turning him into an enemy of the people. I think it's idiotic, but please don't quote me."

He paused and lit a cigarette. "You all know, of course, that I'm a peeper. Probably this fact has alarmed some of you. You imagine that I'm standing here like some mind-peeping monster, probing your mental plumbing. Well . . . Jo ¼maine wouldn't let me if I could. And frankly, if I could, I wouldn't be standing here. I'd be standing on the throne of the universe practically indistinguishable from God. I notice that none of you have commented on that resemblance so far . . ."

There was a ripple of laughter. Powell smiled disarmingly and continued: "No, mass mind-reading is a trick no peeper can perform. It's difficult enough to probe a single individual. It's impossible when dozens of TP patterns are confusing the picture. And when a group of unique, highly individual people like yourselves is gathered, we find ourselves completely at your mercy."

"And he said I had charm," Reich muttered.

"Tonight," Powell went on, "you were playing a game called 'Sardine.' I wish I had been invited, Madame. You must remember me next time . . ."

"I will," Maria called. "I will, dear Prefect . . ."

"In the course of that game, old D'Courtney was killed. We're almost positive it was premeditated murder. We'll be certain after Lab has finished its work. But let's assume that it is a Triple-A Felony. That will enable us to play another game . . . a game called 'Murder.' "

There was an uncertain response from the guests. Powell continued on the same casual course, carefully turning the most shocking crime in seventy years into a morsel of unreality.

"In the game of 'Murder,' " he said, "A make-believe victim is killed. A make-believe detective must discover who killed the victim. He asks questions of the make-believe suspects. Everyone must tell the truth, except the killer who is permitted to lie. The detective compares stories, deduces who is lying, and uncovers the killer. I thought you might enjoy playing this game."

A voice asked: "How?"

Another called: "I'm just one of the tourists."

More laughter.

"A murder investigation," Powell smiled, "explores three facets of a crime. First, the motive. Second, the method. Third, the opportunity. Our Lab people are taking care of the second two. The first we can discover in our game. And if we do, we'll be able to crack the second two problems that have Lab stumped now. Did you know that they can't figure out what killed D'Courtney? Did you know that D'Courtney's daughter has disappeared? She left the house while you were playing 'Sardine.' Did you know that D'Courtney's guards were mysteriously short-circuited? Yes, indeed. Somebody robbed them of a full hour in time. We'd all like to know just how."

They were hanging at the very edge of the trap, breathless, fascinated. It had to be sprung with infinite caution.

"Death, disappearance, and time-theft . . . we can find out all about them through motive. I'll be the make-believe detective. You'll be the make-believe suspects. You'll tell me the truth . . . all except the killer, of course. We'll expect him to lie. But we'll trap him and bring this party to a triumphant finish if you'll give me permission to make a telepathic examination of each of you."

"Oh!" cried Maria in alarm.

"Wait, Madame. Understand me. All I want is your permission. I won't have to peep. Because, you see, if all the innocent suspects grant permission, then the one who refuses must be the guilty. He alone will be forced to protect himself from peeping."

"Can he pull that?" Reich whispered to ¼maine.

¼maine nodded.

"Just picture the scene for a moment." Powell was building the drama for them, turning the room into a stage. "I ask formally: 'Will you permit me to make a TP examination?' Then I go around this room . . ." He began a slow circuit, bowing to each of the guests in turn. "And the answers come . . . 'Yes . . . Yes . . . Of course . . . Why not? . . . Certainly . . . Yes . . . Yes . . .' And then suddenly a dramatic pause." Powell stopped before Reich, erect, terrifying. " 'You, sir,' I repeat. 'Will you give me your permission to peep?' "

They all watched, hypnotized. Even Reich was aghast, transfixed by the pointing finger and the fierce scowl.

"Hesitation. His face flushes red, then ghastly white as the blood drains out. You hear the tortured refusal: 'No!' . . ." The Prefect turned and enveloped them all with an electrifying gesture: "And in that thrilling moment, we know we have captured the killer!"

He almost had them. Almost. It was daring, novel, exciting; a sudden display of ultra violet windows through clothes and flesh into the soul . . . But Maria's guests had bastardy in their souls . . . perjury . . . adultery—the Devil. And the shame within all of them rose up in terror.

"No!" Maria cried. They all shot to their feet and shouted "No! No! No!"

"It was a beautiful try, Linc, but there's your answer. You'll never get motive out of these hyenas."

Powell was still charming in defeat. "I'm sorry, ladies and

gentlemen, but I really can't blame you. Only a fool would trust a cop." He sighed. "One of my assistants will tape the oral statements from those of you who care to make statements. Mr. ¼maine will be on hand to advise and protect you."

He glanced dolefully at ¼maine: "And louse me."

"Don't pull at my heart-strings like that, Linc. This is the first Triple-A Felony in over seventy years. I've got my career to watch. This can make me."

"I've got my own career to watch, Jo. If my department doesn't crack this, it can break me."

"Then it's every peeper for himself. Here's thinking at you, Linc."

"Hell," Powell said. He winked at Reich and sauntered out of the room.

Lab was finished in the orchid Wedding Suite. De Santis, abrupt, testy, harassed, handed Powell the reports and said in an overwrought voice: "This is a bitch!"

Powell looked down at D'Courtney's body. "Suicide?" he snapped. He was always peppery with De Santis who was comfortable in no other relationship.

"Tcha! Not a chance. No weapon."

"What killed him?"

"We don't know."

"You still don't know? You've had three hours!"

"We don't know," De Santis raged. "That's why it's a bitch."

"Why, he's got a hole in his head you could jet through."

"Yes, yes, yes, of course. Entry above the uvula. Exit below the fontanelle. Death instantaneous. But what produced the wound? What drilled the hole through his skull? Go ahead, ask me."

"Hard Ray?"

"No burn."

"Crystallization?"

"No freeze."

"Nitro vapor charge?"

"No ammonia residue."

"Acid?"

"Too much shattering. Acid spray might needle a wound like that, but it couldn't burst the back of his skull."

"Thrusting weapon?"

"You mean a dirk or a knife?"

"Something like that."

"Impossible. Have you any idea how much force is necessary to penetrate like this? Couldn't be done."

59

"Well . . . I've just about exhausted penetrating weapons. No wait. What about a projectile?"

"How's that?"

"Ancient weapon. They used to shoot bullets with explosives. Noisy and smelly."

"Not a chance here."

"Why?"

"Why?" De Santis spat. "Because there's no projectile. None in the wound. None in the room. Nothing nowhere."

"Damnation!"

"I agree."

"Have you got anything for me? Anything at all?"

"Yes. He was eating candy before his death. Found a fragment of gel in his mouth . . . bit of standard candy wrapping."

"And?"

"No candy in the suite."

"He might have eaten it all."

"No candy in his stomach. Anyway, he wouldn't be eating candy with his throat."

"Why not?"

"Psychogenic cancer. Bad. He couldn't talk, let alone eat gook."

"Hell and damnation. We need that weapon . . . whatever it is."

Powell fingered the sheaf of field reports, staring at the waxen body, whistling a crooked tune. He remembered hearing an audio-book once about an Esper who could read a corpse . . . like that old myth about photographing the retina of a dead eye. He wished it could be done.

"Well," he sighed at last. "They licked us on motive, and they've licked us on method. Let's hope we can get something on opportunity, or we'll never bring Reich down."

"What Reich? Ben Reich? What about him?"

"It's Gus Tate I'm worried about most," Powell murmured. "If he's mixed up in this . . . What? Oh, Reich? He's the killer, De Santis. I slicked Jo ¼maine down in Maria Beaumont's study. Reich made a slip. I staged an act and misdirected Jo while I peeped to make sure. This is off the record, of course, but I got enough to convince me Reich's our man."

"Holy Christ!" De Santis exclaimed.

"But that's a long way from convincing a court. We're a long way from Demolition, brother. A long, long way."

Moodily, Powell took leave of the Lab Chief, loafed through the anteroom and descended to field headquarters in the picture gallery.

"And I like the guy," he muttered.

In the picture gallery outside the Orchid Suite where temporary headquarters had been set up, Powell and Beck met for a conference. Their mental exchange took exactly thirty seconds in the lightning tempo typical of telepathic talk:

Well, it's Reich for Demolition, Jax. We tripped him up in that talk, and I sneaked a peep in Maria's study just to make sure. Ben's our boy.

You'll never prove it, Linc.

Can the guards help?

Not a chance. They've lost one solid hour. De Santis says their retinal rhodopsin was destroyed. That's the visual purple . . . what you see with in your eye. As far as the guards are concerned, they were on duty and alert. Nothing happened until the mob suddenly blew in, and Maria was screeching at them for falling asleep on the job . . . which they emphatically swear they did not.

Uh-huh.

Nothing much!

And how The Gilt Corpse can screech.

But we know it was Reich.

You know it was Reich. Nobody else does.

He went up there while the guests were playing the Sardine game. He destroyed the guards' visual purple some way and robbed them of an hour of time. He went into the Orchid Suite and killed D'Courtney. The girl got mixed up in it; somehow, which is why she ran.

How?

How did he kill D'Courtney?

And last of all: why did he kill D'Courtney?

I don't know. I don't know any of the answers . . . yet.

You'll never get a Demolition that way.

That I do know.

You've got to show motive, method, and opportunity,

Uh-huh.

objectively. All you've got is a peeper's knowledge that Reich killed D'Courtney.

Uh-huh.

Did you peep how or why?.

Couldn't gct in dccp enough . . . not with Jo ¼maine watching me.

And you'll probably never get in. Jo's too careful.

Hell & Damnation! Jackson, we need the girl.

Barbara D'Courtney?

Yes. She's the key. If she can tell us what she saw and why she ran, we'll satisfy a court. Collate everything we've got so far and file it. It won't do us any good without the girl. Let everyone go. They won't do us any good without the girl. We'll have to backtrack on Reich . . . see what collateral evidence we can dig up, but—

I agree.

Right.

I'm beginning to hate her.

But it won't help without that goddam girl.

Times like this, Mr. Beck, I hate women too. For Christ's sake, why are they all trying to get me married?

Image of a horse laughing.

Sar(censored)castic retort.

Sar(censored)donic reply.

(censored)

Having had the last word, Powell got to his feet and left the picture gallery. He crossed the overpass, descended to the music room and entered the main hall. He saw Reich, ¼maine, and Tate standing alongside the fountain, deep in conversation. Once again he fretted over the frightening problem of Tate. If the little peeper really was mixed up with Reich, as Powell had suspected at his party the week before, he might be mixed up in this killing.

The idea of a 1st class Esper, a pillar of the Guild, participating in murder was unthinkable; yet, if actually the fact, a son of a bitch to prove. Nobody ever got anything from a 1st without full consent. And if Tate was (incredible . . . impossible . . . 100-1 against) working with Reich, Reich himself might prove impregnable. Resolving on one last propaganda attack before he was forced to resort to police work, Powell turned toward the group.

He caught their eyes, and directed a quick command to the peepers: "Jo. Gus. Jet off. I want to say something to Reich I don't want you to hear. I won't peep him or record his words. That's a pledge."

¼maine and Tate nodded, muttered to Reich and quietly departed. Reich watched them go with curious eyes and then looked at Powell. "Scare 'em off?" he inquired.

"Warned them off. Sit down, Reich."

They sat on the edge of the basin, looking at each other in a friendly silence.

"No," Powell said after a pause, "I'm not peeping you."

"Didn't think you were. But you did in Maria's study, eh?"

"Felt that?"

"No. Guessed. It's what I would have done."

"Neither of us is very trustworthy, eh?"

"Pfutzl!" Reich said emphatically. "We don't play girl's rules. We play for keeps, both of us. It's the cowards and weaklings and sore-losers who hide behind rules and fair play."

"What about honor and ethics?"

"We've got honor in us, but it's our own code . . . not the make-believe rules some frightened little man wrote for the rest of the frightened little men. Every man's got his own honor and ethics, and so long as he sticks to 'em, who's anybody else to point the finger? You may not like his ethics, but you've no right to call him unethical."

Powell shook his head sadly. "You're two men, Reich. One of them's fine; and the other's rotten. If you were all killer, it wouldn't be so bad. But there's half louse and half saint in you, and that makes it worse."

"I knew it was going to be bad when you winked," Reich grinned. "You're tricky, Powell. You really scare me. I never can tell when the punch is coming or which way to duck."

"Then for God's sake stop ducking and get it over with," Powell said. His voice burned. His eyes burned. Once again he terrified Reich with his intensity. "I'm going to lick you on this one, Ben. I'm going to strangle the lousy killer in you, because I admire the saint. This is the beginning of the end, for you. You know it. Why don't you make it easier for yourself?"

For an instant, Reich wavered on the verge of surrender. Then he mustered himself to meet the attack. "And give up the best fight of my life? No. Never in a million years, Linc. We're going to slug this out straight down to the finish."

63

Powell shrugged angrily. They both arose. Instinctively, their hands met in the four-way clasp of final farewell.

"I lost a great partner in you," Reich said.

"You lost a great man in yourself, Ben."

"Enemies?"

"Enemies."

It was the beginning of Demolition.

7

The Police Prefect of a city of seventeen and one half millions cannot be tied down to a desk. He does not have files, memoranda, notes, and reels of red tape. He has three Esper secretaries, memory wizards all, who carry within their minds the minutiae of his business. They accompany him around headquarters like a triple index. Surrounded by his flying squad (nicknamed Wynken, Blynken, and Nod by the staff) Powell jetted through Center Street, assembling the material for his fight.

To Commissioner Crabbe he laid out the broad outlines once more. "We need motive, method, and opportunity, Commissioner. We've got possible opportunity so far, but that's all. You know Old Man Mose. He's going to insist on hard fact evidence."

"Old Man who?" Crabbe looked startled.

"Old Man Mose," Powell grinned. "That's our nickname for the Mosaic Multiplex Prosecution Computor. You wouldn't want us to use his full name, would you? We'd strangle."

"That confounded adding machine!" Crabbe snorted.

"Yes, sir. Now, I'm ready to go all out on Ben Reich and Monarch to get that evidence for Old Man Mose. I want to ask you a straight question. Are you willing to go all out too?"

Crabbe, who resented and hated all Espers, turned purple and shot up from the ebony chair behind the ebony desk in his ebony-and-silver office. "What the hell is that supposed to mean, Powell?"

"Don't sound for undercurrents, sir. I'm merely asking if you're tied to Reich and Monarch in any way. Will you be embarrassed when the heat's on? Will it be possible for Reich to come to you and get our rockets cooled?"

"No, it will not, damn you."

"Sir:" Wynken shot at Powell. "On December 4th last, Commissioner Crabbe discussed the Monolith Case with you. Extract follows:

POWELL: There's a tricky financial angle to this business, Commissioner. Monarch may hold us up with a Demurrer.

CRABBE: Reich's given me his word he won't; and I can always depend on Ben Reich. He backed me for County Attorney.

End quote."

"Right, Wynk. I thought there was something in Crabbe's file." Powell switched his tactics and glared at Crabbe. "What the devil are you trying to hand me? What about your campaign for County D. A.? Reich backed you for that, didn't he?"

"He did."

"And I'm supposed to believe he hasn't continued supporting you?"

"Damn you, Powell—Yes, you are. He backed me then. He has not supported me since."

"Then I have the beacon on the Reich murder?"

"Why do you insist that Ben Reich killed that man? It's ridiculous. You've got no proof. Your own admission."

Powell continued to glare at Crabbe.

"He didn't kill him. Ben Reich wouldn't kill anybody. He's a fine man who—"

"Do I have your beacon on this murder?"

"All right, Powell. You do."

"But with strong reservations. Make a note, boys. He's scared to death of Reich. Make another note. So am I."

To his staff, Powell said: "Now look—You all know what a cold-blooded monster Old Man Mose is. Always screaming for facts—facts—evidence—unassailable proof. We'll have to produce evidence to convince that damned machine he ought to prosecute. To do that we're going to pull the Rough & Smooth on Reich. You know the method. We'll assign a clumsy operative and a slick one to every subject. The cluck won't know the smoothie is on the job. Neither will the subject. After he's shaken the Rough Tail he'll imagine he's clear. That makes it a cinch for the slicker. And that's what we're going to do to Reich."

"Check," said Beck.

"Go through every department. Pull out a hundred low-grade cops. Put 'em in plainclothes and assign 'em to the Reich case. Go up to Lab and get hold of every crackpot tracer-robot that's been submitted in the last ten years. Put all the gadgets to work on the Reich case. Make this whole package a Rough tail . . . the kind he won't have any trouble shaking, but the kind he'll have to work to shake."

"Any specific areas?" Beck inquired.

"Why were they playing 'Sardine'? Who suggested the game? The Beaumont's secretaries went on record that Reich couldn't be peeped because he had a song kicking around in his skull. What song? Who wrote it? Where'd Reich hear it? Lab says the guards were blasted with some kind of Visual Purple Ionizer. Check all research on that sort of thing. What killed D'Courtney? Let's have lots of weapon research. Back-track on Reich's relations with D'Courtney. We know they were commercial rivals. Were they deadly enemies? Was it a profitable murder? A terrified murder? What and how much does Reich stand to win by D'Courtney's death?"

"Jesus!" Beck exclaimed. "All this Rough? We'll louse the case, Linc."

"Maybe. I don't think so. Reich's a successful man. He's had a string of victories that's made him cocky. I think he'll bite. He'll imagine he's outsmarting us every time he out-maneuvers one of our decoys. Keep him thinking that. We're going to run into some brutal public relations. The news'll tear us apart. But play along with it. Rave. Rant. Make outraged statements. We're all going to be blundering, outwitted cops . . . and while Reich's eating himself fat on that diet—"

"You'll be eating Reich," Beck grinned. "What about the girl?"

"She's the one exception to the Rough Routine. We level with her. I want a description and photo sent to every police officer in the country within one hour. On the bottom of the stat we announce that the man who locates her will automatically be jumped five grades."

"Sir: Regulations forbid elevation of more than three ranks at any time." Thus spake Nod.

"To hell with Regulations," Powell snapped. "Five grades to the man who finds Barbara D'Courtney. I've got to get that girl."

In Monarch Tower, Ben Reich shoved every piezo crystal off his desk into the startled hands of his secretaries.

"Get the hell out of here and take all this slok with you," he growled. "From now on the office coasts without me. Understand? Don't bother me."

"Mr. Reich, we'd understood you were contemplating taking over the D'Courtney interests now that Craye D'Court-ney's dead. If you—"

"I'm taking care of that right now. That's why I don't want to be bothered. Now beat it. Jet!"

He herded the terrified squad toward the door, pushed them out, slammed the door and locked it. He went to the phone, punched BD-12,232 and waited impatiently. After too long a time, the image of Jerry Church appeared against a background of pawnshop debris.

"You?" Church snarled and reached for the cut-off.

"Me. On business. Still interested in reinstatement?"

Church stared. "What about it?"

"You've made yourself a deal. I'm starting action on your reinstatement at once. And I can do it, Jerry. I own the league of Esper Patriots. But I want a lot in return."

"For God's sake, Ben. Anything. Just ask me."

"That's what I want."

"Anything?"

"And everything. Unlimited service. You know the price I'm paying. Are you selling?"

"I'm selling, Ben. Yes."

"And I want Keno Quizzard too."

"You can't want him, Ben. He isn't safe. Nobody gets anything from Quizzard."

"Set up a meeting. Same old place. Same time. This is like it used to be, eh, Jerry? Only this time it's going to have a happy ending."

The usual line was assembled in the anteroom of the Esper Guild Institute when Lincoln Powell entered. The hopeful hundreds, all ages, all sexes, all classes, each dreaming that he had the magic quality that could make life the fulfillment of fantasy, unaware of the heavy responsibility that quality entailed. The naivete of those dreams always made Powell smile. *Read minds and make a killing on the market . . .* (Guild Law forbade speculation or gambling by peepers) *Read minds and know the answers to all exam questions . . .* (That was a schoolboy, unaware that Esper Proctors were hired by Examination Boards to prevent that kind of peeper-cheating) *Read minds and know what people really think of me . . . Read minds and know which girls are willing . . . Read minds and be like a King . . .*

At the desk, the receptionist wearily broadcast on the widest TP band: *If you can hear me, please go through the door on the left marked EMPLOYEES ONLY. If you can hear me, please go through the door on the left marked EMPLOYEES ONLY . . .*

To an assured young socialite with a checkbook in her hand, she was saying: "No, Madame. The Guild does not

67

charge for training and instruction, your offer is worthless. Please go home, Madame. We can do nothing for you."

Deaf to the basic test of the Guild, the woman turned away angrily, to be succeeded by the schoolboy.

If you can hear me, please go through the door on the left . . .

A young Negro suddenly detached himself from the line, glanced uncertainly at the receptionist, and then walked to the door marked EMPLOYEES ONLY. He opened it and entered. Powell was excited. Latent Espers turned up infrequently. He'd been fortunate to arrive at this moment.

He nodded to the receptionist and followed the Latent through the door. Inside, two of the Guild staff were enthusiastically shaking the surprised man's hand and patting him on the back. Powell joined them for a moment and added his congratulations. It was always a happy day for the Guild when they unearthed another Esper.

Powell walked down the corridor toward the president's suite. He passed a kindergarten where thirty children and ten adults were mixing speech and thought in a frightful patternless mish-mash. Their instructor was patiently broadcasting: *"Think, class. Think. Words are not necessary. Think. Remember to break the speech reflex. Repeat the first rule after me . . ."*

And the class chanted: "Eliminate the Larynx."

Powell winced and moved on. The wall opposite the kindergarten was covered by a gold plaque on which was engraved the sacred words of the Esper Pledge:

> I will look upon him who shall have taught me this Art as one of my parents. I will share my substance with him, and I will supply his necessities if he be in need. I will regard his offspring even as my own brethren and I will teach them this Art by precept, by lecture, and by every mode of teaching; and I will teach this Art to all others. The regimen I adopt shall be for the benefit of mankind according to my ability and judgment, and not for hurt or wrong. I will give no deadly thought to any, though it be asked of me.
> Whatsoever mind I enter, there will I go for the benefit of man, refraining from all wrong-doing and corruption. Whatsoever thoughts I see or hear in the mind of man which ought not to be made known, I will keep silence thereon, counting such things to be as sacred secrets.

In the lecture hall, a class of 3rds was earnestly weaving simple basket patterns while they discussed current events. There was one little overdue 2nd, a twelve-year-old, who was adding zig-zag ad libs to the dull discussion and peaking every zig with a spoken word. The words rhymed and were barbed comments on the speakers. It was amusing and amazingly precocious.

Powell found the president's suite in an uproar. All the office doors were open, and clerks and secretaries were scurrying. Old T'sung H'sai, the president, a portly mandarin with shaven skull and benign features, stood in the center of his office and raged. He was so angry he was shouting, and the shock of the articulated words made his staff shake.

"I don't care what the scoundrels call themselves," T'sung H'sai roared. "They're a gang of selfish, self-seeking reactionaries. Talk to me about purity of the race, will they? Talk to me about aristocracy, will they? I'll talk to them. I'll fill their ears. Miss Prinn! Miss Pr-i-nnnn!"

Miss Prinn crept into T'sung's office, horrified at the prospect of oral dictation.

"Take a letter to these devils. To the League of Esper Patriots. Gentlemen. . . . *Good morning, Powell. Haven't seen you in eons . . . How's Dishonest Abe?* The organized campaign of your clique to cut down Guild taxation and appropriations for the education of Espers and the dissemination of Esper training to mankind is conceived in a spirit of treachery and fascism. Paragraph . . ."

T'sung wrenched himself from his diatribe and winked profoundly at Powell. "*And have you found the peeper of your dreams yet?*"

"*Not yet, sir.*"

"Confound you, Powell. Get married!" T'sung bellowed. "I don't want to be stuck with this job forever. Paragraph, Miss Prinn: You speak of the hardships of taxation, of preserving the aristocracy of Espers, of the unsuitability of the average man for Esper training . . . *What do you want, Powell?*"

"*I want to use the grapevine, sir.*"

"*Well don't bother me. Speak to my #2 girl.* Paragraph, Miss Prinn: Why don't you come out into the open? You parasites want Esper powers reserved for an exclusive class so you can turn the rest of the world into a host for your bloodsucking! You leeches want to—"

Powell tactfully closed the door and turned to T'sung's second secretary, who was quaking in a corner.

"*Are you really scared?*"

Image of an eye winking.

Image of a question mark quaking.

"*When Papa T'sung blows his top we like him to think we're petrified. Makes him happier. He hates to be reminded that he's a Santa Claus.*"

"*Well, I'm Santa Claus too. Here's something for your stocking.*" Powell dropped the official police description and

69

portrait of Barbara D'Courtney on the secretary's desk.

"What a beautiful girl!" she exclaimed.

"I want this sent out on the grapevine. Marked urgent. A reward goes with it. Pass the word that the peeper who locates Barbara D'Courtney for me will have his Guild taxes remitted for a year."

"Jeepers!" the secretary sat bolt upright. "Can you do that?"

"I think I'm big enough in Council to swing it."

"This'll make the grapevine jump."

"I want it to jump. I want every peeper to jump. If I want anything for Xmas, I want that girl."

Quizzard's Casino had been cleaned and polished during the afternoon break . . . the only break in a gambler's day. The EO and Roulette tables were brushed, the Birdcage sparkled, the Hazard 'and Bank Crap boards gleamed green and white. In crystal globes, the ivory dice glistened like sugar cubes. On the cashier's desk, sovereigns, the standard coin of gambling and the underworld, were racked in tempting stacks. Ben Reich sat at the billiard table with Jerry Church and Keno Quizzard, the blind croupier. Quizzard was a giant pulp-like man, fat, with flaming red beard, dead white skin, and malevolent dead white eyes.

"Your price," Reich told Church, "you know already. And I'm warning you, Jerry. If you know what's good for you, don't try to peep me. I'm poison. If you get into my head you're getting into Demolition. Think about it."

"Jesus," Quizzard murmured in his sour voice. "As bad as that? I don't hanker for a Demolition, Reich."

"Who does? What do you hanker for, Keno?"

"A question." Quizzard reached back and with sure fingers pulled a rouleau of sovereigns off the desk. He let them cascade from one hand to the other. "Listen to what I hanker for."

"Name the best price you can figure, Keno."

"What's it for?"

"To hell with that. I'm buying unlimited service with expenses paid. You tell me how much I've got to put up to get it—guaranteed."

"That's a lot of service."

"I've got a lot of money."

"You got a hundred Ms laying around?"

"One hundred thousand. Right? That's the price."

"For the love of . . ." Church popped upright and stared at Reich. "A hundred thousand?"

"Make up your mind, Jerry," Reich growled. "Do you want money or reinstatement?"

"It's almost worth—No. Am I crazy? I'll take reinstatement."

"Then stop drooling." Reich turned to Quizzard. "The price is one hundred thousand."

"In sovereigns?"

"What else? Now, d'you want me to put the money up in advance or can we get to work right off?"

"Oh, for Christ's sake, Reich," Quizzard protested.

"Frab that," Reich snapped. "I know you, Keno. You've got an idea you can find out what I want and then shop around for higher bids. I want you committed right now. That's why I let you set the price."

"Yeah," Quizzard said slowly. "I had that idea, Reich." He smiled and the milk-white eyes disappeared in folds of skin. "I still got that idea."

"Then I'll tell you right now who'll buy from you. A man named Lincoln Powell. Trouble is, I don't know what he'd pay."

"Whatever it is, I don't want it," Quizzard spat.

"It's me against Powell, Keno. That's the whole auction. I've placed my bid. I'm still waiting to hear from you."

"It's a deal," Quizzard replied.

"All right," Reich said, "now listen to this. First job. I want a girl. Her name is Barbara D'Courtney."

"The killing?" Quizzard nodded heavily. "I thought so."

"Any objections?"

Quizzard jingled gold from one hand to the other and shook his head.

"I want the girl. She blew out of the Beaumont House last night and no one knows where she landed. I want her, Keno. I want her before the police get her."

Quizzard nodded.

"She's about twenty-five. About five-five. Around a hundred and twenty pounds. Stacked. Thin waist. Long legs . . ."

The fat lips smiled hungrily. The dead white eyes glistened.

"Yellow hair. Black eyes. Heart shaped face. Full mouth and a kind of aquiline nose . . . She's got a face with character. It jabs out at you. Electric."

"Clothes?"

"She was wearing a silk dressing gown last time I saw her. Frosty white and translucent . . . like a frozen window. No shoes. No stockings. No hat. No jewelry. She was off her beam . . . Crazy enough to tear out into the streets and disappear. I want her." Something compelled Reich to add: "I want her undamaged. Understand?"

71

"With her hauling a freight like that? Have a heart, Reich." Quizzard licked his fat lips. "You don't stand a chance. She don't stand a chance."

"That's what a hundred Ms are for. I stand a good chance if you get her fast enough."

"I may have to slush for her."

"Then slush. Check every bawdy house, bagnio, Blind Tiger, and frab-joint in the city. Pass the word down the grapevine. I'm willing to pay. I don't want any fuss. I just want the girl. Understand?"

Quizzard nodded, still jingling the gold. "I understand."

Suddenly Reich reached across the table and slashed Quizzard's fat hands with the edge of his palm. The sovereigns chimed into the air and clattered into the four corners.

"And I don't want any double-cross," Reich growled in a deadly voice. "I want the girl."

8

Seven days of combat.

One week of action and reaction, attack and defense, all fought on the surface while deep below the agitated waters Powell and Augustus Tate swam and circled like silent sharks awaiting the onset of the real war.

A patrol officer, now in plainclothes, believed in the surprise attack. He waylaid Maria Beaumont during a theater intermission, and before her horrified friends bellowed: "It was a frame. You was in cahoots with the killer. You set up the murder. That's why you was playin' that Sardine game. Go ahead and answer me."

The Gilt Corpse squawked and ran. As the Rough Tail set off in hot pursuit, he was peeped deeply and thoroughly.

Tate to Reich: The cop was telling the truth. His department believes Maria was an accomplice.

Reich to Tate: All right. We'll throw her to the wolves. Let the cops have her.

In consequence, Madame Beaumont was left unprotected. She took refuge, of all places, in the Loan Brokerage that was the source of the Beaumont fortune. The patrol officer located her there three hours later and subjected her to a merciless grilling in the office of the peeper Credit Supervisor. He was unaware that Lincoln Powell was just outside the office, chatting with the Supervisor.

72

Powell to staff: She got the game out of some ancient book Reich gave her. Probably purchased at Century. They handle that stuff. Pass the word. Did he ask for it specifically? Also, check Graham, the appraiser. How come the only intact game in the book was 'Sardine'? Old Man Mose'll want to know. And where's that girl?

A traffic officer, now in plainclothes, was going to come through on his Big Chance with the suave approach. To the manager and staff of the Century Audio-bookstore, he drawled: "I'm in the market for old game books . . . The kind my very good friend, Ben Reich, asked for last week."

Tate to Reich: I've been peeping around. They're going to check that book you sent Maria.

Reich to Tate: Let 'em. I'm covered. I've got to concentrate on that girl.

The manager and staff carefully explained matters at great length in response to the Rough Tail's suave questions. Many clients lost patience and left the store. One sat quietly in a corner, too wrapt in a crystal recording to realize he was left unattended. Nobody knew that Jackson Beck was completely tone-deaf.

Powell to staff: Reich apparently found the book accidentally. Stumbled over it while he was looking for a present for Maria Beaumont. Pass the word. And where's that girl?

In conference with the agency that handled copy for the Monarch Jumper ("the only Family Air-Rocket on the market"), Reich came up with a new advertising program.

"Here's the slant," Reich said. "People always anthropomorphize the products they use. They attribute human characteristics to them. They give 'em pet names and treat 'em like family pets. A man would rather buy a Jumper if he can feel affectionate toward it. He doesn't give a damn for efficiency. He wants to love that Jumper."

"Check, Mr. Reich. Check!"

"We're going to anthropomorphize our Jumper," Reich said. "Let's find a girl and vote her the Monarch Jumper Girl. When a consumer buys one, he's buying the girl. When he handles one, he's handling her."

"Check!" the account man cried. "Your idea has a sense of solar scope that dwarfs us, Mr. Reich. This is a wrap-up and blast!"

"Start an immediate campaign to locate the Jumper Girl.

73

Get every salesman onto it. Comb the city. I want the girl to be about twenty-five. About five-five tall; weighing a hundred and twenty pounds. I want her built. Lots of appeal."

"Check, Mr. Reich. Check."

"She ought to be a blonde with dark eyes. Full mouth. Good strong nose. Here's a sketch of my idea of the Jumper Girl. Look it over, have it reproduced and passed out to your crew. There's a promotion for the man who locates the girl I have in mind."

Tate to Reich: I've been peeping the police. They're sending a man into Monarch to dig up collusion between you and that appraiser, Graham.

Reich to Tate: Let 'em. There isn't anything, and Graham's left town on a buying spree. Something between me and Graham! Powell couldn't be that dumb, could he? Maybe I've been overrating him.

Expense was no object to a squadman, now in plainclothes, who believed in the disguises of plastic surgery. Freshly equipped with mongoloid features, he took a job in Monarch Utilities' Accounting-city and attempted to unearth Reich's financial relations with Graham, the appraiser. It never occurred to him that his intent had been peeped by Monarch's Esper Personnel Chief, reported upstairs, and that upstairs was quietly chuckling.

Powell to staff: Our stooge was looking for bribery recorded in Monarch's books. This should lower Reich's opinion of us by fifty per cent; which makes him fifty per cent more vulnerable. Pass the word. Where's that girl?

At the board meeting of "The Hour," the only round-the-clock paper on earth, twenty-four editions a day, Reich announced a new Monarch charity.

"We're calling it 'Sanctuary'," he said. "We offer aid and comfort and sanctuary to the city's submerged millions in their time of crisis. If you've been evicted, bankrupted, terrorized, swindled . . . If you're frightened for any reason and don't know where to turn . . . If you're desperate . . . Take Sanctuary."

"It's a terriffic promotion," the managing editor said, "but it'll cost like crazy. What's it for?"

"Public Relations," Reich snapped. "I want this to hit the next edition. Jet!"

Reich left the board room, went down to the street and located a public phone booth. He called "Recreation" and gave careful instructions to Ellery West. "I want a man placed in every Sanctuary office in the city. I want a full description and photo of every applicant relayed to me at once. At once, Ellery. As they come in."

"I'm not asking any questions, Ben, but I wish I could peep you on that."

"Suspicious?" Reich snarled.

"No. Just curious."

"Don't let it kill you."

As Reich left the booth, a man clothed in an air of inept eagerness accosted him.

"Oh, Mr. Reich. Lucky I bumped into you. I just heard about Sanctuary and I thought a human interest interview with the originator of this wonderful new charity might—"

Lucky he bumped into him! The man was the "Industrial Critic's" famous peeper reporter. Probably tailed him down and—*Tenser, said the Tensor. Tenser, said the Tensor. Tension, apprehension, and dissention have begun.*

"No comment," Reich mumbled. *Eight, sir; seven, sir; six, sir; five, sir . . .*

"What childhood episode in your life brought about the realization of this crying need for—"

Four, sir; three, sir; two, sir; one . . .

"Was there ever a time when you didn't know where to turn? Were you ever afraid of death or murder? Were—"

Tenser, said the Tensor. Tenser, said the Tensor. Tension, apprehension, and dissention have begun.

Reich dove into a Public Jumper and escaped.

Tate to Reich: The cops are really after Graham. They've got their entire Lab looking for the appraiser. God knows what kind of red-herring Powell's following, but it's away from you. I think the safety margin's increasing.

Reich to Tate: Not until I've found that girl.

Marcus Graham had left no forwarding address and was pursued by half a dozen impractical tracer-robots dug up by the police lab. They were accompanied by their impractical inventors to various parts of the solar system. In the meantime, Marcus Graham had arrived on Ganymede where Powell located him at an auction of rare primitive books conducted at breakneck speed by a peeper auctioneer. The books had been part of the Drake estate, inherited by Ben Reich from his mother. They had been unexpectedly dumped on the market.

Powell interviewed Graham in the foyer of the auction room, before a crystal port overlooking the arctic tundra of Ganymede with the belted red-brown bulk of Jupiter filling the black sky. Then Powell took the Fortnighter back to Earth, and Dishonest Abe was inspired by a pretty stewardess to disgrace him. Powell was not a happy man when he arrived at headquarters, and Wynken, Blynken, and Nod did some salacious wynking, blynking and nodding.

> Powell to staff: No hope. I don't know why Reich even bothered to decoy Graham to Ganymede with that sale.

> Beck to Powell: What about the game book?

> Powell to Beck: Reich bought it, had it appraised, and sent it as a gift. It was in bad condition and the only game Maria could select was 'Sardine.' We'll never get Mose to pin anything on Reich with that. I know how that machine's mind works. Damn it! Where's that girl!

Three low-grade operatives in succession were smitten with Miss Duffy Wyg& and retired in disgrace to don their uniforms once more. When Powell finally reached her, she was at the "4,000" Ball. Miss Wyg& was delighted to talk.

> Powell to staff: I called Ellery West down at Monarch and he supports Miss Wyg&'s story. West did complain about gambling and Reich bought a psych-song to stop it. It looks like he picked up that mind-block by accident. What about that gimmick Reich used on the guards? And what about that girl?

In response to bitter criticism and loud laughter, Commissioner Crabbe gave an exclusive press interview in which he revealed that Police Laboratories had discovered a new investigation technique which would break the D'Courtney Case within 24 hours. It involved photographic analysis of the Visual Purple in the corpse's eyes which would reveal a picture of the murderer. Rhodopsin researchers were being requisitioned by the police.

Unwilling to run the risk of having Wilson Jordan, the physiologist who had developed the Rhodopsin Ionizer for Monarch picked up and questioned by the police; Reich phoned Keno Quizzard and devised a ruse to get Dr. Jordan off the planet.

"I've got an estate on Callisto," Reich said. "I'll relinquish title and let a court throw it up for grabs. I'll make sure the cards are stacked for Jordan."

"And I tell Jordan?" Quizzard asked in his sour voice.

"We won't be that obvious, Keno. We can't leave a back-trail. Call Jordan. Make him suspicious. Let him find out the rest for himself."

As a result of that conversation, an anonymous person with a sour voice phoned Wilson Jordan and casually attempted to purchase Dr. Jordan's interest in the Drake estate on Callisto for a small sum. The sour voice sounded suspicious to Dr. Jordan, who had never heard of the Drake estate, and he called a lawyer. He was informed that he had just become the probable legatee to half a million credits. The astonished physiologist jetted for Callisto one hour later.

> Powell to staff: We've flushed Reich's man into the open. Jordan must be our lead on the Rhodopsin angle. He's the only Visual Physiologist to disappear after Crabbe's announcement. Pass the word to Beck to tail him to Callisto and handle it. What about that girl?

Meanwhile, the slick side of operation Rough & Smooth was quietly in progress. While Maria Beaumont was occupying Reich's attention with her squawking flight, a bright young attorney from Monarch's legal department was deftly decoyed to Mars and held there anonymously on a valid, if antiquated, vice charge. An astonishing duplication of that young attorney went to work for him.

> Tate to Reich: Check your legal department. I can't peep what's going on, but something's fishy. This is dangerous.

Reich brought in an Esper 1 Efficiency Expert, ostensibly for a general check-up, and located the substitution. Then he called Keno Quizzard. The blind croupier produced a plaintiff who suddenly appeared and sued the bright young attorney for barratry. That ended the substitute's connection with Monarch painlessly and legitimately.

> Powell to staff: Damn it! We're being licked. Reich's slamming every door in our face . . . Rough & Smooth. Find out who's doing the legwork for him, and find that girl.

While the squadman was cavorting around Monarch Tower with his brand new mongolian face, one of Monarch's scientists who had been badly hurt in a laboratory explosion, apparently left the hospital a week early and reported back for duty. He was heavily bandaged, but eager for work. It was the old Monarch spirit.

> Tate to Reich: I've finally figured it. Powell isn't dumb. He's running his investigation on two levels. Don't pay any attention to the one that shows. Watch out for the one underneath. I've peeped something about a hospital. Check it.

Reich checked. It took three days and then he called Keno Quizzard again. Monarch was promptly burgled of Cr. 50,000 in laboratory platinum and the Restricted Room was destroyed in the process. The newly returned scientist was unmasked as an imposter, accused of complicity in the crime, and handed over to the police.

Powell to staff: Which means we'll never prove Reich got that Rhodopsin stuff from his own lab. How in God's name did he un-slick our trick? Can't we do anything on any level? Where's that girl?

While Reich was laughing at the ludicrous robot search for Marcus Graham, his top brass was greeting the Continental Tax Examiner, an Esper 2, who had arrived for a long delayed check on Monarch Utilities & Resources' books. One of the new additions to the Examiner's squad was a peeper ghost-writer who prepared her chief's reports. She was an expert in official work . . . mainly police work.

Tate to Reich: I'm suspicious of that Examiner's squad. Don't take any chances.

Reich smiled grimly and turned his public books over to the squad. Then he sent Hassop, his Code Chief, to Spaceland on that promised vacation. Hassop obligingly carried a small spool of exposed film with his regular photographic equipment. That spool contained Monarch's secret books, cased in a thermite seal which would destroy all records unless it was properly opened. The only other copy was in Reich's invulnerable safe at home.

Powell to staff: And that just about ends everything. Have Hassop double-tailed; Rough & Smooth. He's probably got vital evidence on him, so Reich's probably got him beautifully protected. Damn it, we're licked. I say it. Old Man Mose would say it. You know it. For Christ's sake! Where is that goddamn missing girl?

Like an anatomical chart of the blood system, colored red for the arteries and blue for the veins, the underworld and overworld spread their networks. From Guild headquarters the word passed to instructors and students, to their families, to their friends, to their friends' friends, to casual acquaintances, to strangers met in business. From Quizzard's Casino the word was passed from croupier to gamblers, to confidence men, to the heavy racketeers, to the light thieves, to hustlers, steerers, and suckers, to the shadowy fringe of the semi-crook and near-honest.

On Friday morning, Fred Deal, Esper 3, awoke, arose, bathed, breakfasted, and departed to his regular job. He was Chief Guard on the floor of the Mars Exchange Bank down on Maiden Lane. Stopping to buy a new commutation ticket at the Pneumatique, he passed the time with an Esper 3, on duty at the Information Desk, who passed Fred the word about Barbara D'Courtney. Fred memorized the TP picture she flashed him. It was a picture framed in credit signs.

On Friday morning, Snim Asj was awakened by his landlady, Chooka Frood, with a loud scream for back rent.

"For chrissakes, Chooka," Snim mumbled. "You already makin' a frabby fortune with 'at loopy yella head girl you pick up. You runnin' a golmine withat spook stuff down-inna basement. Whaddya want from me?"

Chooka Frood pointed out to Snim that: A) The yellow-headed girl was not crazy. She was a genuine medium. B) She (Chooka) did not run rackets. She was a legitimate fortune teller. C) If he (Snim) did not come through with six weeks roof and rolls, she (Chooka) would be able to tell his fortune without any trouble at all. Snim would be out on his asphalt.

Snim arose, and already dressed, descended into the city to pick up a few credits. It was too early to run up to Quizzard's and work the sob on the more prosperous clients. Snim tried to sneak a ride uptown on the Pneumatique. He was thrown out by the peeper change clerk and walked. It was a long haul to Jerry Church's hockshop, but Snim had a gold and pearl pocket-pianino up there and he was hoping to cadge Church into advancing another sovereign on it.

Church was absent on business and the clerk could do nothing for Snim. They passed the time. Snim told the sob to the clerk about his bitch landlady crowning herself every day with the new spook-shill she was using in her palm-racket and still trying to milk him when she was rolling. The clerk would not weep even for the price of coffee. Snim departed.

When Jerry Church returned to the hockshop for a brief time-out in his wild quest for Barbara D'Courtney, the clerk reported Snim's visit and conversation. What the clerk did not report, Church peeped. Nearly fainting, he tottered to the phone and called Reich. Reich could not be located. Church took a deep breath and called Keno Quizzard.

Meanwhile, Snim was growing a little desperate. Out of that desperation arose his crazy decision to work the bank teller graft. Snim trudged downtown to Maiden Lane and cased the banks in that pleasant esplanade around Bomb Inlet. He was not too bright and made the mistake of selecting the Mars Exchange as his battlefield. It looked dowdy and provincial. Snim had not learned that it is only the powerful and efficient institutions that can afford to look second-rate.

Snim entered the bank, crossed the crowded main floor to the row of desks opposite the tellers' cages, and stole a handful of deposit slips and a pen. As Snim left the bank, Fred Deal glanced at him once, then motioned wearily to his staff.

"See that little louse?" He pointed to Snim who was disappearing through the front door. "He's getting ready to pull the 'Adjustment' routine."

"Want us to send him, Fred?"

"What the hell's the use? He'll only try it on someone else. Let him go ahead with it. We'll pick him up after he's got the money and get a conviction. Stash him for keeps. There's plenty of room in Kingston."

Unaware of this, Snim lurked outside the bank, watching the tellers' cages closely. A solid citizen was making a withdrawal at Cage Z. The teller was passing over big chunks of paper cash. This was the fish. Snim hastily removed his jacket, rolled up his sleeves, and tucked the pen in his ear.

As the fish came out of the bank, counting his money, Snim slipped behind him, darted up and tapped the man's shoulder.

"Excuse me, sir," he said briskly. "I'm from Cage Z. I'm afraid our teller made a mistake and short-counted you. Will you come back for the adjustment please?" Snim waved his sheaf of slips, gracefully swept the money from the fish's fins and turned to enter the bank. "Right this way, sir," he called pleasantly. "You have another hundred coming to you."

As the surprised solid citizen followed him, Snim darted busily across the floor, slipped into the crowd and headed for the side exit. He would be out and away before the fish realized he'd been gutted. It was at this moment that a rough hand grasped Snim's neck. He was swung around face to face with a Bank Guard. In one chaotic instant, Snim contemplated fight, flight, bribery, pleas, Kingston Hospital, the bitch Chooka Frood and her yellow-headed ghost girl, his pocket-pianino and the man who owned it. Then he collapsed and wept.

The peeper guard flung him to another uniform and shouted: "Take him, boys. I've just made myself a mint!"

"Is there a reward for this little guy, Fred?"

"Not for him. For what's in his head. I've got to call the Guild."

At nearly the same moment late Friday afternoon, Ben Reich and Lincoln Powell received the identical information: "Girl answering to the description of Barbara D'Courtney can be found in Chooka Frood's Fortune Act, 99 Bastion West Side."

Bastion West Side, famous last bulwark in the Siege of New York, was dedicated as a war memorial. Its ten torn acres were to be maintained in perpetuity as a stinging denunciation of the insantiy that produced the final war. But the final war, as usual, proved to be the next-to-the-final, and Bastion West Side's shattered buildings and gutted alleys were patched into a crazy slum by squatters.

Number 99 was an eviscerated ceramics plant. During the war a succession of blazing explosions had burst among the stock of thousands of chemical glazes, fused them, and splashed them into a wild rainbow reproduction of a lunar crater. Great splotches of magenta, violet, bice green, burnt umber, and chrome yellow were burned into the stone walls. Long streams of orange, crimson, and imperial purple had erupted through windows and doors to streak the streets and surrounding ruins with slashing brush strokes. This became the Rainbow House of Chooka Frood.

The top floors had been patched and subdivided into a warren of cells so complicated and confused that only Chooka understood the pattern of the maze, and even Chooka herself was in doubt at times. A man could drift from cell to cell while the floors were being searched, and easily slip through the meshes of the finest dragnet. This unusual complexity netted Chooka large profits each year.

The lower floors were given over to Chooka's famous Frab Joint, where, for a sufficient sum, a consummate expert graciously MC'd the well-known vices for the hungry and upon occasion invented new vices for the satiated. But the cellar of Chooka Frood's house was the phenomenon that had inspired her most lucrative industry.

The war explosions that had turned the building into a rainbow crater had also fused the ceramic glazes, the metals, glasses, and plastics in the old plant; and a molten conglomerate had oozed down through the floors to settle on the floor of the lowest vault and harden into shimmering pavement, crystal in texture, phosphorescent in color, strangely vibrant and singing.

It was worth the hazardous trip to Bastion West Side. You threaded your way through twisting streets until you reached the streak of jagged orange that pointed to the door of Chooka's Rainbow House. At the door you were met by a solemn person in XXth Century formal costume who asked:

"Frab or Fortune, sir?" If you replied "Fortune" you were conducted to a sepulchral door where you paid a gigantic fee and were handed a phosphor candle. Holding the candle aloft, you walked down a steep stone staircase. At the very bottom it turned sharply and abruptly disclosed a broad, long, arched cellar filled with a lake of singing fire.

You stepped onto the surface of that lake. It was smooth and glassy. Under the surface glowed and flickered a constant play of pastel borealis. At every step the crystal hummed sweet chords, throbbing like the prolonged over-tones of bronze bells. If you sat motionless, the floor still sang, responding to vibrations from distant streets.

Around the rim of the cellar, on stone benches, sat the other fortune-seekers, each holding his phosphor candle. You looked at them, sitting silent and awed, and suddenly you realized that each of them looked saintly, glowing with the aura of the floor; and each of them sounded saintly, their bodies echoing the music of the floor. The candles looked like stars on a frosty night.

You joined the throbbing, burning silence and sat quietly, until at last there came the high chime of a silver bell repeated over and over. The entire floor took up the resonance, and the strange relationship of sight and sound made the colors flare up brilliantly. Then, clothed in a cascade of flaming music, Chooka Frood entered the cellar and paced to the center of the floor.

"And there, of course, the illusion ends," Lincoln Powell said to himself. He stared at Chooka's blunt face; the thick nose, flat eyes, and corroded mouth. The borealis flickered around her features and tightly gowned figure, but it could not disguise the fact that although she had ambition, avarice, and ingenuity, she was utterly devoid of sensitivity and clairvoyance.

"Maybe she can act," Powell muttered hopefully.

Chooka stopped in the middle of the floor, looking much like a vulgar Medusa, then lifted her arms in what was intended for a sweeping mystic gesture.

"She can't," Powell decided.

"I am come here to you," Chooka intoned in a hoarse voice, "to help you look into the deeps of your hearts. Look down into your hearts, you which are looking for . . ." Chooka hesitated, then ran on: "You which are looking for revenge on a man named Zerlen from Mars . . . For the love of a red-eyed woman of Callisto . . . For every credit of that rich old uncle in Paris . . . For . . ."

"Why, damn me! The woman's a peeper!"

Chooka stiffened. Her mouth hung open.

"You're receiving me, aren't you, Chooka Frood?"

The telepathic answer came in frightened fragments. It was obvious that Chooka Frood's natural ability had never been trained. "Wha . . . ? Who? Which is . . . you?"

As carefully as if he were communicating with an infant 3rd, Powell spelled it out: "Name: Lincoln Powell. Occupation: Police Prefect. Intent: To question a girl named Barbara D'Courtney. I have heard she's participating in your act." Powell transmitted a picture of the girl.

It was pathetic the way Chooka tried to block. "Get . . . out. Out. Out of here. Get. Get out. Out . . ."

"Why haven't you come to the Guild? Why aren't you in contact with your own people?"

"Get out. Out of here. Peeper! Get out."

"You're a peeper, too. Why haven't you let us train you? What kind of a life is this for you? Mumbo Jumbo . . . Picking sucker brains and turning it all into a Fortune Act. There's real work waiting for you, Chooka."

"Real money?"

Powell repressed the wave of exasperation that rose up in him. It was not exasperation with Chooka. It was anger for the relentless force of evolution that insisted on endowing man with increased powers without removing the vestigial vices that prevented him from using them.

"We'll talk about that later, Chooka. Where's the girl?"

"No girl. There is no girl."

"Don't be an ass, Chooka. Peep the customers with me. That old goat obsessed with the red-eyed woman . . ." Powell explored him gently. "He's been here before. He's waiting for Barbara D'Courtney to come in. You dress her in sequins. You bring her on in half an hour. He likes her looks. She does some kind of trance routine to music. Her dress is slit open and he likes that. She—"

"He's crazy. I never—"

"And the woman who was loused by a man named Zerlen? She's seen the girl often. She believes in her. She's waiting for her. Where's the girl, Chooka?"

"No!"

"I see. Upstairs. Where, upstairs, Chooka? Don't try to block, I'm deep peeping. You can't mis-direct a 1st—I see. Fourth room on the left of the angle turn. That's a complicated labyrinth you've got up there, Chooka. Let's have it again to make sure . . ."

Helpless and mortified, Chooka suddenly shrieked: "Get out of here, you goddam cop! Get the hell out of here!"

"Excuse it, please," said Powell. "I'm on my way."

He rose and left the room.

83

That entire telepathic investigation took place within the second it took Reich to move from the eighteenth to the twentieth step on his way down to Chooka Frood's rainbow cellar. Reich heard Chooka's furious screech and Powell's reply. He turned and shot up the stairs to the main floor.

As he jostled past the door attendant, he thrust a sovereign into the man's hand and hissed: "I wasn't here. Understand?"

"No one is ever here, Mr. Reich."

He made a quick circuit of the frab rooms. *Tenser, said the Tensor. Tenser, said the Tensor-Tension, apprehension, and dissension have begun.* He brushed past the girls who variously solicited him, then locked himself into the phone booth and punched BD-12,232. Church's anxious face appeared on the screen.

"Well, Ben?"

"We're in a jam. Powell's here."

"Oh my God!"

"Where in hell is Quizzard?"

"He isn't there?"

"I can't locate him."

"But I thought he'd be down in the cellar. He—"

"Powell was in the cellar, peeping Chooka. You can bet Quizzard wasn't there. Where in hell is he?"

"I don't know, Ben. He went down with his wife, and—"

"Look, Jerry. Powell must have found the girl's location. I've got maybe five minutes to beat him to her. Quizzard was supposed to do that for me. He isn't in the cellar. He's nowhere in the Frab Joint. He—"

"He must be upstairs in the coop."

"I was going to figure that for myself. Listen, is there a quick way to get up to the coop? A short-cut I can use to beat Powell to her?"

"If Powell peeped Chooka, he peeped the short-cut."

"God damn it, I know that. But maybe he didn't. Maybe he was concentrating on the girl. It's a chance I'll have to take."

"Behind the main stairs. There's a marble bas-relief. Turn the woman's head to the right. The bodies separate and there's a door to a vertical pneumatique."

"Right."

Reich hung up, left the booth, and darted to the main stairs. He turned to the rear of the marble staircase, found the bas-relief, twisted the woman's head savagely and watched the bodies swing apart. A steel door appeared. A panel of buttons was set in the lintel. Reich punched TOP, yanked the door open and stepped into the open shaft. Instantly a metal plate jolted up against his soles and with a hiss of air pressure he was lofted eight storeys to the top floor. A magnetic catch held the plate while he opened the shaft door and stepped out.

He found himself in a corridor that slanted up at an angle of thirty degrees and leaned to the left. It was floored with canvas. The ceiling glowed at intervals with small flickering globes of radon. The walls were lined with doors, none of them numbered.

"Quizzard!" Reich shouted.

There was no answer.

"Keno Quizzard!"

Still no answer.

Reich ran halfway up the corridor, and then at a venture tried a door. It opened to a narrow cubby entirely filled with an oval bed. Reich tripped over the edge of the bed and fell. He crawled across the foam mattress to a door on the opposite side, thrust it open, and fell through. He found himself on a landing. A flight of steps led down to a round anteroom rimmed with doors. Reich tumbled down the steps and stood, breathing heavily, staring at the circle of doors.

"Quizzard!" he shouted again. "Keno Quizzard!"

There was a muffled reply. Reich spun on his heels, ran to a door and pulled it open. A woman with eyes dyed red by plastic surgery was standing just inside and Reich blundered against her. She burst into unaccountable laughter, raised both fists and beat his face. Blinded and bewildered, Reich backed away from the powerful red-eyed woman, reached for the door, apparently missed it and seized the knob of another, for when he backed out of the room it was not into the circular foyer. His heels caught in three inches of plastic quilting. He tumbled over backwards, slamming the door as he fell, and struck his head a stunning blow against the edge of a porcelain stove.

When his vision cleared he found himself staring up into the angry face of Chooka Frood.

"What the hell are you doing in my room?" Chooka screamed.

Reich shot to his feet. "Where is she?" he said.

"You get to hell out of here, Ben Reich."

"I asked you where is she? Barbara D'Courtney. Where is she?"

Chooka turned her head and yelled: "Magda!"

The red-eyed woman came into the room. She held a neuron scrambler in her hand and she was still laughing; but the gun was trained on his skull and never wavered.

"Get out of here," Chooka repeated.

"I want the girl, Chooka. I want her before Powell gets her. Where is she?"

85

"Get him out of here, Magda!" Chooka screamed.

Reich clubbed the woman across the eyes with the back of his hand. She fell backward, dropping the gun, and twitched in a corner, still laughing. Reich ignored her. He picked up the scrambler and rammed it against Chooka's temple.

"Where's the girl?"

"You go to hell, you—"

Reich pulled the trigger back into first notch. The radiation charged Chooka's nervous system with a low induction current. She stiffened and began to tremble. Her skin glistened with sudden sweat, but she still shook her head. Reich yanked the trigger back to second notch. Chooka's body was thrown into a break-bone ague. Her eyes started. Her throat emitted the brute groans of a tortured animal. Reich held her in it for five seconds, then cut the gun.

"Third notch is death notch," he growled. "The Big D. I don't give a curse, Chooka. It's Demolition for me one way or the other if I don't get that girl. Where is she?"

Chooka was almost completely paralysed. "Through . . . door," she croaked. "Fourth room . . . Left . . . After turn."

Reich dropped her. He ran across the bedroom, through the door, and came to a corkscrewed ramp. He mounted it, took a sharp turn, counted doors and stopped before the fourth on the left. He listened for an instant. No sound. He thrust open the door and entered. There was an empty bed, a single dresser, an empty closet, a single chair.

"Gulled, by God!" he cried. He stepped to the bed. It showed no sign of use. Neither did the closet. As he turned to leave the room, he yanked at the middle dresser drawer and tore it open. It contained a frost white silk gown and a stained steel object that looked like a malignant flower. It was the murder weapon; the knife-pistol.

"My God!" Reich breathed. "Oh my God."

He snatched up the gun and inspected it. Its chambers still contained the emasculated cartridges. The one that had blown the top of Craye D'Courtney's head out was still in place under the hammer.

"It isn't Demolition yet," Reich muttered. "Not by a damned sight. No, by Christ, not by a damned sight!" He folded up the knife-pistol and thrust it into his pocket. At that moment he heard the sound of distant laughter . . . a sour laugh. Quizzard's laugh.

Reich stepped quickly to the twisted ramp and followed the sound of the laughter to a plush door hung open on brass hinges and deep set in the wall. Gripping the scrambler at the alert with the trigger set for Big D, Reich stepped through the door. There was a hiss of compressed air and it closed behind him.

He was in a small round room, walled and ceilinged in midnight velvet. The floor was transparent crystal, and gave a clear uninterrupted view of a boudoir on the floor below. It was Chooka's Voyeur Chamber.

In the boudoir, Quizzard sat in a deep chair, his blind eyes glazing. The D'Courtney girl was perched on his lap wearing an astonishing slit gown of sequins. She sat quietly, her yellow hair smooth, her deep dark eyes staring placidly into space, while Quizzard fondled her brutally.

"How does she look?" Quizzard's sour voice came distinctly. "How does she feel?"

He was speaking to a small faded woman who stood across the boudoir from him with her back against the wall and an incredible expression of agony on her face. It was Quizzard's wife.

"How does she look?" the blind man repeated.

"She doesn't know what's happening," the woman answered.

"She knows," Quizzard shouted. "She isn't that far gone. Don't tell me she don't know what's happening. Christ! If I only had my eyes!"

The woman said: "I'm your eyes, Keno."

"Then look for me. Tell me!"

Reich cursed and aimed the scrambler at Quizzard's head. It could kill through the crystal floor. It could kill through anything. It was going to kill now. Then Powell entered the boudoir.

The woman saw him at once. She emitted a blood-curdling scream: "Run, Keno! Run!" She thrust herself from the wall and darted toward Powell, her hands clawing at his eyes. Then she tripped and fell prone. Apparently, the fall knocked her unconscious for she never moved. As Quizzard surged up from the chair with the girl in his arms, his blind eyes staring, Reich came to the appalled conclusion that the woman's fall was no accident; for Quizzard suddenly dropped in his tracks. The girl tumbled out of his arms and fell into the chair.

There was no doubt that Powell had accomplished this on a TP level, and for the first time in their war, Reich was afraid of Powell . . . physically afraid. Again he aimed the scrambler, this time at Powell's head as the peeper walked to the chair.

Powell said: "Good evening, Miss D'Courtney."

Reich muttered: "Goodbye, Mr. Powell," and tried to hold his trembling hand steady on Powell's skull.

87

Powell said: "Are you all right, Miss D'Courtney?" When the girl failed to answer, he bent down and stared into her blank, placid face. He touched her arm and repeated: "Are you all right, Miss D'Courtney? Miss D'Courtney! Do you need help?"

At the word "help" the girl whipped upright in the chair in a listening attitude. Then she thrust out her legs and leaped from the chair. She ran past Powell in a straight line, stopped abruptly and reached out as though grasping a door-knob. She turned the knob, thrust an imaginary door open and burst forward, yellow hair flying, dark eyes wide with alarm . . . A lightning flash of wild beauty.

"Father!" she screamed. "For God's sake! Father!"

She ran forward, then stopped short and backed away as though eluding someone. She darted to the left and ran in a half circle, screaming wildly, her eyes fixed.

"No!" she cried. "No! For the love of Christ! Father!"

She ran again, then stopped and struggled with imaginary arms that held her. She fought and screamed, her eyes still fixed, then stiffened and clapped her hands to her ears as though a violent sound had pierced them. She fell forward to her knees and crawled across the floor, moaning in pain. Then she stopped, snatched at something on the floor, and remained crouched on her knees, her face once again placid, doll-like and dead.

With sickening certainty, Reich knew what the girl had just done. She had relived the death of her father. She had relived it for Powell. And if he had peeped her . . .

Powell went to the girl and raised her from the floor. She arose as gracefully as a dancer, as serenely as a somnambulist. The peeper put his arm around her and took her to the door. Reich followed him all the way with the muzzle of the scrambler, waiting for the best shooting angle. He was invisible. His unsuspecting enemies were below him, easy targets for the death-notch. He could win safety with a shot. Powell opened the door, then suddenly swung the girl around, held her close to him and looked up. Reich caught his breath.

"Go ahead," Powell called. "Here we are. An easy shot. One for the both of us. Go ahead!" His lean face was suffused with anger. The heavy jet brows scowled over the dark eyes. For half a minute he stared up at the invisble Reich, waiting, hating, daring. At last Reich lowered his eyes and turned his face away from the man who could not see him.

Then Powell took the docile girl through the door and closed it quietly behind him, and Reich knew he had permitted safety to slip through his fingers. He was halfway to Demolition.

10

Conceive of a camera with a lens distorted into wild astigmatism so that it can only photograph the same picture over and over—the scene that twisted it into shock. Conceive of a bit of recording crystal, traumatically warped so that it can only reproduce the same fragment of music over and over, the one terrifying phrase it cannot forget.

"She's in a state of Hysterical Recall," Dr. Jeems of Kingston Hospital explained to Powell and Mary Noyes in the living room of Powell's house. "She responds to the key word 'help' and relives one terrifying experience . . ."

"The death of her father," Powell said.

"Oh? I see. Outside of that . . . Catatonia."

"Permanent?" Mary Noyes asked.

Young Doctor Jeems looked surprised and indignant. He was one of the brighter young men of Kingston Hospital despite the fact that he was not a peeper, and was fanatically devoted to his work. "In this day and age? Nothing is permanent except physical death, Miss Noyes, and up at Kingston we've started working on that. Investigating death from the symptomatic point of view, we've actually—"

"Later, Doctor," Powell interrupted. "No lectures to-night. We've got work. Can I use the girl?"

"Use her how?"

"Peep her."

Jeems considered. "No reason why not. I gave her the Déjà Éprouvé Series for catatonia. That shouldn't get in the way."

"The Déjà Éprouvé Series?" Mary asked.

"A great new treatment," Jeems said excitedly. "Developed by Gart . . . one of your peepers. Patient goes into catatonia. It's an escape. Flight from reality. The conscious mind cannot face the conflict between the external world and its own unconscious. It wishes it had never been born. It attempts to revert back to the foetal stage. You understand?"

Mary nodded. "So far."

"All right. Déjà Éprouvé is an old XIXth Century psychiatric term. Literally, it means: 'something already experienced, already tried.' Many patients wish for something so strongly that finally the wish makes them imagine that the act or the experience in which they never engaged has already happened. Get it?"

"Wait a minute," Mary began slowly. "You mean I—"

"Put it this way," Jeems interrupted briskly. "Pretend you had a burning wish to . . . oh, say, to be married to Powell here and have a family. Right?"

Mary flushed. In a rigid voice she said: "Right." For a moment Powell yearned to blast this well-meaning clumsy young normal.

"Well," Jeems continued in blithe ignorance. "If you lost your balance you might come to believe that you'd married Powell and had three children. That would be Déjà Éprouvé. Now what we do is synthesize an artificial Déjà Éprouvé for the patient. We make the catatonic wish to escape come true. We make the experience they desire actually happen. We dissociate the mind from the lower levels, send it back to the womb, and let it pretend it's being born to a new life all over again. Got that?"

"Got it." Mary tried to smile as her control returned.

"On the surface of the mind . . . in the conscious level . . . the patient goes through development all over again at an accelerated rate. Infancy, childhood, adolescence, and finally maturity."

"You mean Barbara D'Courtney is going to be a baby . . . learn to speak . . . walk . . . ?"

"Right. Right. Right. Takes about three weeks. By the time she catches up with herself, she'll be ready to accept the reality she's trying to escape. She'll have grown up to it, so to speak. Like I said, this is only on the conscious level. Below that, she won't be touched. You can peep her all you like. Only trouble is . . . she must be pretty scared down there. Mixed up. You'll have trouble getting what you want. Of course, that's your specialty. You'll know what to do."

Jeems stood up abruptly. "Got to get back to the shop." He made for the front door. "Delighted to be of service. Always delighted to be called in by peepers. I can't understand the recent hostility toward you people . . ." He was gone.

"Ummm. That was a significant parting note."

"What'd he mean, Linc?"

"Our great & good friend, Ben Reich. Reich's been backing an Anti-Esper campaign. You know . . . peepers are clannish, can't be trusted, never become patriots, Interplanetary conspirators, eat little Normal babies, &c."

"Ugh! And he's supporting the League of Patriots too. He's a disgusting, dangerous man."

"Dangerous but not disgusting, Mary. He's got charm. That's what makes him doubly dangerous. People always expect villains to look villainous. Well, maybe we can take care of Reich before it's too late. Bring Barbara down, Mary."

Mary brought the girl downstairs and seated her on the low dais. Barbara sat like a calm statue. Mary had dressed her

90

in blue leotards and combed her blonde hair back, tying it into a fox-tail with blue ribbon. Barbara was polished and shining; a lovely wax-work doll.

"Lovely outside; mangled inside. Damn Reich!"

"What about him?"

"I told you, Mary. I was so mad at Chooka Frood's coop, I handed it to that red slug Quizzard and his wife . . . And when I peeped Reich upstairs, I threw it in his teeth. I—"

"What did you do to Quizzard?"

"Basic Neuro-Shock. Come up to the Lab sometime and we'll show you. It's new. If you make 1st we'll teach you. It's like the scrambler but psychogenie."

"Fatal?"

"Forgotten the Pledge? Of course not."

"And you peeped Reich through the floor? How?"

"TP reflection. The Voyeur Chamber wasn't wired for sound. It had open acoustical ducts. Reich's mistake. He was transmitting down the channel and I swear I was hoping he had the guts to shoot. I was going to blast him with a Basic that would have made Case History."

"Why didn't he shoot?"

"I don't know, Mary. I don't know. He thought he had every reason to kill us. He thought he was safe . . . Didn't know about the Basic, even though Quizzard's Decline & Fall jolted him . . . But he couldn't."

"Afraid?"

"Reich's no coward. He wasn't afraid. He just couldn't. I don't know why. Maybe next time it'll be different. That's why I'm keeping Barbara D'Courtney in my house. She'll be safe here."

"She'll be safe in Kingston Hospital."

"But not quiet enough for the work I've go to do."

"?"

"She's got the detailed picture of the murder locked up in her hysteria. I've got to get at it . . . piece by piece. When I've got it, I've got Reich."

Mary arose. "Exit Mary Noyes."

"Sit down, peeper! Why d'you think I called you? You're staying here with the girl. She can't be left alone. You two can have my bedroom. I'll convert the study for myself."

"Choke it, Linc. Don't jet off like that. You're embarrassed. Let's see if I can't maybe thread-needle through that mind block."

"Listen—"

"No you don't, Mr. Powell." Mary burst into laughter. "So that's it. You want me for a chaperone. Victorian word, isn't? So are you, Linc. Positively atavistic."

91

"I brand that as a lie. In toffy circles I'm known as the most progressive—"

"And what's that image? Oh. Knights of the Round Table. Sir Galahad Powell. And there's something underneath that. I—" Suddenly she stopped laughing and turned pale.

"What'd you dig?"

"Forget it."

"Oh, come on, Mary."

"Forget it, Linc. And don't peep me for it. If you can't reach it yourself, you'd better not get it second-hand. Especially from me."

He looked at her curiously for a moment, then shrugged. "All right, Mary. Then we'd better go to work."

To Barbara D'Courtney he said: "Help, Barbara."

Instantly she whipped upright on the dais in a listening attitude, and he probed delicately . . . Sensation of bedclothes . . . Voice calling dimly . . . Whose voice, Barbara? Deep in the preconscious she answered: "Who is that?" A friend, Barbara. "There's no one. No one. I'm alone." And she was alone, racing down a corridor to thrust a door open and burst into an orchid room to see—"What, Barbara?" "A man. Two men." Who? "Go away. Please go away. I don't like voices. There's a voice screaming. Screaming in my ears . . ." And she was screaming while instincts of terror made her dodge from a dim figure that clutched at her to keep her from her father. She turned and circled . . . What is your father doing, Barbara? "He—No. You don't belong here. There's only the three of us. Father and me and—" And the dim figure caught her. A flash of his face. No more. Look again, Barbara. Sleek head. Wide eyes. Small chiselled nose. Small sensitive mouth. Like a scar. Is that the man? Look at the picture. Is that the man? "Yes. Yes. Yes." And then all was gone.

And she was kneeling again, placid, doll-like, dead.

Powell wiped perspiration from his face and took the girl back to the dais. He was badly shaken . . . worse than Barbara D'Courtney. Hysteria cushioned the emotional impact for her. He had nothing. He was reliving her terror, her horror, her torture, naked and unprotected.

"It was Ben Reich, Mary. Did you get the picture, too?"

"Couldn't stay in long enough, Linc. Had to run for cover."

"It was Reich, all right. Only question is, how in hell did he kill her father? What did he use? Why didn't old D'Courtney put up a fight to defend himself? Have to try again. I hate to do this to her . . ."

"I hate you to do this to yourself."

92

"*Have to.*" He took a deep breath and said: "Help, Barbara."

Again she whipped upright on the dais in a listening attitude. He slipped in quickly. *Gently, dear. Not so fast. There's plenty of time.* "You again?" *Remember me, Barbara?* "No, No, I don't know you. Get out." *But I'm part of you, Barbara. We're running down the corridor together. See? We're opening the door together. It's so much easier, together. We help each other.* "We?" *Yes, Barbara, you and I.* "But why don't you help me now?" *How can I, Barbara?* "Look at father! Help me stop him. Stop him. Stop him. Help me scream. Help me! For pity's sake, help me!"

She knelt again, placid, doll-like, dead.

Powell felt a hand under his arm and realized he was not supposed to be kneeling too. The body before him slowly disappeared; the orchid room disappeared, and Mary Noyes was straining to raise him.

"You first this time," she said grimly.

He shook his head and tried to help Barbara D'Courtney. He fell to the floor.

"*All right, Sir Galahad. Cool a while.*"

Mary raised the girl and led her to the dais. Then she returned to Powell. "*Ready for help now, or don't you think it's manly?*"

"*The word is virile. Don't waste your time trying to help me up. I need brain power. We're in trouble.*"

"*What'd you peep?*"

"*D'Courtney wanted to be murdered.*"

"*No!*"

"*Yep. He wanted to die. For all I know he may have committed suicide in front of Reich. Barbara's recall is confused. That point's got to be cleared up. I'll have to see D'Courtney's physician.*"

"*That's Sam @kins. He and Sally went back to Venus last week.*"

"*Then I'll have to make the trip. Do I have time to catch the ten o'clock rocket? Call Idlewild.*"

Sam @kins, E.M.D. 1, received Cr. 1,000 per hour of analysis. The public knew that Sam earned two million credits per year, but it did not know that Sam was efficiently killing himself with charity work. @kins was one of the burning lights of the Guild long-range education plan, and leader of the Environment Clique which believed that telepathic ability was not a congenital characteristic, but rather a latent quality of every living organism which could be developed by suitable training.

As a result, Sam's desert house in the brilliant arid Mesa outside Venusburg was overrun by charity cases. He invited everyone in the low income brackets to trek their problems out to him, and while he was solving them, he was carefully attempting to foster telepathy in his patients. Sam's reasoning was quite simple. If, say, peeping were a question of developing unused muscles, it might well be that the majority of people had been too lazy or lacked opportunity to do so. But when a man is caught up in the press of a crisis, he can not afford to be lazy; and Sam was there to offer opportunity and training. So far, his results had been the discovery of 2% Latent Espers, which was under the average of the Guild Institute interviews. Sam remained undiscouraged.

Powell found him charging through the rock garden of his desert home vigorously destroying desert flowers under the impression that he was cultivating, and conducting simultaneous conversations with a score of depressed people who followed him about like puppies. The perpetual clouds of Venus radiated dazzling light. Sam's bald head was burned pink. He was snorting and shouting at plants and patients alike.

"Damn it! Don't you tell me that's a Glow-wart. It's a weed. Don't I know a weed when I see it? Hand me the rake, Bernard."

A small man in black handed him the rake and said: "My name is Walter, Dr. @kins."

"And that's your whole trouble," @kins grunted, tearing out a clump of rubbery red. It changed colors in prismatic hysteria and emitted a plaintive wail which proved it was neither weed nor Glow-wort but the disconcerting Pussy-Willow of Venus.

@kins eyed it with disfavor, watching the collapsing air-bladders cry. Then he glared at the small man. "Semantic escape, Bernard. You live in terms of the label, not the object. It's your escape from reality. What are you running away from, Bernard?"

"I was hoping you'd tell me, Dr. @kins," Walter replied.

Powell stood quietly, enjoying the spectacle. It was like an illustration from a primitive Bible. Sam, an ill-tempered Messiah, glowering at his humble disciples. Around them the glittering silica stones of the rock-garden, crawling with the dry motley-colored Venus plants. Overhead, the blinding nacre glow; and in the background, as far as the eye could reach, the red, purple, and violet Bad-Lands of the planet.

@kins snorted at Walter/Bernard: "You remind me of the redhead. Where is that make-believe courtesan anyway?"

A pretty red-headed girl jostled through the crowd and smirked: "Here I am, Dr. @kins."

"Well, don't preen yourself, because I labelled you."
@kins frowned at her and continued on the TP level:
"You're delighted with yourself because you're a woman, aren't
you? It's your substitute for living. It's your phantasy. 'I'm a
woman,' you tell yourself. 'Therefore, men desire me. It's
enough to know that thousands of men could have me if I'd
let them. That makes me real.' Nonsense! You can't escape
that way. Sex isn't make-believe. Life isn't make-believe. Vir-
ginity isn't an apotheosis."

@kins waited impatiently for a response, but the girl
merely smirked and postured before him. Finally he burst out:
"Didn't any of you hear what I told her?"

"I did, teacher."

"Lincoln Powell! No! What are you doing here?
Where'd you sneak up from?"

"From Terra, Sam. Came for a consultation and can't
stay long. Got to jet back on the next rocket."

"Couldn't you phone Interplanetary?"

"It's complicated, Sam. Has to be done peeper-wise. It's
the D'Courtney case."

"Oh. Ah. Hm. Right. Be with you in a minute. Go get
something to drink." @kins let out a warning blast. "SALLY.
COMPANY."

One of @kins' flock unaccountably flinched and Sam
turned on the man excitedly. "You heard that, didn't you?"

"No sir. I didn't hear nothing."

"Yes you did. You picked up a TP broadcast."

"No, Dr. @kins."

"Then why did you jump?"

"A bug bit me."

"It did not," @kins roared. "There are no bugs in my
garden. You heard me yell to my wife." And then he began a
frightful racket. "YOU CAN ALL HEAR ME. DON'T SAY
YOU CAN'T. DON'T YOU WANT TO BE HELPED?
ANSWER ME. GO AHEAD. ANSWER ME!"

Powell found Sally @kins in the cool, spacious living
room of the house. The ceiling was open to the sky. It never
rained on Venus. A plastic dome was enough to provide shade
from the sky that blazed through the seven hundred hour-
long Venus day. And when the seven hundred hour night began its deadly chill, the @kinses simply packed up and returned to their heated city-unit in Venusburg. Everyone on
Venus lived in thirty-day cycles.

Sam came bouncing into the living room and engulfed
a quart of ice-water. "Ten credits down the drain, black market," he shot at Powell. "You know that? We've got a water
black market on Venus. And what the devil are the police do-

ing about it? Never mind, Linc. I know it's out of your juris-
diction. What's with D'Courtney?"

Powell presented the problem. Barbara D'Courtney's
hysterical recall of the death of her father was susceptible of
two interpretations. Either Reich had killed D'Courtney, or
merely been a witness to D'Courtney's suicide. Old Man Mose
would insist on that being cleared up.

"I see. The answer is yes. D'Courtney was suicidal."

"Suicidal? How?"

"He was crumbling. His adaptation pattern was shattering. He was regressing under emotional exhaustion and
on the verge of self-destruction. That's why I rushed over to
Terra to cut him off."

"Hmmm. That's a blow, Sam. Then he could have blown
the back of his head out, eh?"

"What? Blown the back of his head out?"

"Yes. Here's the picture. We don't know what the
weapon was, but—"

"Wait a minute. Now I can give you something definite. If D'Courtney died that way he certainly did not commit suicide."

"Why not?"

"Because he had a poison fixation. He was set on killing himself with narcotics. You know suicides, Linc. Once
they've fixed on a particular form of death, they never change
it. D'Courtney must have been murdered."

"Now we're jetting places, Sam. Tell me, why was
D'Courtney set on suicide by poison?"

"You supposed to be funny? If I knew, he wouldn't have
been. I'm not too happy about all this, Powell. Reich turned
my case into a failure. I could have saved D'Courtney. I—"

"You made any guesses why D'Courtney's pattern was
crumbling?"

"Yes. He was trying to take drastic action to escape deep
guilt sensations."

"Guilt about what?"

"His child."

"Barbara? How? Why?"

"I don't know. He was fighting irrational symbols of
abandonment . . . desertion . . . shame . . . loathing . . .
cowardice. We were going to work on that. That's all I know."

"Could Reich have figured and counted on all this?
That's something Old Man Mose is going to fuss about. When
we present him the case."

"Reich might have guessed—No. Impossible. He'd need
expert help to—"

"Hold it, Sam. You've got something hidden under that.
I'd like to get it if I can . . ."

"Go ahead. I'm wide open."

"Don't try to help me. You're just mixing everything. Easy, now . . . association with festivity . . . party . . . conversation at—my party. Last month. Gus Tate, an expert himself, but needing help on a similar patient of his own, he said. If Tate needed help, you reasoned, Reich certainly would need help." Powell was so upset he spoke aloud. "Well how about that peeper!"

"How about what?"

"Gus Tate was at the Beaumont party the night D'Courtney was killed. He came with Reich, but I kept hoping—"

"Linc, I don't believe it!"

"Neither did I, but there it is. Little Gus Tate was Reich's expert. Little Gus laid it out for him. He pumped you and turned his information over to a killer. Good old Gus. What price the Esper Pledge now?"

"What price Demolition!" @kins answered fiercely.

From somewhere inside the house came an announcement from Sally @kins: "Linc. Phone."

"Hell! Mary's the only one who knows I'm here. Hope nothing's happened to the D'Courtney girl."

Powell loped down a hall toward the v-phone alcove. In the distance he saw Beck's face on the screen. His lieutenant saw him at the same moment and waved excitedly. He began talking before Powell was within earshot.

" . . . gave me your number. Lucky I caught you, boss. We've got twenty-six hours."

"Wait a minute. Take it from the top, Jax."

"Your Rhodopsin man, Dr. Wilson Jordan, is back from Callisto. Now a man of property by courtesy of Ben Reich. I came back with him. He's on earth for twenty-six hours to settle his affairs, and then he rockets back to Callisto to live on his brand new estate forever. If you want anything from him, you'd better come quick."

"Will Jordan talk?"

"Would I call you Interplanetary if he would? No, boss. He's got money-measles. Also he's grateful to Reich who (I am now quoting) generously stepped out of the legal picture in favor of Dr. Jordan and justice. If you want anything, you'd better come back to Terra and get it yourself."

"And this," Powell said, "is our Guild Laboratory, Dr. Jordan."

Jordan was impressed. The entire top floor of the Guild building was devoted to laboratory research. It was a circular floor, almost a thousand feet in diameter, domed with a double layer of controlled quartz that could give graded illumination from full to total darkness including monochrome light to within one tenth of an angstrom. Now, at noon, the sunlight was modulated slightly so that it flooded the tables and benches, the crystal and silver apparatus, the cover-all'd workers with a gentle peach radiance.

"Shall we stroll?" Powell suggested pleasantly.

"I haven't much time, Mr. Powell, but . . ." Jordan hesitated.

"Of course not. Very kind of you to give us an hour, but we need you desperately."

"If it's anything to do with D'Courtney," Jordan began.

"Who? Oh yes. The murder. Whatever put that into your mind?"

"I've been hounded," Jordan said grimly.

"I assure you, Dr. Jordan. We're asking for research guidance, not information on a murder case. What's murder to a scientist? We're not interested."

Jordan unfolded a little. "Very true. You have only to look at this laboratory to realize that."

"Shall we tour?" Powell took Jordan's arm. To the entire laboratory he broadcast: *Stand by, peepers! We're pulling a fast one.*

Without interrupting their work, the lab technicians responded with loud razzberries. And amid a hail of derisory images came the raucous cry of a backbiter: *Who stole the weather, Powell?* This apparently referred to an obscure episode in Dishonest Abe's lurid career which no one had ever succeeded in peeping, but which never failed to make Powell blush. It did not fail now. A silent cackle filled the room.

No. This is serious, peepers. My whole case hangs on something I've got to coax out of this man.

Instantly the silent cackle was stilled.

This is Dr. Wilson Jordan, Powell announced. *He specializes in visual physiology and he's got information I want him to volunteer. Let's make him feel paternal. Please fake obscure visual problems and beg for help. Make him talk.*

They came by ones, by twos, in droves. A red-headed researcher, actually working on a problem of a transistor which would record the TP impulse, hastily invented the fact that TP optical transmission was astigmatic and humbly requested enlightenment. A pair of pretty girls, engrossed in the infuriating dead-end of long range telepathic communication, demanded of Dr. Jordan why transmission of visual images always showed color aberration, which it did not. The Japanese team, experts on the extra sensory Node, center of TP perceptivity, insisted that the Node was in circuit with the Optic

Nerve (it wasn't within two millimeters of same) and besieged Dr. Jordan with polite hissings and specious proofs.

At 1:00 P.M., Powell said: "I'm sorry to interrupt, Doctor, but your hour is finished and you've got important business to—"

"Quite all right. Quite all right," Jordan interrupted. "Now my dear doctor, if you would try a transection of the optic—" &c.

At 1:30 P.M. Powell gave the time-signal again. "It's half past one, Dr. Jordan. You jet at five. I really think—"

"Plenty of time. Plenty of time. Women and rockets, you know. There's always another. The fact is, my dear sir, your admirable work contains one significant flaw. You have never checked the living Node with a vital dye. Ehrlich Röt, perhaps, or Gentian Violet. I would suggest . . ." &c.

At 2:00 P.M. a buffet luncheon was served without interrupting the feast of reason.

At 2:30 P.M., Dr. Jordan, flushed and ecstatic, confessed that he loathed the idea of being rich on Callisto. No scientists there. No meetings of the minds. Nothing on the level of this extraordinary seminar.

At 3:00 P.M., he confided to Powell how he had inherited his foul estate. Seemed that Craye D'Courtney originally owned it. The old Reich (Ben's father) must have swindled it one way or another, and placed it in his wife's name. When she died, it went to her son. That thief Ben Reich must have had conscience qualms for he threw it into open court, and by some legal hokey-pokey Wilson Jordan came up with it.

"And he must have plenty more on his conscience," Jordan said. "The things I saw when I worked for him! But all financiers are crooks. Don't you agree?"

"I don't think that's true of Ben Reich," Powell replied, striking the noble note. "I rather admire him."

"Of course. Of course," Jordan agreed hastily. "After all, he does have a conscience. That's admirable indeed. I wouldn't want him to think that I—"

"Naturally." Powell became a fellow-conspirator and captivated Jordan with a grin. "As fellow scientists we can deplore; but as men of the world we can only praise."

"You do understand." Jordan shook Powell's hand effusively.

And at 4:00 P.M., Dr. Jordan informed the genuflecting Japanese that he would gladly volunteer his most secret work on Visual Purple to these fine youngsters to aid them in their own research. He was handing on the torch to the next generation. His eyes moistened and his throat choked with sentiment as he spent twenty minutes carefully describing the Rhodopsin Ionizer he had developed for Monarch.

At 5:00 P.M., the Guild scientists escorted Dr. Jordan by launch to his Callisto Rocket. They filled his stateroom with gifts and flowers; they filled his ears with grateful testimonials, and he accelerated toward Jupiter's IVth Satellite with the pleasant knowledge that he had materially benefited science and never betrayed that fine and generous patron, Mr. Benjamin Reich.

Barbara was in the living room on all-fours, crawling energetically. She had just been fed and her face was eggy.

"Hajajajajaja," she said. "Haja."

"Mary! Come quick! She's talking!"

"No!" Mary ran in from the kitchen. "What'd she say?"

"She called me Dada."

"Haja." said Barbara. "Hajajajahajaja."

Mary blasted him with scorn. "She said nothing of the kind. She said Haja." She returned to the kitchen.

"She meant Dada. Is it her fault if she's too young to articulate?" Powell knelt alongside Barbara. "Say Dada, baby. Dada? Dada? Say Dada."

"Haja." Barbara replied with an enchanting drool.

Powell gave it up. He went down past the conscious level to the preconscious.

Hello, Barbara.

"You again?"

Remember me?

"I don't know."

Sure you do. I'm the guy who pries into your private little turmoil down here. We fight it out together.

"Just the two of us?"

Just the two of us. Do you know who you are? Would you like to know why you're buried way down here in this solitary existence?

"I don't know. Tell me."

Well, dear infant, once upon a time you were like this before . . . an entity merely existing. Then you were born. You had a mother and a father. You grew up into a lovely girl with blonde hair and dark eyes and a sweet graceful figure. You traveled from Mars to earth with your father and you were—

"No. There's no one but you. Just the two of us together in the darkness."

There was your father, Barbara.

"There was no one. There is no one else."

I'm sorry dear. I'm really sorry, but we must go through the agony again. There's something I have to see.

100

"No. No. . . . please. It's just the two of us alone to-gether. Please, dear spook . . ."

It'll be just the two of us together, Barbara. Stay close, dear. There was your father in the other room . . . the orchid room . . . and suddenly we heard something . . . Powell took a deep breath and cried: "Help. Barbara. Help!"

And they whipped upright in a listening attitude. Sensation of bedclothes. Cool floor under running feet and the endless corridor until at last they burst through the door into the orchid room and screamed and dodged the startled grasp of Ben Reich while he raised something to father's mouth. Raised what? Hold that image. Photograph it. Christ! That horrible muffled explosion. The back of the head burst out and the loved, the adored, the worshipped figure crumpling unbelievably, tearing at their hearts while they moaned and crawled across the floor to snatch a malignant steel flower from the waxen—

"Get up, Linc! For heaven's sake!"

Powell found himself dragged to his feet by Mary Noyes. The air was crackling with indignation.

"Can't I leave you alone for a minute? Idiot!"

"Have I been kneeling here long, Mary?"

"At least a half hour. I came in and found you two like this . . ."

"I got what I was after. It was a gun, Mary. An ancient explosive weapon. Clear picture. Take a look . . ."

"Mmmmm. That's a gun?"

"Yes."

"Where'd Reich get it? Museum?"

"I don't think so. I'm going to play a long shot. Kill two birds. Leave me at the phone . . ."

Powell lurched to the phone and dialed BD-12,232. Presently, Church's twisted face appeared on the screen.

"Hi, Jerry."

"Hello . . . Powell." Cautious. Guarded.

"Did Gus Tate buy a gun from you, Jerry?"

"Gun?"

"Explosive weapon. XXth Century style. Used in the D'Courtney murder."

"No!"

"Yes indeed. I think Gus Tate is our killer, Jerry. I was wondering if he bought the gun from you. I'd like to bring the picture of the gun over and check with you." Powell hesitated and then stressed the next words gently: "It'd be a big help, Jerry, and I'll be extremely appreciative. Extremely. Wait for me. I'll be up in half an hour."

Powell hung up. He looked at Mary. Image of an eye

winking. "That ought to give little Gus time to hustle over to Church's place."

"Why Gus? I thought Ben Reich was—" She caught the picture Powell had sketched in at @kins' house. "Oh. I see. It's a trap for both Tate and Church. Church sold the gun to Reich."

"Maybe. It's a long-shot. But he does run a hockshop, and that's next door to a museum."

"And Tate helped Reich use the gun on D'Courtney? I don't believe it."

"Almost a certainty, Mary."

"So you're playing one against the other."

"And both against Reich. We've failed on the Objective Level all the way down the line. From here on in it's got to be peeper tricks or I'm through."

"But suppose you can't play them against Reich? What if they call Reich in?"

"They can't. We lured Reich out of town. Scared Keno Quizzard into running for his life, and Reich's out somewhere trying to cut him off and gag him."

"You really are a thief, Linc. I bet you did steal the weather."

"No," he said. "Dishonest Abe did." He blushed, kissed Mary, kissed Barbara D'Courtney, blushed again and left the house in confusion.

11

The pawnshop was in darkness. A single lamp burned on the counter, sending out its sphere of soft light. As the three men spoke, they leaned in and out of the illumination, their faces and gesticulating hands suddenly appearing and disappearing in staccato eclipses.

"No," Powell said sharply. "I didn't come here to peep anybody. I'm sticking to straight talk. You two peepers may consider it an insult to have words addressed to you. I consider it evidence of good faith. While I'm talking, I'm not peeping."

"Not necessarily," Tate answered. His gnome face popped into the light. "You've been known to finesse, Powell."

"Not now. Check me. What I want from you two, I want objectively. I'm working on a murder. Peeping isn't going to do me any good."

"What do you want, Powell?" Church cut in.

"You sold a gun to Gus Tate."

"The hell he did." Tate said.

"Then why are you here?"

"Am I supposed to take an outlandish accusation like that lying down?"

"Church called you because he sold you the gun and he knows how it was used."

Church's face appeared. "I sold no gun, peeper, and I don't know how any gun was used. That's my objective evidence. Eat it."

"Oh, I'll eat it," Powell chuckled. "I know you didn't sell the gun to Gus. You sold it to Ben Reich."

Tate's face came back into the light. "Then why'd you—"

"Why?" Powell stared into Tate's eyes. "To get you here for a talk, Gus. Let it wait a minute. I want to finish with Jerry." He turned toward Church. "You had the gun, Jerry. It's the kind of thing you would have. Reich came here for it. It's the only place he could come. You did business together before. I haven't forgotten the Chaos Swindle . . ."

"God damn you!" Church shouted.

"It swindled you out of the Guild," Powell continued. "You risked and lost everything for Reich . . . just because he asked you to peep and squeal on four members of the Stock Exchange. He made a million out of that swindle . . . just by asking a dumb peeper for a favor."

"He paid for that favor!" Church cried.

"And now all I'm asking for is the gun," Powell answered quietly.

"Are you offering to pay?"

"You know me better than that, Jerry. I threw you out of the Guild because I'm mealy-mouthed Preacher Powell, didn't I? Would I make a shady offer?"

"Then what are you paying for the gun?"

"Nothing, Jerry. You'll have to trust me to do the fair thing; but I'm making no promises."

"I've got a promise," Church muttered.

"You do? Ben Reich, probably. He's long on promise. Sometimes he's short on delivery. You'll have to make up your mind. Trust me or trust Ben Reich. What about the gun?"

Church's face disappeared from the light. After a pause, he spoke from the darkness. "I sold no gun, peeper, and I don't know how any gun was used. That's my objective evidence for the court."

"Thanks, Jerry." Powell smiled, shrugged, and turned again to Tate. "I just want to ask you one question, Gus. Skipping over the fact that you're Ben Reich's accessory . . . that you pumped Sam @kins about D'Courtney and got the orbits set for him . . . Skipping over the fact that you went to the Beaumont party with Reich, ran interference for him and've been running interference ever since—"

103

"*Wait a minute, Powell—*"

"Don't get panicky, Gus. All I want to know is whether I've guessed Reich's bribe correctly. He couldn't bribe you with money. You make too much. He couldn't bribe you with position. You're one of the top peepers in the Guild. He must have bribed you with power, eh? Is that it?"

Tate was peeping him hysterically, and the calm assurance he found in Powell's mind; the casual acceptance of Tate's ruin as an accomplished fact jolted the little peeper with a series of shocks too sudden for adjustment. And he was communicating his panic to Church. All this Powell had planned in preparation for one crucial moment that was to come later.

"Reich could offer you power in his world," Powell continued conversationally, "but it isn't likely. He wouldn't give up any of his own, and you wouldn't want any of his kind. So he must have offered you power in the Esper world. How could he do that? Well, he finances the League of Esper Patriots. My guess is he offered you power through the League . . . A coup d'état, maybe? A dictatorship in the Guild? Probably you're a member of the League."

"*Listen, Powell . . .*"

"That's my guess, Gus." Powell's voice hardened. "And I've got a hunch I can make my guess good. Did you imagine we'd let you and Reich smash the Guild as easily as that?"

"*You'll never prove anything. You'll—*"

"Prove? What?"

"*Your word against mine. I—*"

"You little fool. Haven't you ever been at a peeper trial? We don't run 'em like a court of law, where you swear and then I swear and then a jury tries to figure who's lying. No, little Gus. You stand up there before the board and all the 1sts start probing. You're a 1st, Gus. Maybe you could block two . . . Possibly three . . . But not all. I tell you, you're dead."

"*Wait a minute, Powell. Wait!*" The mannequin face was twitching with terror. "*The Guild takes confession into account. Confession before the fact. I'll give you everything right now. Everything. It was an aberration. I'm sane now. Tell the Guild. When you get mixed up with a damned psychotic like Reich, you fall into his pattern. You identify yourself with it. But I'm out of it. Tell the Guild. Here's the whole picture . . . He came to me with a nightmare about a Man With No Face. He—*"

"He was a patient?"

"*Yes. That's how he trapped me. He dragooned me! But I'm out of it now. Tell the Guild I'm cooperating. I've recanted. I'm volunteering everything. Church is your witness . . .*"

"I'm not witness," Church shouted. "You dirty squealer. After Ben Reich promised—"

"Shut up. You think I want permanent exile? Like you? You were crazy enough to trust Reich. Not me, thank you. I'm not that crazy."

"You whining yellow peeper. Do you think you'll get off? Do you think you'll—"

"I don't give a damn!" Tate cried. "I don't take that kind of medicine for Reich. I'll bust him first. I'll walk into court and sit on the witness stand and do everything I can to help Powell. Tell that to the Guild, Linc. Tell them that—"

"You'll do nothing of the kind," Powell snapped.

"What?"

"You were trained by the Guild. You're still in the Guild. Since when does a peeper squeal on a patient?"

"It's the evidence you need to get Reich, isn't it?"

"Sure, but I'm not taking it from you. I'm not letting any peeper disgrace the rest of us by walking into court and blabbing."

"It could mean your job if you don't get him."

"To hell with my job. I want it, and I want Reich . . . but not at this price. Any peeper can be a right pilot when the orbit's easy; but it takes guts to hold to the Pledge when the heat's on. You ought to know. You didn't have the guts. Look at you now . . ."

"But I want to help you, Powell."

"You can't help me. Not at the price of ethics."

"But I was an accessory!" Tate shouted. "You're letting me off. Is that ethics? Is that—?"

"Look at him," Powell laughed. "He's begging for Demolition. No, Gus. We'll get you when we get Reich. But I can't get him through you. I'll play this according to the Pledge." He turned and left the circle of light. As he walked through the darkness toward the front door, he waited for Church to take the bait. He had played the entire scene for this moment alone . . . but so far there was no action on his hook.

As Powell opened the door, flooding the pawnshop with the cold argent street light, Church suddenly called: "Just a minute."

Powell stopped, silhouetted against the door. "Yes?"

"What have you been handing Tate?"

"The Pledge, Jerry. You ought to remember it."

"Let me peep you on that."

"Go ahead. I'm wide open." Most of Powell's blocks opened. What was not good for Church to discover was carefully jumbled and camouflaged with tangentional associations

105

and a kaleidoscopic pattern, but Church certainly could not locate a suspicious block.

"I don't know," Church said at last. "I can't make up my mind."

"About what, Jerry? I'm not peeping you."

"About you and Reich and the gun. God knows, you're a mealy-mouthed preacher, but I think maybe I'd be smarter to trust you."

"That's nice, Jerry. I told you, I can't make any promises."

"Maybe you're the kind that doesn't have to make promises. Maybe the whole trouble with me is that I've always been looking for promises instead of—"

At that moment, Powell's restless radar picked up death out on the street. He whirled and slammed the door. "*Get off the floor. Quick.*" He took three steps back toward the globe of light and vaulted onto the counter. "*Up here with me. Jerry, Gus. Quick, you fools!*"

A queasy shuddering seized the pawnshop and shook it into horrible vibration. Powell kicked the light globe and extinguished it.

"*Jump for the ceiling light bracket and hold on. It's a Harmonic gun. Jump!*" Church gasped and leaped up into the darkness. Powell gripped Tate's shaking arm. "*Too short, Gus? Hold out your hands. I'll toss you.*" He flung Tate upward and followed himself, clawing for the steel spider arms of the bracket. The three hung in space, cushioned against the murderous vibrations enveloping the store . . . vibrations that created shattering harmonics in every substance in contact with the floor. Glass, steel, stone, plastic . . . all screeched and burst apart. They could hear the floor cracking, and the ceiling thundered. Tate groaned.

"*Hang on, Gus. It's one of Quizzard's killers. Careless bunch. They've missed me before.*"

Tate blacked out. Powell could sense every conscious synapse losing hold. He probed for Tate's lower levels: "*Hang on. Hang on. Hang on. HOLD. HOLD. HOLD!*"

Destruction loomed up in the little peeper's subconscious and in that instant Powell realized that no Guild conditioning could ever have prevented Tate from destroying himself. The death compulsion struck. Tate's hands relaxed and he dropped to the floor. The vibrations ceased an instant later, but in that second Powell heard the thick, gravid choke of bursting flesh. Church heard it too and started to scream.

"*Quiet, Jerry! Not yet. Hang on!*"

"*D-did you hear him? DID YOU HEAR HIM?*"

"*I heard. We're not safe yet. Hang on!*"

The pawnshop door opened a slit. A razor edge of light

shot in and searched the floor. It found a broad red and gray organic puddle of flesh, blood, and bones, hovered for three seconds, then blinked out. The door closed.

"All right, Jerry. They think I'm dead again. You can have your hysterics now."

"I can't get down, Powell. I can't step on . . ."

"I don't blame you." Powell held himself with one hand, took Church's arm and swung him toward the counter. Church dropped and shuddered. Powell followed him and fought hard against nausea.

"Did you say that was one of Quizzard's killers?"

"Sure. He owns a squad of psychgoons. Every time we round 'em up and send 'em to Kingston, Quizzard gets another batch. They follow the dope trail to his place."

"But what have they got against you? I—"

"Clever-up, Jerry. They're Ben's deputies. Ben's getting panicky."

"Ben? Ben Reich? But it was in my shop. I might have been here."

"You were here. What the hell difference did that make?"

"Reich wouldn't want me killed. He—"

"Wouldn't he?" Image of a cat smiling.

Church took a deep breath. Suddenly he exploded: "The son of a bitch! The goddam son of a bitch!"

"Don't feel like that, Jerry. Reich's fighting for his life. You can't expect him to be too careful."

"Well, I'm fighting, too, and that bastard's made up my mind for me. Get ready, Powell. I'm opening up. I'm going to give you everything."

After he finished with Church and returned from Headquarters and the Tate nightmare, Powell was grateful for the sight of the blonde urchin in his home. Barbara D'Courtney had a black crayon in her right hand and a red crayon in her left. She was energetically scribbling on the walls, her tongue between her teeth and her dark eyes squinted in concentration.

"Baba!" he exclaimed in a shocked voice. "What are you doing?"

"Drawrin pitchith," she lisped. "Nicth pitchith for Dada."

"Thank you, sweetheart," he said. "That's a lovely thought. Now come and sit with Dada."

"No," she said, and continued scribbling.

"Are you my girl?"

"Yeth."

"Doesn't my girl always do what Dada asks?"

She thought that one over. "Yeth," she said. She de-

107

posited the crayons in her pocket, her bottom on the couch alongside Powell, and her grubby paws in his hands.

"Really, Barbara," Powell murmured. "That lisping is beginning to worry me. I wonder if your teeth need braces?"

The thought was only half a joke. It was difficult to remember that this was a woman seated alongside him. He looked into the deep dark eyes shining with the empty brilliance of a crystal glass awaiting its fulfilling measure of wine.

Slowly he probed through the vacant conscious levels of her mind to the turbulent preconscious, heavily hung with obscuring clouds like a vast dark nebula in the heavens. Behind the clouds was the faint flicker of light, isolated and childlike, that he had grown to like. But now, as he threaded his way down, that flicker of light was the faint spicule of a star that burned with the hot roar of a nova.

Hello, Barbara. You seem to—

He was answered with a burst of passion that made him backtrack fast.

"Hey, Mary!" he called. "Come quick!"

Mary Noyes popped out of the kitchen. "You in trouble again?"

"Not yet. Soon maybe. Our patient's on the mend."

"I haven't noticed any difference."

"Come on inside with me? She's made contact with her Id. Down on the lowest level. Almost had my brains burned out."

"What do you want? A chaperone? Someone to protect the secrets of her sweet girlish passions?"

"Are you comic? I'm the one who needs protection. Come and hold my hand."

"You've got both of yours in hers."

"Just a figure of speech." Powell glanced uneasily at the calm doll face before him and the cool relaxed hands in his. "Let's go."

He went down the black passages again toward the deep-seated furnace that was within the girl . . . that is within every man . . . the timeless reservoir of psychic energy, reasonless, remorseless, seething with the never-ending search for satisfaction. He could sense Mary Noyes mentally tiptoeing behind him. He stopped at a safe distance.

Hi, Barbara.

"Get out!"

This is the spook.

Hatred lashed out at him.

You remember me?

The hatred subsided into the turbulence to be replaced by a wave of hot desire.

108

"Linc, you'd better jet. If you get trapped inside that pleasure-pain chaos, you're gone."

"I'd like to locate something."

"You can't find anything in there except raw love and raw death."

"I want her relations with her father. I want to know why he had those guilt sensations about her."

"Well, I'm getting out."

The furnace fumed over again. Mary fled.

Powell teetered around the edge of the pit, feeling, exploring, sensing. It was like an electrician gingerly touching the ends of exposed wires to discover which of them did not carry a knock-out charge. A blazing bolt surged near him. He touched it, was stunned, and stepped aside to feel a blanket of instinctual self-preservation choke him. He relaxed, permitted himself to be drawn down into a vortex of associations and began sorting. He struggled to maintain his frame of reference that was crumbling in that chaos of energy.

Here were the somatic messages that fed the cauldron; cell reactions by the incredible billion, organic cries, the muted drone of muscletone, sensory sub-currents, blood-flow, the wavering superheterodyne of blood pH . . . all whirling and churning in the balancing pattern that formed the girl's psyche. The never-ending make-and-break of synapses contributed a crackling hail of complex rhythms. Packed in the changing interstices were broken images, half-symbols, partial references . . . The ionized nuclei of thought.

Powell caught part of Plosive image, followed it to the letter P . . . to the sensory association of a kiss, then by cross circuit to the infant's sucking reflex at the breast . . . to an infantile memory of . . . her mother? No. A wet-nurse. That was encrusted with parental associations . . . Negation. Minus Mother . . . Powell dodged an associated flame of infantile rage and resentment, the Orphan's Syndrome. He picked up P again, searched for a related Pa . . . Papa . . . Father.

Abruptly he was face to face with himself.

He stared at the image, teetered on the verge of disintegration, then scrambled back to sanity.

Who the hell are you?

The image smiled beautifully and was gone.

P . . . Pa . . . Papa . . . Father. Heat-of-love-and-devotion-associated-with . . . He was face to face with his image again. This time it was nude, powerful; its outlines haloed with an aura of love and desire. Its arms outstretched.

Get lost. You embarrass me.

The image disappeared. *Damn it! Has she fallen in love with me?*

"Hi, spook."

There was her picture of herself, pathetically caricatured, the blonde hair in strings, the dark eyes like blotches, the lovely figure drawn into flat, ungracious planes. . . It faded, and abruptly the image of Powell-Powerful-Protective-Paternal rushed at him, torrentially destructive. He stayed with it, grappling. The back of the head was D'Courtney's face. He followed the Janus image down to a blazing channel of doubles, pairs, linkages and duplicities to—Reich? Imposs—Yes, Ben Reich and the caricature of Barbara, linked side to side like Siamese twins, brother and sister from the waist upward, their legs turning and twisting separately in a sea of complexity below. B linked to B. B & B. Barbara & Ben. Half joined in blood. Half—

"Linc!"

A call far off. Directionless.

"Lincoln!"

It could wait a second. That amazing image of Reich had to—

"Lincoln Powell! This way, you fool!"

"Mary?"

"I can't find you."

"Be out in a few minutes."

"Linc, this is the third time I've tried to locate you. If you don't come out now, you're lost."

"The third time?"

"In three hours. Please, Linc . . . While I've got the strength."

He permitted himself to wander upward. He could not find upward. The timeless, spaceless chaos roared around him. The image of Barbara D'Courtney appeared, now a caricature of the sexual siren.

"Hi, spook."

"Lincoln, for the love of God!"

In momentary panic, he plunged in any direction until his peeper training reasserted itself. Then the Withdrawal Technique went into automatic operation. The blocks banged down in steady sequence; each barrier a step backward toward the light. Halfway up, he sensed Mary alongside him. She stayed with him until he was once more in his living room, seated alongside the urchin, her hands in his. He dropped the hands as though they were red hot.

"Mary, I located the weirdest association with Ben Reich. Some kind of linkage that—"

Mary had an iced towel. She slapped his face with it smartly. He realized that he was shaking.

"Only trouble is . . . Trying to make sense out of frag-

110

ments in the Id is like trying to run a qualitative analysis in the middle of a sun . . ."

The towel flicked again.

"You aren't working with unit elements. You're working with ionized particles . . . " He dodged the towel and stared at Barbara. "My God, Mary, I think this poor kid's in love with me."

Image of a cockeyed turtle dove.

"No kidding. I kept meeting myself down there. I—"

"And what about you?"

"Me?"

"Why do you think you refused to send her to Kingston Hospital?" she said. "Why do you think you've been peeping her twice a day since you brought her here? Why did you have to have a chaperone? I'll tell you, Mr. Powell . . ."

"Tell me what?"

"You're in love with her. You've been in love with her since you found her at Chooka Frood's."

"Mary!"

She stung him with a vivid picture of himself and Barbara D'Courtney and that fragment she had peeped days ago . . . The fragment that had made her turn pale with jealousy and anger. Powell knew it was true.

"Mary, dear . . ."

"Never mind me. To hell with me. You're in love with her, and the girl isn't a peeper. She isn't even sane. How much of her are you in love with? One tenth? What part of her are you in love with? Her face? Her subconscious? What about the other ninety per cent? Will you love that when you find it? Damn you! I wish I'd let you stay inside her mind until you rotted!" She turned away and began to cry.

"Mary, for the love of—"

"Shut up," she sobbed. "Damn you, shut up! I . . . There's a message for you. From headquarters. You're to jet for Spaceland as soon as possible. Ben Reich's there, and they've lost him. They need you. Everybody needs you. So why should I complain?"

12

It was years since Powell had last visited Spaceland. He sat in the police launch that had picked him off the luxury ship "Holiday Queen," and as the launch dropped, Powell stared through the port at Spaceland glittering below like a patchwork quilt worked in silver and gold. He smiled as he always did at the identical image that came to him each time he saw the playground in space. It was a vision of a shipload of explorers from a far galaxy, strange creatures, solemn and studious, who stumbled on Spaceland and researched it. He always tried to imagine how they'd report it and always failed.

"It's a job for Dishonest Abe," he muttered.

Spaceland had started several generations back with a flat plate of asteroid rock half a mile in diameter. A mad health cultist had raised a transparent hemisphere of Air-Gel on the plate, installed an atmosphere generator, and started a colony. From that, Spaceland had grown into an irregular table in space, extending hundreds of miles. Each new entrepreneur had simply tacked another mile or so onto the shelf, raised his own transparent hemisphere, and gone into business. By the time engineers got around to advising Spaceland that the spherical form was more efficient and economical, it was too late to change. The table just went on proliferating.

As the launch swung around, the sun caught Spaceland at an angle, and Powell could see the hundreds of hemispheres shimmering against the blue-black of space like a mass of soap bubbles on a checkered table. The original health colony was now in the center and still in business. The others were hotels, amusement parks, health resorts, nursing homes, and even a cemetery. On the Jupiter side of the table was the giant fifty-mile hemisphere that covered the Spaceland Nature Reservation which guaranteed more natural history and more weather per square mile than any natural planet.

"Let's have the story," Powell said.

The police sergeant gulped. "We followed instructions," he said. "Rough Tail on Hassop. Slickie following him. The Rough got taken out by Reich's girl . . ."

"It was a girl, eh?"

"Yeah. Cute little trick named Duffy Wyg&."

"Damnation!" Powell jerked bolt upright. The sergeant stared at him. "Why I questioned that girl myself. I never—" He caught himself. "Seems like I did some lousing myself. Shows you. When you meet a pretty girl . . ." He shook his head.

"Well, like I say," the sergeant continued, "she takes out the Rough, and just when the Slickie moves in, Reich jets into Spaceland with a commotion."

"Like?"

"Private yacht. Has a crash in space and limps in hollerin' emergency. One killed. Three injured, including Reich. Front of the yacht stove in. Derelict or meteor stray. They take Reich to the hospital where we figure he's planted for a little. When we turn around, Reich's gone. Hassop too. I grab a peeper interpreter and go looking in four languages. No dice."

112

"Hassop's luggage?"

"Gone likewise."

"Damnation! We've got to pinch Hassop and that luggage. They're our Motive. Hassop is Monarch's Code Chief. We need him for that last message Reich sent to D'Courtney and the reply . . ."

"Monday before the murder?"

"Yes. That exchange probably ignited the killing. And Hassop may have Reich's financial records with him. They can probably tell a court why Reich had a hell of a motive for murdering D'Courtney."

"Such as, for instance?"

"The talk around Monarch is that D'Courtney had Reich with his back to the wall."

"You got Method and Opportunity?"

"Yes and no. I opened up Jerry Church and got everything, but it's ticklish. We can show Reich had the opportunity. It'll stand if the other two stand. We can show the murder method. It'll stand if the other two stand. Same goes for Reich's Motive. They're like three wigwam poles. Each of them needs the other two. No one can stand alone. That's Old Man Mose's opinion. And that's why we need Hassop."

"I'll swear they ain't left Spaceland. That efficient I still am."

"Don't hang your head because Reich outsmarted you. He's outsmarted plenty. Me included."

The sergeant shook his head gloomily.

"I'll start peeping Spaceland for Reich and Hassop at once," Powell said as the launch drifted down for the passage through the air-lock, "but I want to check a hunch first. Show me the corpse."

"What corpse?"

"From Reich's crash."

In the police mortuary, displayed on an air-cushion in the stasis-freeze, the corpse was a mangled figure with dead white skin and a flaming red beard.

"Uh-huh," Powell muttered. "Keno Quizzard."

"You know him?"

"A gimpster. Was working for Reich and turned too hot to be useful. What'll you bet that crash was a cover-up for a killing."

"Hell!" the cop exploded, "those two other guys are hurt bad. Reich might have been faking. Admitted. But the yacht was ruined, and those two other guys—"

"So they were hurt. And the yacht was ruined. So what? Quizzard's mouth is shut for keeps and Reich's that much safer. Reich took care of him. We'll never prove it, but we won't have to if we locate Hassop. That'll be enough to walk friend Reich into Demolition."

Wearing the fashionable spray-gun-tights (Spaceland sport clothes were being painted on, this year), Powell began a lightning tour of the bubbles . . . Victoria Hotel, Sportsman's Hotel, Magic, Home From Home, Ye New Neu Babblesberg, The Martian (very chic), the Venusberg (very bawdy), and the other dozens . . . Powell struck up conversations with strangers, described his dear old friends in half a dozen languages, and peeped gently to make sure they had the precise picture of Reich and Hassop before they answered. And then the answers. Negative. Always negative.

The peepers were easy . . . and Spaceland was filled with them, at work and at play . . . but always the reply was negative.

A Revival Meeting at Solar Rheims . . . hundreds of chanting, genuflecting devotees participating in a kind of hopped-up Midsummer Morn festival. Reply Negative. Sailing Races in Mars From Home . . . Cat boats and sloops skipping over the water in long hops like scaled stones. Reply Negative. The Plastic Surgery Resort . . . hundreds of bandaged faces and bodies. Reply Negative. Free-Flight Polo. Reply Negative. Hot Sulphur Springs, White Sulphur Springs, Black Sulphur Springs, No Sulphur Springs . . . Replies Negative.

Discouraged and depressed, Powell dropped into Solar Dawn Cemetery. The cemetery looked like an English garden . . . all flagged paths and oak, ash and elm trees with tiny little plots of green grass. Muted music from costumed robot string quartets sawing away in strategic pavilions. Powell began to smile.

There was a faithful reproduction of the Notre Dame Cathedral in the center of the cemetery. It was painstakingly labeled: Ye Wee Kirk O' Th' Glen. From the mouth of one of the gargoyles in the tower, a syrupy voice roared: "SEE THE DRAMA OF THE GODS PORTRAYED IN VIBRANT ROBOT-ACTION IN YE WEE KIRK O TH' GLEN. MOSES ON MT. SINAI, THE CRUCIFIXION OF CHRIST, MOHAMMED AND THE MOUNTAIN, LAO TSE AND THE MOON, THE REVELATION OF MARY BAKER EDDY, THE ASCENSION OF OUR LORD BUDDHA, THE UNVEILING OF THE TRUE AND ONLY GOD GALAXY . . ." Pause, and then a little more matter-of-factly: "OWING TO THE SACRED NATURE OF THIS EXHIBIT, ADMISSION IS BY TICKET ONLY. TICKETS MAY BE PURCHASED FROM THE BAILIFF." Pause. Then another voice, injured and pleading: "ATTENTION ALL WORSHIPERS. ATTENTION ALL WORSHIPERS. NO LOUD TALKING OR LAUGHTER . . .

PLEASE!" A click, and another gargoyle began in another language. Powell burst out laughing.

"You ought to be ashamed of yourself," a girl said behind him.

Without turning, Powell replied: "I'm sorry. 'No Loud Talking or Laughter.' But don't you think this is the most ludicrous—" Then the pattern of her psyche hit him and he spun around. He was face to face with Duffy Wyg&.

"Well, Duffy!" he said.

Her frown changed to a look of perplexity, then to a quick smile. "Mr. Powell," she exclaimed. "The boy-sleuth. You still owe me a dance."

"I owe you an apology," Powell said.

"Delighted. Can't have enough of them. What's this one for?"

"Underestimating you."

"The story of my life." She linked arms and drew him along the path. "Tell me how reason has finally prevailed. You took another look at me, and—?"

"I realized you're the cleverest person Ben Reich has working for him."

"I am clever. I did do some work for Ben . . . but your compliment seems to have deep brooding undertones. Is there something?"

"The tail we had on Hassop."

"Just a little more accent on the down-beat, please."

"You took out our tail, Duffy. Congratulations."

"Ah-ha! Hassop is your pet horse. A childhood accident robbed him of a horse's crowning glory. You substituted an artificial one which—"

"Clever-up, Duffy. That isn't going to travel far."

"Then, boy-wonder, will you ream your tubes?" Her pert face looked up at him, half serious, half amused. "What in hell are you talking about?"

"I'll spell it out. We had a tail on Hassop. A tail is a shadow, a spy, a secret agent assigned to the duty of following and watching a suspect . . ."

"Contents noted. What's a Hassop?"

"A man who works for Ben Reich. His Code Chief."

"And what did I do to your spy?"

"Following instructions from Ben Reich, you captivated the man, enravished him, turned him into a derelict from duty, kept him at a piano all day, day after day, and—"

"Wait a minute!" Duffy spoke sharply. "I know that one. The little bem. Let's square this off. He was a cop?"

"Now Duffy, if—"

"I asked a question."

"He was a cop."

115

"Following this Hassop?"

"Yes."

"Hassop . . . Bleached man? Dusty hair? Dusty blue eyes?"

Powell nodded.

"The louse," Duffy muttered. "The low-down louse!" She turned on Powell furiously. "And you think I'm the kind that does his dirty work, do you! Why, you — you peeper! You listen to me, Powell. Reich asked me to do him a favor. Said there was a man up here working on an interesting musical code. Wanted me to check him. How the hell was I supposed to know he was your goon? How was I supposed to know your goon was masquerading as a musician?"

Powell stared at her. "Are you claiming that Reich tricked you?"

"What else?" She glared back. "Go ahead and peep me. If Reich wasn't in the Reservation you could peep that double-crossing —"

"Hold it!" Powell interrupted sharply. He slipped past her conscious barrier and peeped her precisely and comprehensively for ten seconds. Then he turned and began to run.

"Hey!" Duffy yelled. "What's the verdict?"

"Medal of Honor," Powell called over his shoulder. "I'll pin it on as soon as I bring a man back alive."

"I don't want a man. I want you."

"That's your trouble, Duffy. You want anybody."

"Whooooo?"

"An-y-bod-y."

"NO LOUD TALKING OR LAUGHTER . . . PLEASE!"

Powell found his police sergeant in the Spaceland Globe Theater where a magnificent Esper actress stirred thousands with her moving performances—performances that owed as much to her telepathic sensitivity to audience response as to her exquisite command of stage technique. The cop, immune to the star's appeal, was gloomily inspecting the house, face by face. Powell took his arm and led him out.

"He's in the Reservation," Powell told him. "Took Hassop with him. Took Hassop's luggage too. Perfect alibi. He was shaken up by the crash and he needs a rest. Also company. He's eight hours ahead of us."

"The Reservation, huh?" the sergeant pondered. "Twenty-five hundred square miles of more damned animals, geography, and weather than you ever see in three lives."

"What's the odds Hassop has a fatal accident, if he hasn't had one already?"

"No takers at any price."

"If we want to get Hassop out we'll have to grab a Helio and do some fast hunting."

"Uh-uh. No mechanical transportation allowed in the Reservation."

"This is an emergency. Old Man Mose has got to have Hassop!"

"Go let that damn machine argue with the Spaceland Board. You could get special permission in maybe three four weeks."

"By which time Hassop'd be dead and buried. What about Radar or Sonar? We could work out Hassop's pattern and —"

"Uh-uh. No mechanical devices outside of cameras allowed in the Reservation."

"What the hell plays with that Reservation?"

"Hundred per cent guaranteed pure nature for the eager beavers. You go in at your own risk. Element of danger adds spice to your trip. Get the picture? You battle the elements. You battle the wild animals. You feel primitive and refreshed again. That's what the ads say."

"What do they do in there? Rub sticks together?"

"Sure. You hike on your own feet. You carry your own food. You take one Defensive Barrier Screen with you so's the bears don't eat you. If you want a fire you got to build it. If you want to hunt animals, you got to make your own weapons. If you want to catch fish, likewise. You versus nature. And they make you sign a release in case nature wins."

"Then how are we going to find Hassop?"

"Sign a release and go hike for him."

"The two of us? Cover twenty-five hundred square miles of geography? How many squadmen can you spare?"

"Maybe ten."

"Adding up to two hundred and fifty square miles per cop. Impossible."

"Maybe you could persuade the Spaceland Board — No. Even if you could, we wouldn't be able to get the Board together under a week. Wait a minute! Could you get 'em together by peeping 'em? Send out urgent messages or something? How do you peepers work that anyway?"

"We can only pick you up. We can't transmit to anybody except another peeper, so — Hey! Ho! That's an idea!"

"What's an idea?"

"Is a human being a mechanical device?"

"Nope."

"Is he a civilized invention?"

"Not lately."

"Then I'm going to do some fast co-opting and take my own Radar into the Reservation."

117

Which is why a sudden craving for nature overtook a prominent lawyer in the midst of delicate contractual negotiations in one of Spaceland's luxurious conference rooms. The same craving also came upon the secretary of a famous author, a judge of domestic relations, a job analyst screening applicants for the United Hotel Association, an industrial designer, an efficiency engineer, the Chairman of Amalgamated Union's Grievance Committee, Titan's Superintendent of Cybernetics, a Secretary of Political Psychology, two Cabinet members, five Parliamentary Leaders, and scores of other Esper clients of Spaceland at work and at play.

They filed through the Reservation Gate in a unified mood of holiday festivity and assorted gear. Those that had gotten word on the grapevine early enough were in sturdy camping clothes. Others were not; and the astonished gate guards, checking and inspecting for illicit baggage, saw one lunatic in full diplomatic regalia march through with a pack on his back. But all the nature-lovers carried detailed maps of the Reservation carefully zoned into sectors.

Moving swiftly, they spread out and beat forward across the miniature continent of weather and geography. The TP Band crackled as comments and information swept up and down the line of living radar in which Powell occupied the central position.

"Hey. No fair, I've got a mountain dead ahead."

"Snowing here. Full b-b-blizzard."

"Swamps and (ugh!) mosquitoes in my sector."

"Hold it. Party ahead, Linc. Sector 21."

"Shoot a picture."

"Here it is . . ."

"Sorry. No sale."

"Party ahead, Linc. Sector 9."

"Let's have the picture."

"Here it comes . . ."

"Nope. No sale."

"Party ahead, Linc. Sector 17."

"Shoot a picture."

"Hey! It's a goddam bear!"

"Don't run! Negotiate!"

"Party ahead, Linc. Sector 12."

"Shoot a picture."

"Here it comes . . ."

"No sale."

"AAAAAAA-choo!"

"That the blizzard?"

"No. I'm a cloud-burst."

"Party ahead, Linc. Sector 41."

"Shoot a picture."

"Here it is."

"Not them."

"How do you climb a palm tree?"

"You shinny up."

"Not up. Down."

"How'd you get up, your honor?"

"I don't know. A moose helped me."

"Party ahead, Linc. Sector 37."

"Let's have the picture."

"Here it comes."

"No sale."

"Party ahead, Linc. Sector 60."

"Go ahead."

"Here's the picture . . ."

"Pass 'em by."

"How long do we have to keep on travelling?"

"They're at least eight hours ahead."

"No. Correction, peepers. They've got eight hours start but they may not be eight hours ahead."

"Spell that out, will you, Linc."

"Reich may not have trekked straight ahead. He may have circled around to a favorite spot close to the gate."

"Favorite for what?"

"For murder."

"Excuse me. How does one persuade a cat not to devour one?"

"Use Political Psychology."

"Use your Barrier screen, Mr. Secretary."

"Party ahead, Linc. Sector 1."

"Shoot a picture, Mr. Superintendent."

"Here it is."

"Pass 'em by, sir. That's Reich and Hassop."

"WHAT!"

"Don't make a fuss. Don't make anybody suspicious. Just pass 'em by. When you're out of sight, circle around to Sector 2. Everybody head back for the Gate and go home. All my thanks. From here on I'll take it alone."

"Leave us in on the kill, Linc."

"No. This needs finesse. I don't want Reich to know I'm abducting Hassop. It's all got to look logical and natural and unimpeachable. It's a swindle."

"And you're the thief to do it."

"Who stole the weather, Powell?"

The departing peepers were propelled by a hot blush.

This particular square mile of Reservation was jungle, humid, swampy, overgrown. As darkness fell, Powell slowly

119

wormed his way toward the glimmering camp fire Reich had built in a clearing alongside a small lake. The water was infested with hippo, crocodile, and swambat. The trees and terrain swarmed with life. The entire junglette was a savage tribute to the brilliance of Reservation ecologists who could assemble and balance nature on the point of a pin. And in tribute to that nature, Reich's Defensive Barrier Screen was in full operation.

Powell could hear mosquitoes whine as they batted against the outer rim of the barrier, and there was an intermittent hail of larger insects caroming off the invisible wall. Powell could not risk operating his own. The screens hummed slightly and Reich had keen ears. He inched forward and peeped.

Hassop was at ease, relaxed, just a little beglamoured by the idea of intimacy with his puissant chief, just a little intoxicated by the knowledge that his film cannister contained Ben Reich's fate. Reich, working feverishly on a crude, powerful bow, was planning the accident that would eliminate Hassop. It was that bow and the sheaf of fire-tipped arrows alongside Reich that had eaten up the eight hours start on Powell. You can't kill a man in a hunting accident unless you go hunting.

Powell lifted to his knees and crawled forward, his senses pinpointed on Reich's perception. He froze again as ALARM clanged in Reich's head. Reich leaped to his feet, bow ready, a featherless arrow at half-cock, and peered intently into the darkness.

"What is it, Ben?" Hassop murmured.

"I don't know. Something."

"Hell. You've got your Barrier, haven't you?"

"I keep forgetting." Reich sank back and built up the fire; but he was not forgetting the Barrier. The wary instinct of the killer was warning him, vaguely, persistently . . . And Powell could only marvel at the intricate survival mechanism of the human mind. He peeped Reich again. Reich was mechanically resorting to the tune-block he associated with crisis: *Tenser, said the Tensor, Tenser, said the Tensor. Tension, apprehension, and dissension have begun.* Behind that there was turmoil; a mounting resolution to kill quickly . . . kill savagely . . . destroy now and arrange the evidence later . . .

As Reich reached for the bow, his eyes carefully averted from Hassop, his mind intent on the throbbing heart that was his target, Powell drove forward urgently. Before he had moved ten feet, ALARM tripped again in Reich's mind and the big man was on his feet once more. This time he whipped a burning branch from the fire and hurled the flare toward the blackness where Powell was concealed. The idea and execution came so quickly that Powell could not anticipate the action. He

120

would have been fully illumined if Reich had not forgotten the Barrier. It stopped the flaming branch in mid-flight and dropped it to the ground.

"Christ!" Reich cried, and swung around abruptly at Hassop.

"What is it, Ben?"

In answer, Reich drew the arrow back to the lobe of his ear and held the point on Hassop's body. Hassop scrambled to his feet.

"Ben, watch out! You're shooting at me!"

Hassop leaped to one side unexpectedly as Reich let the arrow fly.

"Ben! For the love of —" Suddenly Hassop realized the intent. He turned with a strangulated cry and ran from the fire as Reich notched another arrow. Running desperately, Hassop smashed into the barrier and staggered back from the invisible wall as an arrow shot past his shoulder and shattered.

"Ben!" he screamed.

"You son of a bitch," Reich growled, and notched another shaft.

Powell leaped forward and reached the edge of the Barrier. He could not pass it. Inside, Hassop ran screaming across the far side while Reich stalked him with half-cocked bow, closing in for the kill. Hassop again smashed into the Barrier, fell, crawled, and regained his feet to dart off again like a cornered rat, Reich following him doggedly.

"Jesus!" Powell muttered. He stepped back into the darkness, thinking desperately. Hassop's screams had aroused the jungle, and there was a roaring and an echoing rumble in his ears. He reached out on the TP Band, sensing, touching, feeling. There was nothing but blind fear, blind rage, blind instinct around him. The hippos, sodden and viscid . . . the crocodiles, deaf, angry, hungry . . . swambats, as furious as rhinoceri whose size they doubled . . . A quarter mile off were the faint broadcasts of elephant, wapiti, giant cats . . .

"It's worth the chance," Powell said to himself. "I've got to bust that Barrier. It's the only way."

He set his blocks on the upper levels, masking everything except the emotional broadcast, and transmitted: fear, fear, terror, fear . . . driving the emotion down to its most primitive level . . . Fear, Fear. Terror. Fear . . . FEAR - FLIGHT - TERROR - FEAR - FLIGHT - TERROR - flight!

Every bird in every roost awoke screaming. The monkeys screamed back and shook thousands of branches in sudden flight. A barrage of sucking explosions sounded from the lake as the herd of hippos surged up from the shallows in blind terror. The jungle was shaken by the ear-splitting trumpetings of elephants and the crashing thunder of their stampede.

Reich heard and froze in his tracks, ignoring Hassop who still ran and sobbed and screamed from wall to wall of the Barrier.

The hippos hit the barrier first in a blind, blundering rush. They were followed by the swambats and the crocodiles. Then came the elephants. Then the wapiti, the zebra, the gnu . . . heavy, pounding herds. There had never been such a stampede in the history of the Reservation. Nor had the manufacturers of the Defensive Barrier Screen ever anticipated such a concerted mass attack. Reich's Barrier went down with a sound like scissored glass.

The hippos trampled the fire, scattered it and extinguished it. Powell darted through the darkness, seized Hassop's arm, and dragged the crazed creature across the clearing to the piled packs. A wild hoof sent him reeling, but he held on to Hassop and located the precious film cannister. In the frantic blackness Powell could sort the frenzied TP broadcasts of the stampeding animals. Still dragging Hassop, he threaded his way out of the main stream. Behind the thick bole of a *lignum vitae* Powell paused to catch his breath and settle the cannister safely in his pocket. Hassop was still sobbing. Powell sensed Reich, a hundred feet away, back against a fever tree, bow and arrows clutched in his stricken hands. He was confused, furious, terrified . . . but still safe. Above all, Powell wanted to keep him safe for Demolition.

Unhitching his own Defensive Barrier Screen, Powell tossed it across the clearing toward the embers of the fire where Reich would surely find it. Then he turned and led the numb, unresisting Code Chief toward the Gate.

13

The Reich case was ready for final submission to the District Attorney's office. Powell hoped it was also ready for that cold-blooded, cynical monster of facts and evidence, Old Man Mose.

Powell and his staff assembled in Mose's office. A round table had been set up in the center, and on it was constructed a transparent model of the key rooms of Beaumont House, inhabited by miniature android models of the *dramatis personae*. The lab's model division had done a superlative job, and actually had characterized the leading players. The tiny Reich, Tate, Beaumont, and others moved with the characteristic gaits of their originals. Alongside the table was massed the documentation the staff had prepared, ready for presentation to the machine.

Old Man Mose himself occupied the entire circular wall of the giant office. His multitudinous eyes winked and glared coldly. His multitudinous memories whirred and hummed. His mouth, the cone of a speaker, hung open in a kind of astonishment at human stupidity. His hands, the keys of a multiflex typewriter, poised over a roll of tape, ready to hammer out logic. Mose was the Mosaic Multiplex Prosecution Computer of the District Attorney's Office, whose awful decisions controlled the preparation, presentation, and prosecution of every police case.

"We won't bother Mose to start with," Powell told the D.A. "Let's take a look at the models and check them against the Crime Schedule. Your staff has the time sheets. Just watch them while the dolls go through the motions. If you catch anything our gang's missed, make a note and we'll kick it around."

He nodded to De Santis, the harassed Lab Chief, who inquired in an overwrought voice: "One to one?"

"That's a little fast. Make it one to two. Half slow motion."

"The androids look unreal at that tempo," De Santis snarled. "It can't do them justice. We slaved for two weeks and now you—"

"Never mind. We'll admire them later."

De Santis verged on mutiny, then touched a button. Instantly the model was illumined and the dolls came to life. Acoustics had faked a background. There was a hint of music, laughter, and chatter. In the main hall of Beaumont House, a pneumatic model of Maria Beaumont slowly climbed to a dais with a tiny book in her hands.

"The time is 11:09 at that point," Powell said to the D.A.'s staff. "Watch the clock above the model. It's geared to synchronize with the slow motion."

In rapt silence, the legal division studied the scene and jotted notes while the androids reproduced the actions of the fatal Beaumont party. Once again Maria Beaumont read the rules of the Sardine game from the dais in the main hall of Beaumont House. The lights dimmed and went out. Ben Reich slowly threaded his way through the main hall to the music room, turned right, mounted the stairs to the Picture Gallery, passed through the bronze doors leading to the Orchid Suite, blinded and stunned the Beaumont guards, and then entered the suite.

And again Reich met D'Courtney face to face, closed with him, drew a deadly knife-pistol from his pocket and with the blade pried D'Courtney's mouth open while the old man hung weak and unresisting. And again a door of the Orchid Suite burst open to reveal Barbara D'Courtney in a frost-white transparent dressing gown. And she and Reich feinted and dodged until Reich suddenly blew the back of D'Courtney's head out with a shot through the mouth.

"Got that material from the D'Courtney girl," Powell murmured. "Peeped her. It's authentic."

Barbara D'Courtney crawled to the body of her father, seized the gun and suddenly dashed out of the Orchid Suite, followed by Reich. He pursued her down into the darkened house and lost her as she darted out through the front entrance into the street. Then Reich met Tate and they marched to the Projection Room, pretending to play Sardine. The drama came to an end at last with the stampede of the guests up to the Orchid Suite where the dolls burst in and crowded around the tiny dead body. There they froze in a grotesque little tableau.

There was a long pause while the legal staff digested the drama.

"All right," Powell said. "That's the picture. Now let's feed the data to Mose for an opinion. First, Opportunity. You won't deny that the Sardine game provided Reich with perfect opportunity?"

"How'd Reich know they were going to play Sardine?" the D.A. muttered.

"Reich bought the book and sent it to Maria Beaumont. He provided his own Sardine game."

"How'd he know she'd play the game?"

"He knew she liked games. Sardine was the only legible game in the book."

"I don't know . . ." The D.A. scratched his head. "Mose takes a lot of convincing. Feed it to him. Won't do any harm."

The office door banged open and Commissioner Crabbe marched in as though heading a parade.

"Mr. Prefect Powell," Crabbe pronounced formally.

"Mr. Commissioner?"

"It has come to my attention, sir, that you are perverting that mechanical brain for the purpose of implicating my good friend, Ben Reich, in the foul and dastardly murder of Craye D'Courtney. Mr. Powell, such a purpose is grotesque. Ben Reich is an honorable and leading citizen of our country. Furthermore, sir, I have never approved of that mechanical brain. You were chosen by the electorate to exercise your intellectual powers, not bow in slavery to that—"

Powell nodded to Beck, who began feeding the punched data into Mose's ear. "You're absolutely right, Commissioner. Now, about the Method. First question: How'd Reich knock out the guards. De Santis?"

"And furthermore, gentlemen . . ." Crabbe continued.

"Rhodopsin Ionizer," De Santis spat. He picked up a plastic sphere and tossed it to Powell who exhibited it. "Man named Jordan developed it for Reich's private police. I've got the empiric processing formula ready for the Computer, and the sample we mocked up. Anybody care to try it?"

The D.A. looked dubious. "I don't see the use. Mose can make up his own mind about that."

"In addition to which, gentlemen . . ." Crabbe summarized.

"Oh come on," De Santis said with unpleasant cheerfulness. "You'll never believe us unless you see it for yourself. It doesn't hurt. Just makes you non compos for six or seven—"

The plastic bulb shattered in Powell's fingers. A vivid blue light flared under Crabbe's nose. Caught in mid-oration, the Commissioner collapsed like an empty sack. Powell looked around in horror.

"Good Heavens!" he exclaimed. "What have I done? That bulb simply melted in my fingers." He looked at De Santis and spoke severely. "You made the covering too thin, De Santis. Now see what you've done to Commissioner Crabbe."

"What I've done!"

"Feed that data to Mose," the D.A. said in a voice rigid with control. "This I know he'll buy."

They made the Commissioner's body comfortable in a deep chair. "Now, the murder method," Powell continued. "Kindly watch this, gentlemen. The hand is quicker than the eye." He exhibited a revolver from the police museum. From the chambers he removed the shells, and from one of the shells he extracted the bullet. "This is what Reich did to the gun Jerry Church gave him before the murder. Pretended to make it safe. A phoney alibi."

"Phoney, hell! That gun is safe. Is that Church's evidence?"

"It is. Look at your sheet."

"Then you don't have to bother Mose with the problem." The D.A. threw his papers down in disgust. "We haven't got a case."

"Yes we have."

"How can a cartridge kill without a bullet? Your sheet doesn't say anything about Reich reloading."

"He reloaded."

"He did not," De Santis spat. "There was no projectile in the wound or the room. There was nothing."

"There was everything. It was easy once I figured the clue."

"There was no clue!" De Santis shouted.

"Why, you located it, De Santis. That bit of candy gel in D'Courtney's mouth. Remember? And no candy in the stomach."

125

De Santis glared, Powell grinned. He took an eye-dropper and filled a gel capsule with water. He pressed it into the open end of the cartridge above the charge and placed the cartridge in the gun. He raised the gun, aimed at a small wooden block on the edge of the model table, and pulled the trigger. There was a dull, flat explosion and the block leaped into fragments.

"For the love of— That was a trick!" The D.A. exclaimed. "There was something in that shell besides water." He examined the fragments of wood.

"No, there was not. You can shoot an ounce of water with a powder charge. You can shoot it with enough muzzle velocity to blow out the back of a head if you fire through the soft roof of the mouth. That's why Reich had to shoot through the mouth. That's why De Santis found the bit of gel. That's why he found nothing else. The projectile was gone."

"Give it to Mose," the D.A. said faintly. "By God, Powell, I'm beginning to think we've got a case."

"All right. Now, Motive. We picked up Reich's business records, and Accounting's gone through them. D'Courtney had Reich with his back to the wall. With Reich it was 'if you can't lick 'em, join 'em.' He tried to join D'Courtney. He failed. He murdered D'Courtney. Will you buy that?"

"Sure I'll buy it. But will Old Man Mose? Feed it in and let's see."

They fed in the last of the punched data, warmed the computor up from 'Idle' to 'Run,' and kicked him into it. Mose's eyes blinked in hard meditation; his stomach rumbled softly; his memories began to hiss and stutter. Powell and the others waited with mounting suspense. Abruptly, Mose hiccupped. A soft bell began to 'Ping-Ping-Ping-Ping-Ping-Ping—' and Mose's type began to flail the virgin tape under it.

"IF IT PLEASE THE COURT," Mose said, "WITH PLEADERING OF NON VULTS AND DEMURERS, LEGAL SIGNATURES. SS. LEADING CASE HAY v. COHOES AND THE RULE IN SHELLEY'S CASE. URP."

"What the—" Powell looked at Beck.

"He gets kittenish," Beck explained.

"At a time like this!"

"Happens now and then. We'll try him again."

They filled the computor's ear again, held the warmup for a good five minutes and then kicked him into it. Once again his eyes blinked, his stomach growled, his memories hissed, and Powell and the two staffs waited anxiously. A month's hard work hung on this decision. The type-hammers began to fall.

"BRIEF #921,088. SECTION C-1. MOTIVE," Mose

said. "PASSION MOTIVE FOR CRIME INSUFFICIENT-
LY DOCUMENTED. CF STATE v. HANRAHAN, 1202
SUP. COURT. 19, AND SUBSEQUENT LINE OF LEAD-
ING CASES."

"Passion motive?" Powell muttered. "Is Mose crazy? It's
a profit motive. Check C-1, Beck."

Beck checked. "No mistake here."

"Try him again."

They ran the computor through it a third time. This
time he spoke to the point: "BRIEF #921,088. SECTION
C-1. MOTIVE. PROFIT MOTIVE FOR CRIME INSUF-
FICIENTLY DOCUMENTED. CF STATE v. ROYAL
1197 SUP. COURT 388."

"Didn't you punch C-1 properly?" Powell inquired.

"We got everything in that we could," Beck replied.

"Excuse me," Powell said to the others, "I've got to peep
this out with Beck. You don't mind, I hope." He turned to
Beck: "Open up, Jackson. I smelled an evasion in them last
words. Let me have it . . ."

"Honestly, Linc, I'm not aware of any —"

"If you were aware, it wouldn't be an evasion. It'd be a
downright lie. Now lemme see . . . Oh. Of course! Idiot.
You don't have to be ashamed because Code's a little slow."
Powell spoke aloud to the staffs: "Beck's missing one small
datum point. Code's still working with Hassop upstairs trying
to bust Reich's private code. So far all we've got is the knowledge that Reich offered merger and was refused. We haven't
got the definite offer and refusal yet. That's what Mose wants.
A cautious monster."

"If you didn't bust the code, how do you know the offer
was made and refused?" the D.A. asked.

"Got that from Reich himself through Gus Tate. It was
one of the last things Tate gave me before he was murdered.
I tell you what, Beck. Add an assumption to the tape. Assuming that our merger evidence is unassailable (which it is) what
does Mose think of the case?"

Beck hand punched a strip, spliced it to the main prob-
lem and fed it in again. By now well warmed up, the Mosaic
Multiplex Computor answered in thirty seconds: "BRIEF
#921,088. ACCEPTING ASSUMPTION, PROBABILITY
OF SUCCESSFUL PROSECUTION 97.0099%."

Powell's staff grinned and relaxed. Powell tore the tape
out of the typewriter and presented it to the D.A. with a flour-
ish. "And there's your case, Mr. District Attorney . . . Sewn
up and delivered."

"By God!" the D.A. said. "Ninety seven per cent! Jesus,
we haven't had one in the ninety bracket all my term. I thought
I was lucky when I broke seventy. Ninety seven per cent . . .

127

Against Ben Reich himself! Jesus!" He looked around at his staff in a kind of wild surmise. "We'll make goddam history!"

The office door opened and two perspiring men darted in waving manuscript.

"Here's Code now," Powell said. "You bust it?"

"We busted it," they said, "and now you're busted, Powell. The whole case is busted."

"What? What the hell are you talking about?"

"Reich knocked off D'Courtney because D'Courtney wouldn't merge, didn't he? He had a nice fat profit motive for killing D'Courtney, didn't he? In a pig's eye he did."

"Oh God!" Beck groaned.

"Reich sent YYJI TTED RRCB UUFE AALK OOBA to D'Courtney. That reads: SUGGEST MERGER BOTH OUR INTERESTS EQUAL PARTNERSHIP."

"Damn it, that's what I've said all along. And D'Courtney replied: WWHG. That was a refusal. Reich told Tate. Tate told me."

"D'Courtney answered WWHG. That reads: ACCEPT OFFER."

"The hell it does!"

"The hell it don't. WWHG. ACCEPT OFFER. It was the answer Reich wanted. It was the answer that gave Reich every reason for keeping D'Courtney alive. You'll never convince any court in the solar system that Reich had a motive for murdering D'Courtney. Your case is washed out."

Powell stood stock still for half a minute, his fists clenched, his face working. Suddenly he turned on the model, reached in and pulled out the android figure of Reich. He twisted its head off. He went to Mose, yanked out the tapes of punched data, crumpled them into a wad and hurled the wad across the room. He strode to Crabbe's recumbent figure and launched a tremendous kick at the seat of the chair. While the staffs watched in an appalled silence, the chair and Commissioner overturned to the floor.

"God damn you! You're always sitting in that God damned chair!" Powell cried in a shaking voice and stormed out of the office.

14

Explosion! Concussion! The cell doors burst open. And far outside, freedom is waiting in the cloak of darkness and flight into the unknown. . . .

Who's that? Who's outside the cell-block? Oh God! Oh Christ! The Man With No Face! Looking. Looming. Silent. Run! Escape! Fly! Fly. . . .

Fly through space. There's safety in the solitude of this silver-lined launch jetting to the deeps of the distant unknown . . . The hatch door! Opening. But it can't. There's no one on this launch to swing it slowly, ominously . . . Oh God! The Man With No Face! Looking. Looming. Silent . . .

But I am innocent, your honor. Innocent. You will never prove my guilt, and I will never stop pleading my case though you pound your gavel until you deafen my ears and—Oh Christ! On the bench. In wig and gown. The Man With No Face. Looking. Looming. Quintessence of vengeance . . .

The pounding gavel dissolved to knuckles on the state-room door. The steward's voice called: "Over New York, Mr. Reich. One hour to debarkation. Over New York, Mr. Reich." The knuckles went on hammering on the door.

Reich found his voice. "All right," he croaked. "I hear you."

The steward departed. Reich climbed out of the liquid bed and found his legs giving way. He clutched at the wall and cursed himself upright. Still in the grip of the nightmare's terror, he went into the bathroom, depilated, showered, steamed, and air-washed for ten minutes. He was still reeling. He stepped into the massage alcove and punched 'Glow-Salt.' Two pounds of moistened, scented salt were sprayed on his skin. As the massage buffers were about to begin, Reich suddenly decided he needed coffee. He stepped out of the alcove to ring Service.

There was a dull concussion and Reich was hurled to his face by the force of the explosion in the alcove. His back was slashed by flying particles. He darted into the bedroom, seized his traveling case, and turned like an animal at bay, his hands automatically opening the case and groping for the cartridge of Detonation Bulbs he always carried. There was no cartridge in the case.

Reich pulled himself together. He was aware of the bite of salt in the cuts in his back and the streaming blood. He was aware that he was no longer trembling. He went back into the bathroom, shut off the massage buffers and inspected the alcove wreckage. Someone had removed the cartridge from his case during the night and planted a bulb in each of the massage buffers. The empty cartridge lay behind the alcove. Only a split-second miracle had saved his life . . . from whom?

He inspected his stateroom door. The lock had evidently been gaffed by a past-master. It showed no sign of tampering. But who? Why?

"Son of a bitch!" Reich growled. With iron nerve he re-
129

turned to the bathroom, washed off the salt and blood, and sprayed his back with coagulent. He dressed, had his coffee, and descended to the Staging Hall where, after a savage skirmish with the peeper Customs Man (*Tension, apprehension, and dissention have begun!*), he boarded the Monarch launch that was waiting to take him down to the city.

From the launch he called Monarch Tower. His secretary's face appeared on the screen.

"Any news of Hassop?" Reich asked.

"No, Mr. Reich. Not since you called from Spaceland."

"Give me Recreation."

The screen herring-boned and then disclosed the chrome lounge of Monarch. West, bearded and scholarly, was carefully binding sheets of typescript into plastic volumes. He looked up and grinned.

"Hello, Ben."

"Don't look so cheerful, Ellery," Reich growled. "Where the hell is Hassop? I thought you'd surely—"

"Not my problem any more, Ben."

"What are you talking about?"

West displayed the volumes. "Just finishing up my work. History of my career with Monarch Utilities & Resources for your files. Said career ended this morning at nine o'clock."

"What!"

"Yep. I warned you, Ben. The Guild's just ruled Monarch out of bounds for me. Company Espionage is unethical."

"Listen, Ellery, you can't quit now. I'm on a hook and I need you bad. Someone tried to booby-trap me on the ship this morning. I beat it by an eyelash. I've got to find out who it is. I need a peeper."

"Sorry, Ben."

"You don't have to work for Monarch. I'll put you under personal contract for private service. The same contract Breen has."

"Breen? A 2nd? The analyst?"

"Yes. My analyst."

"Not any more."

"What!"

West nodded. "The ruling came down today. No more exclusive practice. It limits the service of peepers. We've got to be dedicated to the most good for the most people. You've lost Breen."

"It's Powell!" Reich shouted. "Using every dirty peeper trick he can dig out of the slime to bitch me. He's trying to nail me to the D'Courtney cross, the sneaking peeper! He—"

"Sign off, Ben. Powell had nothing to do with it. Let's break it off friendly, eh? We've always kept it pleasant. Let's break it pleasant. What do you say?"

"I say go to hell!" Reich roared and cut the connection. To the launch pilot he said in the same tone: "Take me home!"

Reich burst into his penthouse apartment, once again awakening the hearts of his staff to terror and hatred. He hurled his traveling case at his valet and went immediately to Breens' suite. It was empty. A crisp note on the desk repeated the information West had already given him. Reich strode to his own rooms, went to the phone and dialed Gus Tate. The screen cleared and displayed a sign:

SERVICE PERMANENTLY DISCONTINUED

Reich stared, broke the connection and dialed Jerry Church. The screen cleared and displayed a sign:

SERVICE PERMANENTLY DISCONTINUED

Reich snapped the contact key up, paced around the study uncertainly, then went to the shimmer of light in the corner that was his safe. He switched the safe into temporal phase, revealing the honeycomb paper rack, and reached for the small red envelope in the upper left-hand pigeon hole. As he touched the envelope he heard the faint click. He doubled up and spun away, his face buried in his arms.

There was a blinding flash of light and a heavy explosion. Something brutal punched Reich in the left side, hurled him across the study and slammed him against the wall. Then a hail of debris followed. He struggled to his feet, bellowing in bewilderment and fury, stripping the ripped clothes from his left side to examine the state of his body. He was badly slashed, and a particularly excruciating pain indicated at least one broken rib.

He heard his staff come running down the corridor and roared: "Keep out! You hear me? Keep out! All of you!"

He stumbled through the wreckage and began sorting over the remains of his safe. He found the neuron scrambler he had taken from Chooka Frood's red-eyed woman. He found the malignant steel flower that was the knife-pistol that had killed D'Courtney. It still contained four unfired shells loaded with water and sealed with gel. He thrust both into the pocket of a new jacket, got a fresh cartridge of Detonation Bulbs from his desk, and tore out of the room, ignoring the servants who stared at him in astonishment.

Reich swore feverishly all the way down from the tower apartment to the cellar garage where he deposited his private Jumper key in the Call slot and waited for the little car. When it came out of storage with the key in the door, another tenant was approaching and even at a distance was staring. Reich turned the key and yanked open the door to jump in. There was a low pressure Rrrrrrip. Reich hurled himself to the ground. The Jumper tank exploded. By some freak, it failed to burst into flame. It erupted a shattering geyser of raw fuel and fragments of twisting metal. Reich crawled frantically, reached the exit ramp, and ran for his life.

On the street level, torn, bleeding, rank with creosote fuel, he searched frantically for a Public Jumper. He couldn't find a coin-Jumper. He managed to flag a piloted machine.

"Where to?" the driver asked.

Reich dabbed dazedly at the blood and oil that smeared him. "Chooka Frood!" he croaked in a hysterical voice.

The cab hopped him to 99 Bastion West.

Reich thrust past the protesting doorman, the indignant reception clerk, and Chooka Frood's highly paid chargé d'affaires to the private office, a Victorian room furnished with stained glass lamps, overstuffed sofas and a roll-top desk. Chooka was seated at the desk, wearing a dingy smock and a dingy expression that changed to alarm when Reich yanked the scrambler out of his pocket.

"For God's sake, Reich!" she exclaimed.

"Here I am, Chooka," he said hoarsely. "So let's have the trail run before we feed it to the dice. I used this scrambler on you once before. I'm warmed up for it again. You warmed me up, Chooka."

She shot up from the desk and screamed: "Magda!"

Reich caught her by the arm and hurled her across the office. She side-swiped the couch and fell across it. The red-eyed bodyguard came running into the office. Reich was ready for her. He clubbed her across the back of the neck, and as she fell forward, he ground his heel into her back and slammed her flat on the floor. The woman twisted and clawed at his leg. Ignoring her he spat at Chooka: "Let's get it squared off. Why the booby-traps?"

"What are you talking about?" Chooka cried.

"What the hell do I look like I'm talking about. Read the blood, lady. I've skinned out of three obituaries running. How long can my luck hold out?"

"Make sense, Reich! I can't—"

"I'm talking about the big D, Chooka, D for death. I came in here and strong-armed the D'Courtney girl out of you. I beat hell out of your girl-friend and I beat hell out of you. So you got frabbed off and set those traps. Right?"

Chooka shook her head dazedly.

"Three of them so far. On the ship coming back from Spaceland. In my study. In my Jumper. How many more, Chooka?"

"It wasn't me, Reich. So help me. I—"

"It has to be you, Chooka. You're the only one with a gripe and the only one who hires gimpsters. That adds up to you, so let's get it squared off." He slapped the safety off the scrambler. "I've got no time for a two-bit hater with coffin-queer friends."

"For God's sake!" Chooka screamed. "What the hell have I got against you? So you rough-housed a little. So you mugged Magda. You wasn't the first. You ain't gonna be the last. Use your head!"

"I used it. If it isn't you, who else?"

"Keno Quizzard. He hires gimpsters too. I heard you and him—"

"Quizzard's out. Quizzard's dead. Who else?"

"Church."

"He hasn't got the guts. If he had he would have tried it ten years ago. Who else?"

"How do I know? There's hundreds hate you enough."

"There's thousands, but who could get into my safe? Who could break a phase combination and—"

"Maybe nobody broke into your safe. Maybe somebody broke into your head and peeped the combination. Maybe—"

"Peeped!"

"Yeah. Peeped. Maybe you added Church up wrong . . . Or some other peeper what's got a eager reason for filling your coffin."

"My God . . ." Reich whispered. "Oh my God . . . Yes."

"Church?"

"No. Powell."

"The cop?"

"The cop. Powell. Yes. Mr. Holy Lincoln Powell. Yes!" The words began pouring out of Reich in a torrent. "Yes, Powell! The son of a bitch is fighting dirty because I've licked him clean. He can't get a case together. He's got nothing but booby-trapping left . . ."

"You're crazy, Reich."

"Am I? Why the hell did he take Ellery West away from me, and Breen? He knows the only defense I've got against a booby-trap is a peeper. It's Powell!"

"But a cop, Reich? A cop?"

"Sure a cop!" Reich shouted. "Why not a cop? He's safe. Who'd suspect him? It's smart. It's what I'd do myself. All right . . . Now I'm going to booby-trap him!"

He kicked the red-eyed woman from him, went to Chooka and yanked her to her feet. "Call Powell."

"What?"

"Call Powell," he yelled. "Lincoln Powell. Call him at his house. Tell him to come down here right away."

"No, Reich . . ."

He shook her. "Listen to me, frab-head. Bastion West is owned by the D'Courtney Cartel. Now that old D'Courtney's dead, I'm going to own the cartel, which means I'll own Bastion. I'll own this house. I'll own you, Chooka. You want to stay in business? Call Powell!"

She stared at his livid face, feebly peeping him, slowly realizing that what he said was true.

"But I got no excuse, Reich."

"Wait a minute. Wait a minute." Reich thought, then yanked the knife-pistol from his pocket and shoved it into Chooka's hands. "Show him this. Tell him the D'Courtney girl left it here."

"What is it?"

"The gun that killed D'Courtney."

"For the love of—Reich!"

Reich laughed. "It won't do him any good. By the time he's got it, he'll be booby-trapped. Call him. Show him the gun. Get him down here." He thrust Chooka toward the phone, followed her and stood alongside the screen out of the line of sight. He hefted the scrambler in his hand meaningfully. Chooka understood.

She dialed Powell's number. Mary Noyes appeared on the screen, listened to Chooka, then called Powell. The prefect appeared, his lean face haggard, his dark eyes heavily shadowed.

"I . . . I got something you might want, maybe, Mr. Powell," Chooka stammered. "I just found it. That girl you took outa my house. She left it behind."

"Left what, Chooka?"

"The gun which killed her father."

"No!" Powell's face was suddenly animated. "Let's see it."

Chooka displayed the knife-pistol.

"That's it, by heaven!" Powell exclaimed. "Maybe I'm going to get a break after all. Stay right where you are, Chooka. I'll be down as fast as a Jumper can jet."

The screen blacked out. Reich ground his teeth and tasted blood. He turned, dashed out of the Rainbow House and located a vacant coin-Jumper. He dropped a half-credit into the lock, opened the door and lurched in. As he took off with a hissing roar, he clattered against a thirtieth storey cornice and nearly capsized. He realized dazedly that he was in no condition to pilot a Jumper or set a booby-trap.

"Don't try to think," he thought. "Don't try to plan.

Leave it to your instincts. You're a killer. A natural killer. Just wait and kill!"

Reich fought himself and the controls all the way to Hudson Ramp, and he fought the Jumper down through the crazy, shifting North River winds. The killer instinct prompted him to crash-land in Powell's back garden. He didn't know why. As he pounded the twisted cabin door open, a canned voice spoke: "Your attention, please. You are liable for any damage to this vehicle. Please leave your name and address. If we are forced to trace you, you will be liable for the costs. Thank you."

"I'm going to be liable for a lot more damage," Reich growled. "You're welcome."

He plunged under a heavy clump of forsythia and waited with the scrambler ready. Then he understood why he had crashed. The girl who answered Powell's phone came out of the house and ran down through the garden toward the Jumper. Reich waited. No one else came from the house. The girl was alone. He surged up out of the brush and the girl spun around before she heard him. A peeper. He pulled the trigger to first notch. She stiffened and trembled . . . helpless.

At the moment when he was about to pull the trigger all the way back to the big D, instinct stopped him again. Suddenly the booby-trap for Powell came to him. Kill the girl inside the house. Seed her body with Detonation Bulbs and leave that bait for Powell. Sweat broke out on the girl's swarthy face. The muscles in her jaws twitched. Reich took her by the arm and led her up the garden to the house. She walked with the stiff-legged gait of a scarecrow.

Inside the house, Reich led the girl through the kitchen to the living room. He found a long, corded modern lounge and thrust the girl down on it. She was fighting him with everything short of her body. He grinned savagely, bent down and kissed her full on the mouth.

"My love to Powell," he said, and stepped back, raising the scrambler. Then he lowered it.

Someone was watching him.

He turned, almost casually, and darted a quick look around the living room. There was no one. He turned back to the girl and asked: "Are you doing that with TP, peeper?" Then he raised the scrambler. Again he lowered it.

Someone was watching him.

This time, Reich prowled around the living room, searching behind chairs, inside closets. There was no one. He checked the kitchen and the bath. No one. He returned to the living room and Mary Noyes. Then thought of the upper floor. He went to the stairs, started to mount them, and then stopped in mid-stride as though he had been pole-axed.

Someone was watching him.

She was at the head of the stairs, kneeling and peeping through the bannisters like a child. She was dressed like a child in tight little leotards with her hair drawn back and tied with ribbon. She looked at him with the droll, mischievous expression of a child. Barbara D'Courtney.

"Hello," she said.

Reich began to shake.

"I'm Baba," she said.

Reich motioned to her faintly.

She arose at once and came down the stairs, holding on to the bannister carefully. "I'm not s'posed to," she said. "Are you Papa's friend?"

Reich took a deep breath. "I . . . I . . ." he croaked.

"Papa had to go away," she prattled. "But he's coming back right away. He told me. If I'm a good girl, he'll bring me a present. I'm trying, but it's awful hard. Are you good?"

"Your father? Coming b-back? Your father?"

She nodded. "Was you playing games with Aunt Mary? You kissed her. I saw it. Papa kisses me. I like it. Does Aunt Mary like it?" She took his hand confidently. "When I grow up I'm going to marry Papa and be his girl for always. Do you have a girl?"

Reich pulled Barbara around and stared into her face. "Are you rocketing?" he said hoarsely. "Do you think I'll fall into that orbit? How much did you tell Powell?"

"That's my papa," she said. "When I ask him why his name is different from my name he looks funny. What's your name?"

"I asked you!" Reich shouted. "How much did you tell him? Who do you think you're fooling with that act? Answer me!"

She looked at him doubtfully, then began to cry, trying to pull away from him. He held on to her.

"Go 'way!" she sobbed. "Let me go!"

"Will you answer me!"

"Let me go!"

He dragged her from the foot of the stairs to the lounge where Mary Noyes still sat paralysed. He threw the girl alongside her and stepped back again, with the scrambler raised. Suddenly, the girl whipped upright in the chair in a listening attitude. Her face lost its childishness and became drawn and taut. She thrust out her legs, leaped from the lounge, ran, stopped abruptly, then appeared to open a door. She ran forward, yellow hair flying, dark eyes wide with alarm . . . a lightning flash of wild beauty.

136

"Father!" she screamed. "For God's sake! Father!"

Reich's heart constricted. The girl ran toward him. He stepped forward to catch her. She stopped short, backed away, then darted to the left and ran in a half circle, screaming wildly, her eyes fixed.

"No!" she cried. "No! For the love of Christ! Father!"

Reich pivoted and clutched at the girl. This time he caught her while she fought and screamed. Reich was shouting too. The girl suddenly stiffened and clutched her ears. Reich was back in the Orchid Suite. He heard the explosion and saw the blood and brains gout out of the back of D'Courtney's head. He shook with galvanic spasms that forced him to release the girl. She fell forward to her knees and crawled across the floor. He saw her crouch over the waxen body.

Reich gasped for breath and beat his knuckles together painfully, fighting for control. When the roaring in his ears subsided, he propelled himself toward Barbara, trying to arrange his thoughts and make split-second alterations in his plans. He had never counted on a witness. God damn Powell. He would have to kill the girl. Could he arrange a double-murder in the— No. Not murder. Booby-trap. Damn Gus Tate. Wait. He wasn't in Beaumont House. He was . . . in . . .

"Thirty-three Hudson Ramp," Powell said from the front door.

Reich jerked around, crouched automatically and whipped the scrambler up under his left elbow as Quizzard's killers had taught him.

Powell side-stepped. "Don't try it," he said sharply.

"You son of a bitch!" Reich shouted. He wheeled on Powell who had already crossed him up and again stepped out of the line of fire. "You God damned peeper! You lousy, sleazy, son of a —"

Powell faked to the left, reversed, closed with Reich and delivered a six-inch jab to the ulnar nerve complex. The scrambler fell to the floor. Reich clinched; punching, clawing, butting, swearing hysterically. Powell hit him with three lightning blows, nape, navel, and groin. The effect was that of a full spinal block. Reich crashed to the floor, retching, blood streaming from his nose.

"Brother, you think only you know how to gut fight," Powell grunted. He went to Barbara D'Courtney, who still knelt on the floor, and raised her.

"All right, Barbara?" he said.

"Hello, Papa. I had a bad dream."

"I know, baby. I had to give it to you. It was an experiment on that big oaf."

"Gimme a kiss."

137

He kissed her forehead. "You're growing up fast," he smiled. "You were just baby-talking yesterday."

"I'm growing up because you promised to wait for me."

"It's a promise, Barbara. Can you go upstairs by yourself or do you have to be carried . . . like yesterday?"

"I can go all by own self."

"All right, baby. Go up to your room."

She went to the stairs, took a firm hold on the bannister and climbed up. Just before she reached the top, she darted a glance at Reich and stuck her tongue out. Then she disappeared. Powell crossed to Mary Noyes, removed the gag, checked her pulse, then made her comfortable on the lounge.

"First notch, eh?" he murmured to Reich. "Painful but she'll recover in an hour." He went back to Reich and stared down at him, anger darkening his drawn face. "I ought to pay you back for Mary; but what's the use? It wouldn't teach you anything. You poor bastard . . . you're just no damned good."

"Kill me!" Reich groaned. "Kill me or let me up and by Christ I'll kill you!"

Powell picked up the scrambler and cocked an eye at Reich. "Try flexing your muscles a little. Those blocks shouldn't last more than a few seconds . . ." He sat down with the scrambler in his lap. "You had a tough break. I wasn't out of the house five minutes when I realized Chooka's story was a phoney. You put her up to it, of course."

"You're the phoney!" Reich shouted. "You and your ethics and your high talk. You and your phoney god-dam—"

"She said the gun killed D'Courtney," Powell continued imperturbably. "It did, but no one knows what killed D'Courtney . . . except you and me. I turned around and came back. It was a long take. Almost too long. Try getting up now. You can't be that sick."

Reich struggled up, his breath hissing horribly. Suddenly he dipped into his pocket and brought out the cartridge of Detonation Bulbs. Powell arched back in the chair and kicked Reich in the chest with his heel. The cartridge went flying. Reich fell back and collapsed on a sofa.

"When will you people learn you can't surprise a peeper?" Powell said. He went to the cartridge and picked it up. "You're quite the arsenal today, aren't you? You're acting more like you're wanted dead or alive than like a free man. Notice I said free. Not innocent."

"Free how long?" Reich said through his teeth. "I never talked about innocence either. But free how long?"

"Forever. I had a perfect case against you. Every detail right. I checked that when I peeped you with Barbara just now. I had every detail except one, and that one flaw blew my case out into deep space. You're a free man, Reich. We've closed your file."

Reich stared. "Closed the file?"

"Yep. No solution. I'm licked. You can disarm, Reich. Go about your business. No one's going to bother you."

"You're a liar! This is one of your peeper tricks. You—"

"Nope. I'll lay it out for you. I know all about you . . . How much you bribed Gus Tate . . . What you promised Jerry Church . . . Where you located that Sardine Game . . . What you did with Wilson Jordan's Rhodopsin Caps . . . How you emptied those cartridges for an alibi and then turned them lethal again with a drop of water . . . So far a perfect chain of evidence. Method and Opportunity. But Motive was the flaw. The courts demand Objective Motive and I can't produce it. That sets you free."

"You liar!"

"Of course I could throw this breaking and entering with deadly intent at you . . . but it's too small a charge. Like shooting a popgun after you misfire with a cannon. You could probably beat it, too. My only witnesses would be a peeper and a sick girl. I—"

"You liar," Reich growled. "You hypocrite. You lying peeper. Am I supposed to believe you? Am I supposed to listen to the rest of it? You had nothing, Powell. Nothing! I licked you on every point. That's why you're booby-trapping me. That's why you—" Reich broke off abruptly and beat his forehead. "And this is probably the biggest booby-trap of all. And I fell into it. What a damned fool I am. What a—"

"Shut up," Powell snapped. "When you rave like that I can't peep you. Now what's all this about booby-traps? Think it through."

Reich uttered a ragged laugh. "As if you don't know . . . My stateroom on the liner . . . My gaffed safe . . . My Jumper . . ."

For almost a minute, Powell focussed on Reich, peeping, absorbing, digesting. Then his face began to pale and his respiration quicken. "My God!" he exclaimed. "My God!" He leaped to his feet and began pacing distractedly. "That's it. . . . That explains it . . . And Old Man Mose was right. Passion motive, and we thought he was kittenish . . . And Barbara's Siamese Twin Image . . . And D'Courtney's guilt . . . . No wonder Reich couldn't kill us at Chooka's . . . But—the murder isn't important any more. It goes deeper. Far deeper. And it's dangerous . . . More than I ever dreamed." He stopped, turned and looked at Reich with blazing eyes.

"If I could kill you," he cried, "I'd twist your head off with my hands. I'd tear you apart and hang you on a Galacti

139

Gallows, and the Universe would bless me. Do you know how dangerous you are? Does a plague know its peril? Is death conscious?"

Reich goggled at Powell in bewilderment. The Prefect shook his head impatiently. "Why ask you?" he muttered. "You don't know what I'm talking about. You'll never know." He went to a sideboard, selected two brandy ampules and popped them into Reich's mouth. Reich attempted to spit them out. Powell held his jaws shut.

"Swallow them," he said crisply. "I want you to pull yourself together and listen to me. Do you want Butylene? Thyric Acid? Can you compose yourself without drugs?"

Reich choked on the brandy and sputtered angrily. Powell shook him silent.

"Get this straight," Powell said. "I'm going to show you half the pattern. Try to understand it. The case against you is closed. It's closed because of those booby-traps. If I'd known about them I'd never have started the case. I'd have broken my conditioning and killed you. Try to understand this, Reich . . ."

Reich stopped sputtering.

"I couldn't find a motive for your murder. That's the flaw. When you offered merger to D'Courtney, he accepted. He sent WWHG in answer. That's acceptance. You had no reason to murder him. You had every objective reason to keep him alive."

Reich went white. His head began to wobble crazily. "No. No. WWHG. Offer refused. Refusal. Refusal!"

"Acceptance."

"No. The bastard refused. He—"

"He accepted. When I learned that D'Courtney accepted your offer, I was finished. I knew I couldn't bring a case to court. But I haven't been trying to booby-trap you. I did not gaff your stateroom lock. I did not plant those Detonation Bulbs. I'm not the man who's trying to murder you. That man is trying to kill you because he knows you're safe from me. He knows you're safe from Demolition. He's always known what I've just discovered . . . that you're the deadly enemy of our entire future."

Reich tried to speak. He struggled up out of the sofa, gesticulating feebly. Finally he said: "Who is it? Who? Who?"

"He's your ancient enemy, Reich . . . A man you'll never escape. You'll never be able to run from him . . . hide from him . . . and I pray to God you'll never be able to save yourself from him."

"Who is it, Powell? WHO IS IT?"

"The Man With No Face."

Reich emitted a guttural cry of pain. Then he turned and staggered out of the house.

15

Tension, apprehension, and dissension have begun.
Tension, apprehension, and dissension have begun.
Tension, apprehension, and dissension have begun.
Tension, apprehension, and dissension have begun.
"Shut up!" Reich cried.
Eight, sir;
      Seven, sir;
            Six, sir;
                  Five, Sir:
"For God's sake! Shut up!"
                      Four, Sir;
            Three, sir;
      Two, sir;
One!
"You've got to think. Why don't you think? What's happened to you? Why don't you think?"
Tension, apprehension and—
"He was lying. You know he was lying. You were right the first time. A giant booby-trap. WWHG. Refusal. Refusal. But why did he lie? How is that going to help him?"
—dissension have begun.
"The Man With No Face. Breen could have told him. Gus Tate could have told him. Think!"
Tension—
"There is no Man With No Face. It's just a dream. A nightmare!"
Apprehension—
"But the booby-traps? What about the booby-traps? He had me cold in his house. Why didn't he pull the switch? Telling me I'm free. What's he up to? Think!"
Dissension—
A hand touched his shoulder.
"Mr. Reich?"
"What?"
"Mr. Reich!"
"What? Who's that?"
Reich's eyes focussed. He became aware that it was raining heavily. He was lying on his side, knees drawn up, arms folded, his cheek buried in mud. He was drenched, shivering with cold. He was in the esplanade of Bomb Inlet. Around him were sighing, sodden trees. A figure was bending over him.

"Who are you?"

"Galen Chervil, Mr. Reich."

"What?"

"Galen Chervil, sir. From Maria Beaumont's party. Can I do you that favor, Mr. Reich?"

"Don't peep me!" Reich cried.

"I'm not, Mr. Reich. We don't usually—" Young Chervil caught himself. "I didn't know you knew I was a peeper. You'd better get up, sir."

He took Reich's arm and pulled. Reich groaned and yanked his arm free. Young Chervil took him under the shoulders and raised him, staring at Reich's frightful appearance.

"Were you mugged, Mr. Reich?"

"What? No. No . . ."

"Accident, sir?"

"No. No, I . . . Oh, for God's sake," Reich burst out, "get the hell away from me!"

"Certainly, sir. I thought you needed help and I owe you a favor, but—"

"Wait," Reich interrupted. "Come back." He grasped the bole of a tree and leaned against it, panting hoarsely. Finally he thrust himself erect and glared at Chervil with bloodshot eyes. "You mean that about the favor?"

"Of course, Mr. Reich."

"No questions asked. No tales told?"

"Certainly not, Mr. Reich."

"My problem's murder, Chervil. I want to find out who's trying to kill me. Will you do me that favor? Will you peep someone for me?"

"I should imagine the police would be able to—"

"The police?" Reich laughed hysterically, then clutched himself in agony as the broken rib caught. "I want you to peep a cop for me, Chervil. A big cop. The Commissioner of cops. D'you understand?" He let go the tree and lurched to Chervil. "I want to visit my friend the Commissioner and ask him a few questions. I want you to be there to tell me the truth. Will you come to Crabbe's office and peep him for me? Will you just do it and forget about it? Will you?"

"Yes, Mr. Reich . . . I will."

"What? An honest peeper! How about that? Come on. Let's jet."

Reich stumbled out of the esplanade with a horrible gait. Chervil followed, overwhelmed by the fury in the man that drove him through injury, through fever, through agony to police headquarters. There, Reich bulled and roared past clerks and guards until the mud-streaked blood-smeared figure burst into Commissioner Crabbe's elaborate ebony and silver office.

"My God, Reich!" Crabbe was aghast. "It is you, isn't it? Ben Reich?"

"Sit down, Chervil," Reich said. He turned to Crabbe. "It's me. Get a full perspective. I'm half a corpse, Crabbe. The red stuff is blood. The rest is slime. I've had a great day . . . a glorious day . . . and I want to know where the hell the police have been? Where's your God Almighty Prefect Powell? Where's your—"

"Half a corpse? What are you telling me, Ben?"

"I'm telling you that I was almost murdered three times today. This boy . . ." Reich pointed to Chervil. "This boy just found me in the Inlet Esplanade more dead than alive. Look at me, for Christ's sake. Look at me!"

"Murdered!" Crabbe thumped his desk emphatically. "Of course. That Powell is a fool. I should never have listened to him. The man who killed D'Courtney is trying to kill you."

Behind his back, Reich motioned savagely to Chervil.

"I told Powell you were innocent. He wouldn't listen to me," Crabbe said. "Even when that infernal adding machine in the District Attorney's office told him you were innocent, he wouldn't listen."

"The machine said I was innocent?"

"Of course it did. There's no case against you. There never was a case against you. And by the sacred Bill of Rights, you'll have the protection from the murderer that any honest law-abiding citizen deserves. I'll see to that at once." Crabbe strode to the door. "And I think this is all I'll need to settle Mr. Powell's hash for good! Don't go, Ben. I want to talk to you about your support for the Solar Senatorship . . ."

The door opened and slammed. Reich reeled and fought his way back to the world. He looked at three Chervils. "Well?" he muttered. "Well?"

"He's telling the truth, Mr. Reich."

"About me? About Powell?"

"Well . . ." Chervil paused judiciously, weighing the truth.

"Jet, you bastard," Reich groaned. "How long do you think I can keep my fuses from blowing."

"He's telling the truth about you," Chervil said quickly. "The Prosecution Computer has declined to authorize any action against you for the D'Courtney murder. Mr. Powell has been forced to abandon the case and . . . well . . . his career is very much in jeopardy."

"Is that true!" Reich staggered to the boy and seized his shoulders. "Is that true, Chervil? I've been cleared? I can go about my business? No one's going to bother me?"

"You've been dropped, Mr. Reich. You can go about your business. No one's going to bother you."

Reich burst into a roar of triumphant laughter. The pain of his bruised and broken body made him groan as he laughed, and his eyes smarted with tears. He pulled himself up, brushed past Chervil and left the Commissioner's office. He was more a Neanderthal vestige as he paraded down headquarters' corridors streaked with blood and mud, laughing and groaning, bearing himself with limping arrogance. He needed a stag's carcass on his shoulders or a cave bear borne in triumph behind him to complete the picture.

"I'll complete the picture with Powell's head," he told himself. "Stuffed and mounted on my wall. I'll complete the picture with the D'Courtney Cartel stuffed into my pockets. By God, give me time I'll complete a picture with the Galaxy inside the frame!"

He passed through the steel portals of headquarters and stood for a moment on the steps gazing at the rain-swept streets . . . at the amusement center across the square, block after block blazing under a single mutual transparent dome . . . at the open shops lining the upper footways, all bustle and brilliance as the city's night shopping began . . . the towering office buildings in the background, great two-hundred storey cubes . . . the lace tracery of skyways linking them together . . . the twinkling running lights of Jumpers bobbing up and down like a plague of crimson-eyed grasshoppers in a field . . .

"And I'll own you!" he shouted, raising his arms to engulf the universe. "I'll own you all! Bodies, passions, and souls!"

Then his eye caught the tall, ominous, familiar figure crossing the square, watching him covertly over its shoulder. A figure of black shadows sparkling with raindrop jewels . . . looking, looming, silent, horrible . . . A Man With No Face.

There was a strangled cry. The fuses blew. Like a blighted tree, Reich fell to the ground.

At one minute to nine, ten of the fifteen members of the Esper Guild Council assembled in President T'sung's office. Emergency business required their attention. At one minute after nine, the meeting was adjourned with the business completed. Within those one hundred and twenty Esper seconds, the following took place:

> A gavel pounding
> A clock face
> Hour hand at 9
> Minute hand at 59
> Second hand at 60

144

EMERGENCY MEETING

To examine a request for Mass Cathexis with Lincoln Powell as the human canal for the Capitalized energy.

(Consternation)

T'sung: You can't be serious, Powell. How can you make such a request? What can possibly require such an extraordinary and dangerous measure?

Powell: An astonishing development in the D'Courtney Case which I would like you all to examine.

(Examination)

Powell: You all know that Reich is our most dangerous enemy. He is supporting the Anti-Esper smear campaign. Unless that is blocked we may suffer the usual history of minority groups. .

@kins: True enough.

Powell: He is also supporting the League of Esper Patriots. Unless that organization is blocked we may be plunged into a civil war and be lost forever in a morass of internal chaos.

Franion: That's true too.

Powell: But there is an addiitonal development which you have all examined. Reich is about to become a Galactic focal point . . . A crucial link between the positive past and the probabᶦe future. He is on the verge of a powerful reorganization at this moment. Time is of the essence. If Reich can readjust and reorient before I can reach him, he will become immune to our reality, invulnerable to our attack, and the deadly enemy of Galactic reason and reality.

(Alarm)

@kins: Surely you're exaggerating, Powell.

Powell: Am I? Inspect the picture with me. Look at Reich's position in time and space. Will not his beliefs become the world's belief? Will not his reality become the world's reality? Is he not, in his critical position of power, energy, and intellect, a sure road to utter destruction?

(Conviction)

T'sung: That's true. Nevertheless I'm reluctant to authorise the Mass Cathexis Measure. You will recall that the MCM has invariably destroyed the human energy canal in past attempts. You're too valuable to be destroyed, Powell.

Powell: I must be permitted to run the risk. Reich is one of the rare Universe-shakers . . . a child as yet, but about to mature. And all reality . . . Espers, Normals, Life, the earth, the solar system, the universe

145

itself . . . all reality hangs precariously on his awakening. He cannot be permitted to awake to the wrong reality. I call the question.

Franion: You're asking us to vote your death.

Powell: It's my death against the eventual death of everything we know. I call the question.

@kins: Let Reich awaken as he will. We have the time and the warning to attack him at another crossroad.

Powell: Question! I call the question!
    (Request granted)
    Meeting adjourned
    Clock face
    Hour hand at 9
    Minute hand at 01
    Second hand at Demolition

Powell arrived home an hour later. He had made his will, paid his bills, signed his papers, arranged everything. There had been dismay at the Guild. There was dismay when he came home. Mary Noyes read what he had done the instant he entered.

"Linc!"

"No fuss. It's got to be done."

"But—"

"There's a chance it won't kill me. Oh . . . One reminder. Lab wants a brain autopsy soon as I'm dead . . . if I die. I've signed all the papers, but I wish you'd help in case there's trouble. They'd like to have the body before rigor. If they can't get the corpse they'll settle for the head. See to it, will you?"

"Linc!"

"Sorry. Now, you'd better pack and take the baby up to Kingston Hospital. She won't be safe here."

"She isn't a baby any more. She—"

Mary turned and ran upstairs, trailing the familiar sensory impact: Snow/mint/tulips/taffeta . . . and now mixed with terror and tears. Powell sighed, then smiled as a highly poised teen-ager appeared at the head of the stairs and came down with grand insouciance. She was wearing a dress and an expression of rehearsed surprise. She paused halfway down to let him take in the dress and the manner.

"Why! It's Mr. Powell, is it not?"

"It is. Good morning, Barbara."

"And what brings you to our little domain this morning?" She came down the rest of the stairs with her fingertips brushing the bannister and tripped on the bottom step. "Oh Pip!" she squawked.

146

Powell caught her. "Pop," he said.

"Bim."

"Bam."

She looked up at him. "You stand right here. I'm going to come down those stairs again and I bet I do it perfect."

"I'll bet you don't."

She turned, trotted up and posed again at the top step. "Dear Mr. Powell, what a scatter-brain you must think me . . ." She began the grand descent. "You must re-evaluate your opinion of me. I am no longer the mere child I was yesterday. I am ages and ages older. You must regard me as an adult from now on." She negotiated the bottom step and regarded him intently. "Re-evaluate? Is that right?"

"Revaluate is sometimes preferred, dear."

"I thought it had an extra sound." Suddenly she laughed, pushed him into a chair, and plumped down on his lap. Powell groaned.

"Gently, Barbara. You're ages older and pounds heavier."

"Listen," she said. "What ever made me think you was . . . Were? Were my father?"

"What's the matter with me as a father?"

"Let's be frank. Real frank."

"Sure."

"Do you feel like a father toward me? Because I don't feel like a daughter toward you."

"Oh? How do you feel?"

"I asked first, so you go first."

"My feelings toward you are those of a loving and dutiful son."

"No. Be serious."

"I have resolved to be a trustworthy son to all women until Vulcan assumes its rightful place in the Commity of Planets."

She flushed angrily and got up from his lap. "I wanted you to be serious, because I need advice. But if you—"

"I'm sorry, Barbara. What is it?"

She knelt alongside him and took his hand. "I'm all mixed up about you."

"How?"

She looked into his eyes with the alarming directness of the young. "You know."

After a pause, he nodded. "Yes. I know."

"And you're all mixed up about me, too. I know."

"Yes, Barbara. That's true. I am."

"Is it wrong?"

Powell heaved up from the chair and began pacing unhappily. "No, Barbara, it isn't wrong. It's . . . mistimed."

"I want you to tell me about it."

"Tell you . . . ? Yes, I suppose I'd better. I . . . I'll put it this way, Barbara. The two of us are four people. There's two of you, and two of me."

"Why?"

"You've been sick, dear. So we had to turn you into a baby and let you grow up again. That's why you're two people. The grown-up Barbara inside, and the baby outside."

"And you?"

"I'm two grown-up people. One of them is me . . . Powell . . . The other is a member of the governing Council of the Esper Guild."

"What's that?"

"It doesn't need explaining. It's the part of me that's got me mixed up . . . God knows, maybe it's the baby part. I don't know."

She considered earnestly, then said slowly. "When I don't feel like a daughter to you . . . which me feels like that?"

"I don't know, Barbara."

"You do know. Why won't you say?" She came to him and put her arms around his neck . . . a grown-up woman with the manner of a child. "If it isn't wrong, why won't you say? If I love you—"

"Who said anything about love!"

"It's what we're talking about, isn't it? Isn't it? I love you and you love me. Isn't that it?"

"*All right,*" Powell thought desperately. "*Here it is. What are you going to do? Admit the truth?*"

"*Yes!*" From the stairs. Mary was descending with a travelling case in her hand. "*Admit the truth.*"

"*She isn't a peeper.*"

"*Forget that. She's a woman and she's in love with you. You're in love with her. Please, Linc, give yourselves a chance.*"

"*A chance for what? An affair if I get out of this Reich mess alive? That's all it could be. You know the Guild won't let us marry normals.*"

"*She'll settle for that. She'll be grateful to settle for that. Ask me. I know.*"

"*And if I don't come out alive? She'll have nothing . . . Nothing but half a memory of half a love.*"

"No, Barbara," he said. "That isn't it at all."

"It is," she insisted. "It is!"

"No. It's the baby part of you talking. The baby thinks she's in love with me. The woman is not."

"She'll grow up into the woman."

"And she'll forget all about me."

"You'll make her remember."

"Why should I, Barbara?"

"Because you feel that way about me, too. I know you do."

Powell laughed. "Baby! Baby! Baby! What makes you think I'm in love with you that way? I'm not. I've never been."

"You are!"

"Open your eyes, Barbara. Look at me. Look at Mary. You're ages older, aren't you? Can't you understand? Do I have to explain the obvious?"

"For God's sake, Linc!"

"Sorry, Mary. Got to use you."

"I'm getting ready to say goodbye . . . Maybe for good . . . Do I have to endure this? Isn't it bad enough for me already?"

"Shhhhh. Gently, dear . . ."

Barbara stared at Mary, then at Powell. She shook her head slowly. "You're lying."

"Am I? Look at me." He put his hands on her shoulders and looked into her face. Dishonest Abe came to his assistance. His expression was kind, tolerant, amused, patronizing. "Look at me, Barbara."

"No!" she cried. "Your face is lying. It's . . . It's hateful! I—" She burst into tears and sobbed: "Oh go away. Why don't you go away?"

"We're going away, Barbara," Mary said. She came forward, took the girl's arm and led her to the door.

"There's a Jumper waiting, Mary."

"There's me waiting, Linc. For you. Always. And the Chervils & @kins & Jordans &&&&&&—"

"I know. I know. I love you all. Kisses. XXXXXX. 𝔅lessings . . ."

Image of four-leaf clover, rabbits' feet, horseshoes . . .

Bawdy response of Powell emerging from slok covered with diamonds.

Faint laughter.

Farewell.

He stood in the doorway whistling a crooked, plaintive tune, watching the Jumper disappear into the steel-blue sky boring north toward Kingston Hospital. He was exhausted. A little proud of himself for having made the sacrifice. Intensely ashamed of himself for feeling proud. Clearly melancholic. Should he take a grain of Potassium Niacate and kick himself up into the manic curve? What the hell was the use? Look at that great foul city of seventeen and one half million souls and not one soul for him. Look at—

The first impulse came. A thin trickle of latent energy. He felt it distinctly and glanced at his watch. Ten-twenty. So soon? So quickly? Good. He'd better get ready.

He turned into the house and darted up the stairs to his

dressing room. The impulses came pattering . . . like the preliminary raindrops before a storm. His psyche began to throb and vibrate as he reached out and absorbed those tiny streams of latent energy. He changed his clothes, dressed for all weather, and—

And what? The pattering had become a drizzle, washing over him, filling his consciousness with ague . . . with grinding emotional flashes . . . with—Yes, nutrient capsules. Hold on to that. Nutrient. Nutrient. Nutrient! He tumbled down the stairs into the kitchen. Found the plastic bulb, cracked it and swallowed a dozen capsules.

The energy came in torrents now. From each Esper in the city, a trickle of latent power that merged and merged into a stream, a river, a swirling sea of Mass Cathexis directed toward Powell, tuned to Powell. He opened all blocks and absorbed it all. His nervous system superheterodyned and screamed and a turbine in his mind whirled faster and faster with a mounting intolerable whine.

He was out of the house, wandering through the streets, blind, deaf, senseless, immersed in that boiling mass of latent energy . . . like a ship with sails caught in the nexus of a typhoon, fighting to convert a whirlpool of wind into the motive power that would lead to safety . . . So Powell fought to absorb that fearful torrent, to Capitalize that latent energy, to Cathectize and direct it toward the Demolition of Reich before it was too late, too late, too late, too late, too late . . .

16

ABOLISH THE LABYRINTH.
DESTROY THE MAZE.
DELETE THE PUZZLE.
($X^2 \phi Y^3 d!$ Space/d! Time)
DISBAND.
(OPERATIONS, EXPRESSIONS, FACTORS, FRACTIONS, POWERS, EXPONENTS, RADICALS, IDENTITIES, EQUATIONS, PROGRESSIONS, VARIATIONS, PERMUTATIONS, DETERMINANTS, AND SOLUTIONS)
EFFACE.
(ELECTRON, PROTON, NEUTRON, MESON AND PHOTON)
ERASE.

(CAYLEY, HENSON, LILLIENTHAL, CHANUTE, LANGLEY, WRIGHT, TURNBUL AND S&ERSON)
EXPUNGE.
(NEBULAE, CLUSTERS, STREAMS, BINARIES, GIANTS, MAIN SEQUENCE, AND WHITE DWARFS)
DISPERSE.
(PISCES, AMPHIBIA, BIRDS, MAMMALS, AND MAN)
ABOLISH.
DESTROY.
DELETE.
DISBAND.
ERASE ALL EQUATIONS.
INFINITY EQUALS ZERO.
THERE IS NO—

"—there is no what?" Reich shouted. "There is no what?" He struggled upward, fighting the bedclothes and the restraining hands. "There is no what?"

"No more nightmares," Duffy Wyg& said.

"Who's that?"

"Me. Duffy."

Reich opened his eyes. He was in a frilly bedroom in a frilly bed with old-fashioned linen and blankets. Duffy Wyg&, starched and fresh, had her hands against his shoulders. Once again she tried to thrust him back against the pillows.

"I'm asleep," Reich said. "I want to wake up."

"You say the nicest things. Lie down and the dream will continue."

Reich fell back. "I was awake," he said somberly. "I was wide awake for the first time in my life. I heard . . . I don't know what I heard. Infinity and zero. Important things. Reality. Then I fell asleep and I'm here."

"Correction," Duffy smiled. "Just for the record. You awoke."

"I'm asleep!" Reich shouted. He sat up. "Have you got a shot? Anything . . . opium, hemp, somnar, lethettes . . . I've got to wake up, Duffy. I've got to get back to reality."

Duffy bent over him and kissed him hard on the mouth. "How about this? Real?"

"You don't understand. It's all been delusions . . . hallucinations . . . everything. I've got to readjust, reorientate, reorganize . . . Before it's too late, Duffy. Before it's too late, too late, too late . . ."

Duffy threw up her hands. "What the hell's happened to medicine!" she exclaimed. "First that damned doctor scares you into a faint. Then he swears you're patched up . . . and

151

now look at you. Psychotic!" She knelt on the bed and shook a finger against Reich's noise. "One more word out of you and I call Kingston."

"What? Who?"

"Kingston, as in hospital. Where they send people like you."

"No. Who did you say scared me into a faint?"

"A doctor friend."

"In the square in front of police headquarters?"

"X marks the spot."

"Sure?"

"I was with him, looking for you. Your valet told me about the explosion and I was worried. We got to the rescue just in time."

"Did you see his face?"

"See it? I've kissed it."

"What's it look like?"

"It's a face. Two eyes. Two lips. Two ears. One nose. Three chins. Listen, Ben, if this is some more of the awake-asleep-reality-infinity lyrics . . . it ain't commercial."

"And you brought me here?"

"Sure. How could I pass up the opportunity? It's the only way I can get you into my bed."

Reich grinned. He relaxed and said: "Duffy, you may now kiss me."

"Mr. Reich, you already been kissed. Or was that when you were still awake?"

"Forget that. Nightmares. Plain nightmares." Reich burst into laughter. "Why the hell should I worry about having nightmares? I have the rest of the world in my hands. I'll take the dreams too. Didn't you once ask to be dragged through the gutter, Duffy?"

"That was a childish whim. I thought I could meet a better class of people."

"You name the gutter and you can have it, Duffy. Gold gutters . . . Jewelled gutters. You want a gutter from here to Mars? You'll have it. You want me to turn the System into a gutter? I'll do it. Christ! I can turn the Galaxy into a gutter if you want it." He jabbed his chest with his thumb. "Want to look at God? Here I am. Go ahead and look."

"Dear man. So modest and so hung-over."

"Drunk? Sure, I'm drunk." Reich thrust his legs out of the bed and stood up, reeling slightly. Duffy came to him at once and he put his arm around her waist for support. "Why shouldn't I be drunk? I've licked D'Courtney. I've licked Powell. I'm forty years old. I've got sixty years of owning the whole world ahead of me. Yes, Duffy . . . the whole damned world!" He began walking around the room with Duffy. It was like a stroll through her ebullient erotic mind. A peeper decorator had reproduced Duffy's psyche perfectly in the decor.

"How'd you like to start a dynasty with me, Duffy?"

"I wouldn't know about starting dynasties."

"You start with Ben Reich. First you marry him. Then—"

"That's enough. When do I start?"

"Then you have children. Boys. Dozens of boys . . ."

"Girls. And only three."

"And you watch Ben Reich take over D'Courtney and merge it with Monarch. You watch the enemies go down . . . like this!" In full stride, Reich kicked the leg of a busty vanity table. It toppled and crashed a score of crystal bottles to the floor.

"After Monarch and D'Courtney become Reich, Incorporated, you watch me eat up the rest . . . the small ones . . . the fleas. Case and Umbrel on Venus. Eaten!" Reich brought his fist down on a torso-shaped side table and smashed it. "United Transaction on Mars. Mashed and eaten!" He crushed a delicate chair. "The GCI Combine on Ganymede, Callisto, and Io . . . Titan Chemical & Atomics . . . And then the smaller lice: the backbiters, the haters, the Guild of Peepers, the moralists, the patriots . . . Eaten! Eaten! Eaten!" He pounded his palm against a marble nude until it toppled from its pedestal and shattered.

"Clever-up, dog," Duffy hung on his neck. "Why waste all that dear violence? Punch me around a little."

He lifted her in his arms and shook her until she squealed. "And parts of the world will taste sweet . . . like you, Duffy; and parts will stink to high heaven . . . but I'll gobble them all." He laughed and crushed her against him. "I don't know much about the God business, but I know what I like. We'll tear it all down, Duffy, and we'll build it all up to suit us . . . You and me and the dynasty."

He carried her to the window, tore away the drapes and kicked open the sashes with a mighty jangle of smashed glass. Outside, the city was in velvet darkness. Only the skyways and streets twinkled with lights, and the scarlet eyes of an occasional Jumper popped up over the jet skyline. The rain had stopped and a slender moon hung pale in the sky. The night wind came whispering in, cutting through the cloy of the spilled perfume.

"You out there!" Reich roared. "Can you hear me? All of you . . . sleeping and dreaming. You'll dream my dreams from now on! You'll—"

Abruptly he was silent. He relaxed his hold on Duffy and permitted her to slide to the floor alongside him. He seized the sides of the window and poked his head far out into the night, twisting his neck to stare up. When he drew his head back into the room, his face wore a bewildered expression.

"The stars," he mumbled. "Where are the stars?"

"Where are the what?" Duffy wanted to know.

"The stars," Reich repeated. He gestured timidly toward the sky. "The stars. They're gone."

Duffy looked at him curiously. "The what are gone?"

"The stars!" Reich cried. "Look up at the sky. The stars are gone. The constellations are gone! The Great Bear . . . The Little Bear . . . Cassiopeia . . . Draco . . . Pegasus . . . They're all gone! There's nothing but the moon! Look!"

"It's the way it always is," Duffy said.

"It is not! Where are the stars?"

"What stars?"

"I don't know their names. . . Polaris and . . . Vega . . . and . . . How the hell should I know their names? I'm not an astronomer. What's happened to us? What's happened to the stars?"

"What are stars?" Duffy asked.

Reich seized her savagely. "Suns . . . Boiling and blazing with light. Thousands of them. Billions of them . . . shining through the night. What the hell's the matter with you? Don't you understand? There's been a catastrophe in space. The stars are gone!"

Duffy shook her head. Her face was terrified. "I don't know what you're talking about, Ben. I don't know what you're talking about."

He shoved her away, turned and ran to the bathroom, and locked himself in. While he was hurriedly bathing and dressing, Duffy pounded on the door and pleaded with him. Finally, she broke off, and seconds later he heard her calling Kingston Hospital, using a guarded voice.

"Let her start explaining about the stars," Reich muttered, halfway between anger and terror. He finished his toilette and came out into the bedroom. Duffy cut the phone off hastily and turned to him.

"Ben," she began.

"Wait here for me," he growled. "I'm going to find out."

"Find out about what?"

"About the stars!" he yelled. "The Christ almighty missing stars!"

He flung out of the apartment and rushed down to the street. On the empty footway, he paused and stared up again. There was the moon. There was one brilliant red point of light . . . Mars. There was another . . . Jupiter. There was nothing else. Blackness. Blackness. Blackness. It hung over his head, enigmatic, unrelieved, terrifying. It pressed downward, by some trick of the eye, oppressive, stifling, deadly.

154

He began to run, still staring upward. He turned a corner of the footway and collided with a woman, knocking her flat. He pulled her to her feet.

"You clumsy bastard!" she screamed, adjusting her feathers. Then in an oily voice: "Lookin' for a good time, pilot?"

Reich held her arm. He pointed up. "Look. The stars are gone. Have you noticed? The stars are gone."

"What's gone?"

"The stars. Don't you see? They're gone."

"I don't know what you're talkin' about, pilot. C'mon. Let's have us a ball."

He tore himself away from her claws and ran. Halfway down the footway was a public v-phone alcove. He stepped in and dialed information. The screen lit and a robot voice spoke: "Question?"

"What's happened to the stars?" Reich asked. "When did it happen? It must have been noticed by now. What's the explanation?"

There was a click, a pause, then another click. "Will you spell the word, please."

"Star!" Reich roared. "S-T-A-R. Star!"

Click, pause, click. "Noun or verb?"

"God damn you! Noun!"

Click, pause, click. "There is no information listed under that heading," the canned voice announced.

Reich swore, then fought to control himself. "Where's the nearest Observatory to the city?"

"Kindly specify city."

"This city. New York."

Click, pause, click. "The Lunar Observatory at Croton Park is situated thirty miles north. It may be reached by Jumper Route North Coordinate 227. The Lunar Observatory was endowed in the year two thousand—"

Reich slammed down the phone. "No information listed under that heading! My God! Are they all crazy?" He ran out into the streets, searching for a Public Jumper. A piloted machine cruised past and Reich signalled. It swooped to pick him up.

"Northco 227," he snapped as he stepped into the cabin. "Thirty miles. The Lunar Observatory."

"Premium trip," the driver said.

"I'll pay it. Jet!"

The cab jetted. Reich restrained himself for five minutes, then began casually: "Notice the sky?"

"Why, mister?"

"The stars are gone."

Sycophantic laugh.

"It's not supposed to be a joke," Reich said. "The stars are gone."

"If it ain't a joke, it needs explaining," the driver said. "What the hell are stars?"

A blasting reply trembled on Reich's lips. Before it could erupt, the cab landed him on the observatory grounds close to the domed roof. He snapped: "Wait for me," and ran across the lawns to the small stone entrance.

The door was ajar. He entered the observatory and heard the low whine of the dome mechanism and the quiet click of the observatory clock. Except for the low glow of the clock-light, the room was in darkness. The twelve-inch refractor was in operation. He could see the observer, a dim outline, crouched over the eyepiece of the guiding telescope.

Reich walked toward him, nervous, strained, flinching at the loud clack of his footsteps in the silence. There was a chill in the air.

"Listen," Reich began in a low voice. "Sorry to bother you but you must have noticed. You're in the star business. You have noticed, haven't you? The stars. They're gone. All of them. What's happened? Why hasn't there been any alarm? Why's everybody pretending? My God! The stars! We always take them for granted. And now they're gone. What's happened? Where are the stars?"

The figure straightened slowly and turned toward Reich. "There are no stars," it said.

It was the Man With No Face.

Reich cried out. He turned and ran. He flew out of the door, down the steps and across the lawn to the waiting cab. He blundered against the crystal cabin wall with a crack that dropped him to his knees.

The driver pulled him to his feet. "You all right, Mac?"

"I don't know," Reich groaned. "I wish I did."

"None of my business," the driver said, "but I think you ought to see a peeper. You're talkin' crazy."

"About the stars?"

"Yeah."

Reich gripped the man. "I'm Ben Reich," he said. "Ben Reich of Monarch."

"Yeah, Mac. I recognized you."

"Good. You know what I can do for you if you do me a favor? Money . . . New job . . . Anything you want . . ."

"You can't do nothin' for me, Mac. I already been adjusted at Kingston."

"Better. An honest man. Will you do me a favor for the love of God or anything you love?"

"Sure, Mac."

"Go into that building. Take a look at the man behind

156

the telescope. A good look. Come back and describe him to me."

The driver departed, was gone five minutes, then returned.

"Well?"

"He's just an ordinary guy, Mac. Sixtyish. Bald. Got lines in his face kinda deep. His ears stick out and he's got what they call a weak chin. You know. It kinda backslides."

"It's nobody . . . nobody," Reich muttered.

"What?"

"About those stars," Reich said. "You never heard of them? You never saw them? You don't know what I'm talking about?"

"Nope."

"Oh God . . ." Reich moaned. "Sweet God . . ."

"Now don't warp your orbit, Mac." The driver thumped him powerfully on the back. "Tell you something. They taught me plenty up at Kingston. One of them things was . . . Well, sometimes you get a crazy notion. It's brand new, see? But you think you always had it. Like . . . oh . . . for instance, that people always had one eye and now all of a sudden they got two."

Reich stared at him.

"So you run around yellin': 'For Chrissakes, where did they all of a sudden get two eyes everybody?' And they say: 'They always got two eyes.' And you say: 'The hell they did. I distinctly remember everybody got one eye.' And by God you believe it. And they have a hell of a time knockin' the notion outa you." The driver thumped him again. "Seems to me, Mac, like you're on a one-eye kick."

"One eye," Reich muttered. "Two eyes. Tension, apprehension, and dissension have begun."

"What?"

"I don't know. I don't know. I've had a rough time the last month. Maybe . . . Maybe you're right. But—"

"You want to go to Kingston?"

"No!"

"You want to stay here and mope about them stars?"

Abruptly, Reich shouted: "What the hell do I care about the stars!" His fear turned to hot rage. Adrenalin flooded his system, bringing with it a surge of courage and high spirits. He leaped into the cab. "I've got the world. What do I care if a few delusions go with it?"

"That's the way, Mac. Where to?"

"The Royal Palace."

"The which?"

Reich laughed. "Monarch," he said, and roared with

157

laughter all the flight through the dawn to Monarch's soaring tower. But it was a semi-hysterical laughter.

The office ran around-the-clock shifts, and the night staff was in the last drowsy stages of the 12-8 shift when Reich bustled in. Although they had not seen much of him in the past month, the staff was accustomed to these visits, and shifted smoothly into high gear. As Reich went to his desk he was followed by secretaries and sub-secretaries carrying the urgent agenda of the day.

"Let all that wait," he snapped. "Call in the entire staff . . . all department heads and organizational supervisors. I'm going to make an announcement."

The flutter soothed him and recaptured his frame of reference. He was alive again, real again. All this was the only reality . . . the hustle, the bustle, the annunciator bells, the muted commands, the quick filling of his office with so many awed faces. All this was a preview of the future when bells would ring on planets and satellites and world supervisors would scuttle to his desk with awe on their faces.

"As you all know," Reich began, pacing slowly and darting piercing glances into the faces that watched him, "We of Monarch have been locked in a death-struggle with the D'Courtney Cartel. Craye D'Courtney was killed some time ago. There were complications that have just been ironed out. You'll be pleased to hear that the road is open for us now. We can commence operation of Plan AA to take over the D'Courtney Cartel."

He paused, waiting for the excited murmur that should respond to his announcement. There was no response.

"Perhaps," he said, "some of you do not comprehend the size of the job and the importance of the job. Let me put it this way . . . in terms you'll understand. Those of you that are city supervisors will become continental supervisors. Continental supervisors will become satellite chiefs. Present satellite chiefs will become planetary chiefs. From now on, Monarch will dominate the solar system. From now on all of us must think in terms of the solar system. From now on . . ."

Reich faltered, alarmed by the blank looks around him. He glanced around, then singled out the chief secretary. "What the hell's the matter?" he growled. "There been news I haven't heard yet? Bad news?"

"N-No, Mr. Reich."

"Then what's eating you? This is something we've all been waiting for. What's wrong with it?"

The chief secretary stammered: "We . . . I . . . I'm s-sorry, sir. I d-don't know what y-you're talking about."

"I'm talking about the D'Courtney Cartel."

"I . . . I've n-never heard of the organization, Mr.
158

Reich, sir. I . . . we . . ." The chief secretary turned around for support. Before Reich's unbelieving eyes the entire staff shook their heads in mystification.

"D'Courtney on Mars!" Reich shouted.

"On where, sir?"

"Mars! Mars! M-A-R-S. One of the ten planets. Fourth from the sun." Gripped by the returning terror, Reich bellowed incoherently. "Mercury, Venus, Earth, Mars, Jupiter, Saturn, Mars! Mars! Mars! A hundred and forty-one million miles from the sun, Mars!"

Again the staff shook their heads. There was a rustle and they backed away slightly from Reich. He darted at the secretaries and tore the sheafs of business papers from their hands. "You've got a hundred memos about D'Courtney on Mars there. You've got to. My God, we've been battling it out with D'Courtney for the last ten years. We—"

He clawed through the papers, throwing them wildly in all directions, filling the office with fluttering snow. There was not one reference to D'Courtney or Mars. There was neither any reference to Venus, Jupiter, the Moon, nor the other satellites.

"I've got memos in my desk," Reich shouted. "Hundreds of them. You lousy liars! Look in my desk . . ."

He darted to the desk and yanked out drawers. There was a stunning explosion. The desk burst asunder. Fragments of flying fruit-wood slashed the staff, and Reich was hurled back against the window by the desk top which smacked him like a giant's hand.

"The Man With No Face!" Reich cried. "Christ Almighty!" He shook his head feverishly, and clung to the paramount obsession. 'Where are the files? I'll show you in the files . . . D'Courtney and Mars and all the rest. And I'll show him, too. The Man With No Face . . . Come on!"

He ran out of his office and burst into the file vaults. He tore out rack after rack; scattering papers, clusters of piezo crystals, ancient wire recordings, microfilm, molecular transcripts. There was no reference to D'Courtney or Mars. There was no reference to Venus, Jupiter, Mercury, the asteroids, the satellites.

And now indeed the office was alive with hustle and bustle, annunciator bells, strident commands. Now the office was stampeding, and three burly gentlemen from Recreation' came trotting into the vaults directed by the bleeding scretary who urged: "You must! You must! I'll take the responsibility!"

"Easy now, easy now, easy now, Mr. Reich," they said with the hissing noise with which hostlers soothe savage stallions. "Easy . . . easy . . . easy . . ."

"Get away from me, you sons of bitches."

"Easy, sir. Easy. It's all right, sir."

They deployed strategically while the hustle and the bustle increased and the bells sounded and voices far off called: "Who's his doctor? Get his doctor. Somebody call Kingston. Did you notify the police? No, don't. No scandal. Get the legal department, will you! Isn't the Infirmary open yet?"

Reich's breath came and went in snarls. He overturned files in the path of the burly gentlemen, put his head down and bulled straight through them. He raced through the office to the outside corridor and the Pneumatique. The door opened; he punched Science-city 57. He stepped into the air-shuttle and was shot over to Science where he stepped out.

He was on the laboratory floor. It was in darkness. Probably the staff imagined he had dropped to the street level. He would have time. Still breathing heavily, he trotted to the lab library, snapped on the lights and went to the reference alcove. A sheet of frosted crystal, cocked like a draft-board, was set before a desk chair. There was a complicated panel of control buttons alongside it.

Reich seated himself and punched READY. The sheet lit up and a canned voice spoke from an overhead speaker.

"Topic?"

Reich punched SCIENCE.

"Section?"

Reich punched ASTRONOMY.

"Question?"

"The universe."

Click-pause-click. "The term universe in its complete physical sense applies to all matter in existence."

"What matter is in existence?"

Click-pause-click. "Matter is gathered into aggregates ranging in size from the smallest atom to the largest collection of matter known to astronomers."

"What is the largest collection of matter known to astronomers?" Reich punched DIAGRAM.

Click-pause-click. "The sun." The crystal plate displayed a dazzling picture of the sun in speed-up action.

"But what about the others? The stars?"

Click-pause-click. "There are no stars."

"The planets?"

Click-pause-click. "There is the earth." A picture of the revolving earth appeared.

"The other planets? Mars? Jupiter? Saturn . . ."

Click-pause-click. "There are no other planets."

"The moon?"

Click-pause-click. "There is no moon."

Reich took a deep trembling breath. "We'll try it again. Go back to the sun."

160

The sun appeared again in the crystal. "The sun is the largest collection of matter known to astronomers," the canned voice began. Suddenly it stopped. Click-pause-click. The picture of the sun began to fade slowly. The voice spoke. "There is no sun."

The model disappeared, leaving behind it an after-image that looked up at Reich . . . looming, silent, horrible . . . The Man With No Face.

Reich howled. He leaped to his feet, knocking the desk chair backward. He picked it up and smashed it down on that frightful image. He turned and blundered out of the library into the lab, and thence to the corridor. At the Vertical Pneumatique, he punched STREET. The door opened, he staggered in and was dropped 57 storeys to the Main Hall of Monarch's Science-city.

It was filled with early workers hurrying to their offices. As Reich pushed past them, he caught the astonished glances at his cut and bleeding face. Then he was aware of a dozen uniformed Monarch guards closing in on him. He ran down the hall and with a frantic burst of speed dodged the guards. He slipped into the revolving doors and whirled through to the footway. There he jerked to a stop as though he had run into white hot iron. There was no sun.

The street lights were lit; the skyways twinkled; Jumper eyes floated up and down; the shops were blazing . . . And overhead there was nothing . . . nothing but a deep, black, fathomless infinity.

"The sun!" Reich shouted. "The sun!"

He pointed upward. The office workers regarded him with suspicious eyes and hurried on. No one looked up.

"The sun! Where's the sun? Don't you understand, you fools? The sun!" Reich plucked at their arms, shaking his fist at the sky. Then the first of the guards came through the revolving door and he took to his heels.

He went down the footway, turned sharp to his right and sprinted through an arcade of brilliant, busy shops. Beyond the arcade was the entrance of a Vertical Pneumatique to the skyway. Reich leaped in. As the door closed behind him, he caught sight of the pursuing guards less than twenty yards off. Then he was lofted seventy storeys and emerged on the skyway.

There was a small car-park alongside him, shelved onto the face of Monarch Tower, with a runway leading into the skyway. Reich ran in, flung credits to the attendant and got into a car. He pressed GO. The car went. At the foot of the runway he pressed LEFT. The car turned left and continued. That was all the control he had. Left, right; stop, go. The rest was automatic. Moreover, cars were strictly limited to the skyways. He might spend hours racing in circles high over the city, trapped like a dog in a revolving cage.

The car needed no attention. He glanced alternately over his shoulder and up at the sky. There was no sun . . . and they went about their business as though there had never been a sun. He shuddered. Was this more of the one-eye kick? Suddenly the car slowed and stopped; and he was marooned in the middle of the skyway, halfway between Monarch Tower and the giant Visiphone & Visigraph Building.

Reich hammered on the control studs. There was no response. He leaped out and raised the tail hood to inspect the pick-up. Then he saw the guards far down the skyway, running toward him, and he understood. These cars were powered by broadcast energy. They'd cut the transmission off at the car-park and were coming after him. Reich turned tail and sprinted toward the V & V Building.

The skyway tunneled through the building and was lined with shops, restaurants, a theater—and there was a travel office! A sure out. He could grab a ticket, get into a one-man capsule and have himself slotted to any of the take-off fields. He needed a little time to reorganize . . . reorient . . . and he had a house in Paris. He leaped across the center island, dodged past cars and ran into the office.

It looked like a miniature bank. A short counter. A grilled window protected by burglar-proof plastic. Reich went to the window, pulling money from his pocket. He slapped credits down on the counter and shoved them under the grille.

"Ticket to Paris," he said. "Keep the change. Which way to the capsules? Jet, man! Jet!"

"Paris?" came the reply. "There is no Paris."

Reich stared through the cloudy plastic and saw . . . looking, looming, silent . . . The Man With No Face. He spun around twice, heart pounding, skull pounding, located the door and ran out. He ran blindly onto the skyway, shied feebly from an oncoming car, and was struck down into enveloping darkness—

ABOLISH.
DESTROY.
DELETE.
DISBAND.
    (MINERALOGY, PETROLOGY, GEOLOGY, PHYS-IOGRAPHY)
DISPERSE.
    (METEOROLOGY, HYDROLOGY, SEISMOLOGY)
ERASE.

$(X^2 \oslash Y^3 \; d:Space/d:Time)$
EFFACE.
THE SUBJECT WILL BE—

"—will be what?"
THE SUBJECT WILL BE—
"—will be what? What? WHAT?"

A hand was placed over his mouth. Reich opened his eyes. He was in a small tiled room, an emergency police station. He was lying on a white table. Around him were grouped the guards, three uniformed police, unidentified strangers. All were writing carefully in report books, murmuring, shifting confusedly.

The stranger removed his hand from Reich's mouth and bent over him. "It's all right," he said gently. "Easy. I'm a doctor . . ."

"A peeper?"

"What?"

"Are you a peeper? I need a peeper. I need somebody inside my head to prove I'm right. My God! I've got to know I'm right. I don't care about the price. I—"

"What's he want?" a policeman asked.

"I don't know. He said a peeper." The doctor turned back to Reich. "What d'you mean by that? Just tell us. What's a peeper?"

"An Esper! A mind reader. A —"

The doctor smiled. "He's joking. Show of high spirits. Many patients do that. They simulate sang froid after accidents. We call it Gallows Humor . . ."

"Listen," Reich said desperately. "Let me up. I want to say something . . ."

They helped him up.

To the police, he said: "My name is Ben Reich. Ben Reich of Monarch. You know me. I want to confess. I want to confess to Lincoln Powell, the police prefect. Take me to Powell."

"Who's Powell?"

"And what y'want to confess?"

"The D'Courtney murder. I murdered Craye D'Courtney last month. In Maria Beaumont's house . . . Tell Powell. I killed D'Courtney."

The police looked at each other in surprise. One of them drifted to a corner and picked up an old-fashioned hand phone: "Captain? Got a character here. Calls himself Ben Reich of Monarch. Wants to confess to some prefect named Powell. Claims he killed a party named Craye D'Courtney last month." After a pause, the policeman called to Reich: "How do you spell that?"

"D'Courtney! Capital D apostrophe Capital C-O-U-R-T-N-E-Y."

The policeman spelled it out and waited. After another pause, he grunted and hung up. "A nut," he said and stowed his notebook in a pocket.

"Listen—" Reich began.

"Is he all right?" the policeman asked the doctor without looking at Reich.

"Just shaken a little. He's all right."

"Listen!" Reich shouted.

The policeman yanked him to his feet and propelled him toward the door of the station. "All right, buddy. Out!"

"You've got to listen to me! I—"

"You listen to me, buddy. There ain't no Lincoln Powell in the service. There ain't no D'Courtney killing in the books. And we ain't takin' no slok from your kind. Now . . . Out!" And he hurled Reich into the street.

The pavement was strangely broken. Reich stumbled, then regained his balance and stood still, numb, lost. It was darker . . . eternally darker. A few street lights were lit. The skyways were extinguished. The Jumpers had disappeared. There were great gaps shorn in the skyline.

"I'm sick," Reich moaned. "I'm sick. I need help . . ."

He began to lurch down the broken streets with arms clutching his belly.

"Jumper!" he yelled. "Jumper! Isn't there anything in this God-forsaken city? Where is everything? Jumper!"

There was nothing.

"I'm sick . . . sick. Got to get home. I'm sick . . ." Again he shouted: "Isn't there anybody can hear me? I'm sick. I need help . . . Help! . . . Help!"

There was nothing.

He moaned again. Then he tittered . . . weakly, inanely. He sang in a broken voice: "Eight, sir . . . Five, sir . . . One, sir . . . Tenser said Tensor . . . Tension . . . 'prehension . . . 'ssention have begun . . ."

He called plaintively: "Where is everybody? Maria! Lights! Ma-ri-aaa! Stop this crazy Sardine game!"

He stumbled.

"Come back!" Reich called. "For God's sake, come back! I'm all alone."

No answer.

He was searching for 9 Park South, looking for the Beaumont Mansion, the site of D'Courtney's death . . . and Maria Beaumont, shrill, decadent, reassuring.

There was nothing.

A bleak tundra. Black sky. Unfamiliar desolation. Nothing.

Reich shouted once . . . a hoarse, inarticulate yell of rage and fright.

No answer. Not even an echo.

"For God's sake!" he cried. "Where is everything? Bring it all back! There's nothing but space . . ."

Out of the enveloping desolation, a figure gathered and grew, familiar, ominous, gigantic . . . A figure of black shadows, looking, looming, silent . . . The Man With No Face. Reich watched it, paralysed, transfixed.

Then the figure spoke: "There is no space. There is nothing."

And there was a screaming in Reich's ears that was his voice, and a hammering pulse that was his heart. He was running down a yawning alien path, devoid of life, devoid of space, running before it was too late, too late, too late . . . running while there was still time, time, time —

He ran headlong into a figure of black shadows. A figure without a face. A figure that said: "There is no time. There is nothing."

Reich backed away. He turned. He fell. He crawled feebly through eternal emptiness shrieking: "Powell! Duffy! Quizzard! Tate! Oh Christ! Where is everybody? Where is everything? For the love of God . . ."

And he was face to face with the Man With No Face who said: "There is no God. There is nothing."

And now there was no longer escape. There was only a negative infinity and Reich and the Man With No Face. And fixed, frozen, helpless in that matrix, Reich at last raised his eyes and stared deep into the face of his deadly enemy . . . the man he could not escape . . . the terror of his nightmares . . . the destroyer of his existence . . .

It was . . .

Himself.

D'Courtney.

Both.

Two faces, blending into one. Ben D'Courtney. Crayc Reich. D'Courtney-Reich. D'R.

He could make no sound. He could make no move. There was neither time nor space nor matter. There was nothing left but dying thought.

"Father?"

"Son."

"You are me?"

"We are us."

"Father and son?"

"Yes."

165

"I can't understand . . . What's happened?"

"You lost the game, Ben."

"The Sardine Game?"

"The Cosmic Game."

"I won. I won. I owned every bit of the world. I —"

"And therefore you lose. We lose."

"Lose what?"

"Survival."

"I don't understand. I can't understand."

"My part of us understands, Ben. You would understand too if you hadn't driven me from you."

"How did I drive you from me?"

"With every rotten, distorted corruption in you."

"You say that? You . . . betrayer, who tried to kill me?"

"That was without passion, Ben. That was to destroy you before you could destroy us. That was for survival. It was to help you lose the world and win the game, Ben."

"What game? What Cosmic Game?"

"The maze . . . the labyrinth . . . all the universe, created as a puzzle for us to solve. The galaxies, the stars, the sun, the planets . . . the world as we knew it. We were the only reality. All the rest was make-believe . . . dolls, puppets, stage-settings . . . pretended passions. It was a make-believe reality for us to solve."

"I conquered it. I owned it."

"And you failed to solve it. We'll never know what the solution is, but it's not theft, terror, hatred, lust, murder, rapine. You failed, and it's all been abolished, disbanded . . ."

"But what's to become of us?"

"We are abolished too. I tried to warn you. I tried to stop you. But we failed the test."

"But why? Why? Who are we? What are we?"

"Who knows? Did the seed know who or what it was when it failed to find fertile soil? Does it matter who or what we are? We have failed. Our test is ended. We are ended."

"No!"

"Perhaps if we had solved it, Ben, it might have remained real. But it is ended. Reality has turned into might-have-been, and you have awakened at last . . . to nothing."

"We'll go back! We'll try it again!"

"There is no going back. It is ended."

"We'll find a way. There must be a way . . ."

"There is none. It is ended."

It was ended.

Now . . . Demolition.

17

They found the two men next morning, far up the island in the gardens overlooking the old Haarlem Canal. Each had wandered all the night, through footway and skyway, unconscious of his surroundings, yet both were drawn inevitably together like two magnetized needles floating on a weed choked pond.

Powell was seated cross-legged on the wet turf, his face shrivelled and lifeless, his respiration almost gone, his pulse faded. He was clutching Reich with an iron grip. Reich was curled into a tight foetal ball.

They rushed Powell to his home on Hudson Ramp where the entire Guild Lab team alternately sweated over him and congratulated themselves on the first successful Mass Cathexis Measure in the history of the Esper Guild. There was no hurry for Reich. In due course and with proper procedure, his inert body was transported to Kingston Hospital for Demolition.

There the matter rested for seven days.

On the eighth day, Powell arose, bathed, dressed, successfully defeated his nurses in single combat, and left the house. He made one stop at Sucre et Cie, emerged with a large mysterious parcel and then proceeded to headquarters to make his personal report to Commissioner Crabbe. On the way up, he poked his head into Beck's office.

"Hi, Jax."

"Bless (and curses) ings, Linc."

"Curses?"

"Bet fifty they'd keep you in bed till next Wed."

"You lose. Did Mose back us up on the D'Courtney motive?"

"Lock, stock & barrel. Trial took one hour. Reich's going into Demolition now."

"Good. Well, I'd better go up and s-p-e-l-l it out for Crabbe."

"What you got under your arm?"

"Present."

"For me?"

"Not today. Here's thinking at you."

Powell went up to Crabbe's ebony and silver office, knocked, heard the imperious: "Come!" and entered. Crabbe was properly solicitous, but stiff. The D'Courtney Case had not improved his relations with Powell. The denouement had come as an additional blow.

"It was a remarkably complex case, sir," Powell began tactfully. "None of us could understand it, and none of us are to blame. You see, Commissioner, even Reich himself was not consciously aware of why he had murdered D'Courtney. The only one who grasped the case was the Prosecution Computor, and we thought it was acting kittenish."

"The machine? It understood?"

"Yes, sir. When we ran our final data through the first time, the Computor told us that the 'passion motive' was insufficiently documented. We'd all been assuming profit motive. So had Reich. Naturally we assumed the Computor was having kinks, and we insisted on computation based on the profit motive. We were wrong . . ."

"And that infernal machine was right?"

"Yes, Commissioner. It was. Reich told himself that he was killing D'Courtney for financial reasons. That was his psychological camouflage for the real passion motive. And it couldn't hold up. He offered merger to D'Courtney. D'Courtney accepted. But Reich was subconsciously compelled to misunderstand the message. He had to. He had to go on believing he murdered for money."

"Why?"

"Because he couldn't face the real motive . . ."

"Which was . . . ?"

"D'Courtney was his father."

"What!" Crabbe stared. "His father? His flesh and blood?"

"Yes, sir. It was all there before us. We just couldn't see it. . . . because Reich couldn't see it. That estate on Callisto, for instance. The one that Reich used to decoy Dr. Jordan off the planet. Reich inherited it from his mother who'd received it from D'Courtney. We all assumed Reich's father had chiseled it out of D'Courtney and placed it in his wife's name. We were wrong. D'Courtney had given it to Reich's mother because they were lovers. It was his love-gift to the mother of his child. Reich was born there. Jackson Beck uncovered all that, once we had the lead."

Crabbe opened his mouth, then closed it.

"And there were so many other signposts. D'Courtney's suicide drive, produced by intense guilt sensations of abandonment. He had abandoned his son. It was tearing him apart. Then, Barbara D'Courtney's deep half-twin image of herself and Ben Reich; somehow she knew they were half-brother and sister. And Reich's inability to kill Barbara at Chooka Frood's. He knew it too, deep down in the unconscious. He wanted to destroy the hateful father who had rejected him, but he could not bring himself to harm his sister."

"But when did you unearth all this?"

"After the case was closed, sir. When Reich attacked me for setting those booby-traps."

"He claimed you did. He— But if you didn't, Powell, who did?"

"Reich himself, sir."

"Reich!"

"Yes, sir. He murdered his father. He discharged his hatred. But his super-ego . . . his conscience, could not permit him to go unpunished for such a horrible crime. Since the police apparently were unable to punish him, his consience took over. That was the meaning of Reich's nightmare image . . . The Man With No Face."

"The Man With No Face?"

"Yes, Commissioner. It was the symbol of Reich's real relationship to D'Courtney. The figure had no face because Reich could not accept the truth . . . that he had recognized D'Courtney as his father. The figure appeared in his dreams when he made the decision to kill his father. It never left him. It was first the threat of punishment for what he contemplated. Then it became the punishment itself for the murder."

"The booby-traps?"

"Exactly. His conscience had to punish him. But Reich had never admitted to himself that he murdered because he hated D'Courtney as the father who had rejected and abandoned him. Therefore, the punishment had to take place on the unconscious level. Reich set those traps for himself without ever realizing it . . . in his sleep, somnambulistically . . . during the day, in short fugues . . . brief departures from conscious reality. The tricks of the mind-mechanism are fantastic."

"But if Reich himself knew none of this . . . how did you get at it, Powell?"

"Well, sir. That was the problem. We couldn't get it by peeping him. He was hostile and you have to have complete cooperation from a subject to get that kind of material. It takes months anyway. Also, if Reich recovered from the series of shocks he'd had, he would be able to readjust, reorient, and become immune to us. That was dangerous, too, because he was in a position of power to rock the solar system. He was one of those rare World-Shakers whose compulsions might have torn down our society and irrevocably committed us to his own psychotic pattern."

Crabbe nodded.

"He very nearly succeeded. These men appear every so often . . . links between the past and the future. If they are permitted to mature . . . If the link is permitted to weld . . . The world finds itself chained to a dreadful tomorrow."

"Then what did you do?"

"We used the Mass Cathexis Measure, sir. It's difficult to explain, but I'll do my best. Every human being has a psyche composed of latent and capitalized energy. Latent energy is our reserve . . . the untapped natural resources of our mind. Capitalized energy is that latent energy which we call up and put to work. Most of us use only a small portion of our latent energy."

"I understand."

"When the Esper Guild uses the Mass Cathexis Measure, every Esper opens his psyche, so to speak, and contributes his latent energy to a pool. One Esper alone taps this pool and becomes the canal for the latent energy. He capitalizes it and puts it to work. He can accomplish tremendous things . . . if he can control it. It's a difficult and dangerous operation. About on a par with jetting to the moon with a stick of dynamite stuck—er—riding on dynamite sticks . . ."

Suddenly Crabbe grinned. "I wish I were a peeper," he said. "I'd like to get the real image in your mind."

"You've got it already, sir." Powell grinned back. A rapport had been established between them for the first time.

"It was necessary," Powell continued, "to confront Reich with The Man With No Face. We had to make him see the truth before we could get the truth. Using the pool of latent energy, I built a common neurotic concept for Reich . . . the illusion that he alone in the world was real."

"Why, I've—Is that common?"

"Oh yes, sir. It's one of the run-of-the-mill escape patterns. When life gets tough, you tend to take refuge in the idea that it's all make-believe . . . a giant hoax. Reich had the seeds of that weakness in him already. I simply forced them and let Reich defeat himself. Life was getting tough for him. I persuaded him to believe that the universe was a hoax . . . a puzzle-box. Then I tore it down, layer by layer. I made him believe that the test was ended. The puzzle was being dismantled. And I left Reich alone with The Man With No Face. He looked into the face and saw himself and his father . . . and we had everything."

Powell picked up his parcel and arose. Crabbe jumped up and escorted him to the door with a friendly hand on his shoulder.

"You've done a phenomenal job, Powell. Really phenomenal. I can't tell you . . . It must be a wonderful thing to be an Esper."

"Wonderful and terrible, sir."

"You must all be very happy."

"Happy?" Powell paused at the door and looked at Crabbe. "Would you be happy to live your life in a hospital, Commissioner?"

170

"A hospital?"

"That's where we live . . . All of us. In the psychiatric ward. Without escape . . . without refuge. Be grateful you're not a peeper, sir. Be grateful that you only see the outward man. Be grateful that you never see the passions, the hatreds, the jealousies, the malice, the sicknesses . . . Be grateful you rarely see the frightening truth in people. The world will be a wonderful place when everyone's a peeper and everyone's adjusted . . . But until then, be grateful you're blind."

He left headquarters, hired a Jumper and was jetted North toward Kingston Hospital. He sat in the cabin with the parcel on his knees, gazing down at the magnificent Hudson valley, whistling a crooked tune. Once he grinned and muttered: "Wow! That was some line I handed Crabbe. But I had to cement our relations. Now he'll feel sorry for peepers . . . and friendly."

Kingston Hospital came into view . . . acre upon rolling acre of magnificent landscaping. Solariums, pools, lawns, athletic fields, dormitories, clinics . . . all in exquisite neo-classic design. As the Jumper descended, Powell could make out the figures of patients and attendants . . . all bronzed, active, laughing, playing. He thought of the vigilant measures the Board of Governors was forced to take to prevent Kingston Hospital from becoming another Spaceland. Too many fashionable malingerers were already attempting to obtain admission.

Powell checked in at the Visitors Office, found Barbara D'Courtney's location and started across the grounds. He was weak, but he wanted to leap hedges, vault gates, run races. He had awakened after seven days' exhaustion with a question —one question to ask Barbara. He felt exhilarated.

They saw one another at the same moment. Across a broad stretch of lawn flanked by field-stone terraces and brilliant gardens. She flew toward him, waving, and he ran toward her. Then as they approached, both were stricken with shyness. They stopped a few feet apart, not daring to look at each other.

"Hello."

"Hello, Barbara."

"I . . . Let's get into the shade, shall we?"

They turned toward the terrace wall. Powell glanced at her from the corner of his eye. She was alive again . . . alive as he had never seen her before. And her urchin expression —the expression that he had imagined was a phase of her Déjà Éprouvé development was still there. She looked inexpressibly mischievous, high-spirited, fascinating. But she was adult. He did not know her.

"I'm being discharged this evening," Barbara said.

"I know."

171

"I'm terribly grateful to you for all you've—"

"Please don't say that."

"For all you've done," Barbara continued firmly. They sat down on a stone bench. She looked at him with grave eyes. "I want to tell you how grateful I am."

"Please, Barbara. You're terrifying me."

"Am I?"

"I knew you so intimately as . . . well, as a child. Now . . ."

"Now I'm grown up again."

"Yes."

"You must get to know me better." She smiled graciously. "Shall we say . . . Tea tomorrow at five?"

"At five . . ."

"Informal. Don't dress."

"Listen," Powell said desperately. "I helped dress you more than once. And comb your hair. And brush your teeth."

She waved her hand airily.

"Your table manners were a caution. You liked fish but you hated lamb. You hit me in the eye with a chop."

"That was ages ago, Mr. Powell."

"That was two weeks ago, Miss D'Courtney."

She arose with magnificent poise. "Really Mr. Powell. I feel it would be best to end the interview. If you feel impelled to cast chronographical aspersions . . ." She stopped and looked at him. The urchin appeared again in her face. "Chronographical?" she inquired.

He dropped the parcel and caught her in his arms.

"Mr. Powell, Mr. Powell, Mr. Powell . . ." she murmured. "Hello, Mr. Powell . . ."

"My God, Barbara . . . Baba, dear. For a moment I thought you meant it."

"I was paying you back for being grown up."

"You always were a revengeful kid."

"You always were a mean daddy." She leaned back and looked at him. "What are you really like? What are we both like? Will we have time to find out?"

"Time?"

"Before . . . Peep me. I can't say it."

"No, dear. You'll have to say it."

"Mary Noyes told me. Everything."

"Oh. She did?"

Barbara nodded. "But I don't care. I don't care. She was right. I'll settle for anything. Even if you can't marry me . . ."

He laughed. The exhilaration bubbled out of him. "You won't have to settle for anything," he said. "Sit down. I want to ask you one question."

She sat down. On his lap.

"I have to go back to that night," he said.

"In Beaumont House?"

He nodded.

"It's not easy to talk about."

"It won't take a minute. Now . . . You were lying in bed, asleep. Suddenly you woke up and rushed into the Orchid room. You remember the rest."

"I remember."

"One question. What was the cry that woke you?"

"You know."

"I know, but I want you to say it. Say it out loud."

"Do you think it's . . . it's going to send me into hysteria again?"

"No. Just say it."

After a long pause, she said in a low voice: "Help, Barbara."

He nodded again. "Who shouted that?"

"Why, it was —" Suddenly she stopped.

"It wasn't Ben Reich. He wouldn't be yelling for help. He didn't need help. Who did?"

"My . . . My father."

"But he couldn't speak, Barbara. His throat was gone . . . Cancer. He couldn't utter a word."

"I heard him."

"You peeped him."

She stared; then she shook her head. "No, I—"

"You peeped him," Powell repeated gently. "You're a latent Esper. Your father cried out on the telepathic level. If I hadn't been such an ass and so intent on Reich, I'd have realized it long before. You were unconsciously peeping Mary and me all the while you were in my house."

She couldn't grasp it.

"Do you love me?" Powell shot at her.

"I love you, of course," she muttered, "but I think you're inventing excuses to—"

"Who asked you?"

"Asked me what?"

"If you loved me."

"Why you just—" She stopped, then tried again. "You said . . . Y-You . . ."

"I didn't say it. Do you understand now? We won't have to settle for anything short of us."

Seconds later, it seemed, but it was actually half an hour, they were separated by a violent crash that sounded from the top of the terrace above their heads. They looked up in astonishment.

A naked thing appeared on the stone wall, gibbering, screaming, twitching. It toppled over the edge and crashed down through the flower beds until it landed on the lawn, crying and jerking as though a steady stream of voltage was pouring through its nervous system. It was Ben Reich, almost unrecognizable, partway through Demolition.

Powell swung Barbara to him with her back to Reich. He took her chin in his hand and said: "Are you still my girl?"

She nodded.

"I don't want you to see this. It isn't dangerous, but it isn't good for you. Will you run back to your pavilion and wait for me? Like a good girl? All right . . . Scamper now! Jet!"

She grabbed his hand, kissed it quickly, and ran across the lawn without once looking back. Powell watched her go, then turned and inspected Reich.

When a man is demolished at Kingston Hospital, his entire psyche is destroyed. The series of osmotic injections begins with the topmost strata of cortical synapses and slowly works down, switching off every circuit, extinguishing every memory, destroying every particle of the pattern that has been built up since birth. And as the pattern is erased, each particle discharges its portion of energy, turning the entire body into a shuddering maelstrom of dissociation.

But this is not the pain; this is not the dread of Demolition. The horror lies in the fact that the consciousness is never lost; that as the psyche is wiped out, the mind is aware of its slow, backward death until at last it too disappears and awaits the rebirth. The mind bids an eternity of farewells; it mourns at an endless funeral. And in those blinking, twitching eyes of Ben Reich, Powell saw the awareness . . . the pain . . . the tragic despair.

"Now how the hell did he fall down there? Do we have to keep him tied?" Dr. Jeems poked his head over the terrace. "Oh. Hi, Powell. That's a friend of yours. Remember him?"

"Vividly."

Jeems spoke over his shoulder: "You go down to the lawn and pick him up. I'll keep an eye on him." He turned to Powell. "He's a lusty lad. We've got great hopes for him."

Reich squalled and twitched.

"How's the treatment coming?"

"Wonderful. He's got the stamina to take anything. We're stepping him up. Ought to be ready for rebirth in a year."

"I'm waiting for it. We need men like Reich. It would have been a shame to lose him."

"Lose him? How's that possible? You think a little fall like that could—"

"No. I mean something else. Three or four hundred years ago, cops used to catch people like Reich just to kill them. Capital punishment, they called it."

"You're kidding."

"Scout's honor."

"But it doesn't make sense. If a man's got the talent and guts to buck society, he's obviously above average. You want to hold on to him. You straighten him out and turn him into a plus value. Why throw him away? Do that enough and all you've got left are the sheep."

"I don't know. Maybe in those days they wanted sheep."

The attendants came trotting across the lawn and picked Reich up. He fought and screamed. They handled him with the deft and gentle Kingston judo while they checked him carefully for breaks and sprains. Then, reassured, they started to lead him away.

"Just a minute," Powell called. He turned to the stone bench, picked up the mysterious parcel and unwrapped it. It was one of Sucre et Cie's most magnificent candy boxes. He carried it to the demolished man and held it out. "It's a present for you, Ben. Take it."

The creature lowered at Powell and then at the box. At last the clumsy hands came out and took the gift.

"Why damn it, I'm just his nursemaid," Powell muttered. "We're all of us nursemaids to this crazy world. Is it worth it?"

Out of the chaos in Reich came an explosive fragment: "Powell-peeper-Powell-friend-Powell-friend . . ."

It was so sudden, so unexpected, so passionately grateful that Powell was overcome with warmth and tears. He tried to smile, then turned away and wandered across the lawn toward the pavilion and Barbara.

"Listen," he cried in exaltation. "*Listen, normals! You must learn what it is. You must learn how it is. You must tear the barriers down. You must tear the veils away. We see the truth you cannot see . . . That there is nothing in man but love and faith, courage and kindness, generosity and sacrifice. All else is only the barrier of your blindness. One day we'll all be mind to mind and heart to heart . . .*"

In the endless universe there has been nothing new, nothing different. What has appeared exceptional to the minute mind of man has been inevitable to the infinite Eye of God. This strange second in a life, that unusual event, those remarkable coincidences of environment, opportunity, and encounter . . . all of them have been reproduced over and over on the planet of a sun whose galaxy revolves once in two hundred million years and has revolved nine times already. There has been joy. There will be joy again.

the end

SIGNET Science Fiction You Will Enjoy

☐ **NEW DIMENSIONS III edited by Robert Silverberg.**
Eleven stories, each one your passport through time,
space and imagination to the infinite realm of science
fiction. Included are stories by Ursula K. Le Guin, R. A.
Lafferty, and Terry Carr. (#Q5805—95¢)

☐ **THE STARS AROUND US: A Science Fiction Anthology
edited by Robert Hoskins.** Ten fascinating short stories
by ten masters of science fiction. (#Q5755—95¢)

☐ **MOON OF MUTINY by Lester del Rey.** Set in the early
days of the moon's colonization, this exciting novel tells
of one man's escapades in a new frontier.
(#Q5539—95¢)

☐ **THE SEEDLING STARS by James Blish.** Future mankind
populates the universe with specially created human
beings who can survive the weirdest conditions on other
planets. (#Q5440—95¢)

☐ **ELEMENT 79 by Fred Hoyle.** A noted astronomer and
science fiction author leads an excursion into a fantastic
—but scientifically possible—future universe in this
engaging collection of stories. (#Q5279—95¢)

THE NEW AMERICAN LIBRARY, INC.,
P.O. Box 999, Bergenfield, New Jersey 07621

Please send me the SIGNET BOOKS I have checked above. I am
enclosing $_____(check or money order—no currency
or C.O.D.'s). Please include the list price plus 25¢ a copy to cover
handling and mailing costs. (Prices and numbers are subject to
change without notice.)

Name_____

Address_____

City_____State_____Zip Code_____
Allow at least 3 weeks for delivery